AUGUST
NIGHTS

ALSO BY HUGH HOOD

Novels:
White Figure, White Ground
The Camera Always Lies
A Game of Touch
You Cant Get There From Here

The New Age/Le nouveau siècle:
The Swing in the Garden
A New Athens
Reservoir Ravine
Black and White Keys
The Scenic Art

Stories:
Flying a Red Kite
Around the Mountain:
Scenes from Montréal Life
The Fruit Man, the Meat Man
and the Manager
Dark Glasses
Selected Stories
None Genuine Without
This Signature

Non-fiction:
Strength Down Centre:
The Jean Béliveau Story
The Governor's Bridge
Is Closed
Scoring: Seymour Segal's
Art of Hockey
Trusting the Tale

HUGH HOOD

AUGUST NIGHTS

Stoddart

FIRST PUBLISHED IN 1985 BY
STODDART PUBLISHING CO. LIMITED

34 Lesmill Road, Toronto, Canada M3B 2T6

The author gratefully acknowledges the invaluable assistance
of the Canada Council and the Ontario Arts Council
in the completion of this work.

Canadian Cataloguing in Publication Data

Hood, Hugh, 1928 –
August Nights

ISBN 0-7737-5046-0

I. Title.

PS8515.049A94 1985   C813'.54   C85-099019-X
PR9199.3.H66A94 1985

Cover design by Brant Cowie/Artplus Ltd.

Printed and bound in Canada

For Jack David and Robert Lecker
in recognition of their services
to Canadian Literature

Some of these stories have already appeared in the following magazines:

Best Canadian Short Stories 1980
The Canadian Forum
The Malahat Review
Prism: International
Waves

Contents

The Small Birds

BY THE BEGINNING OF JUNE THE BLACK FLIES and mosquitoes were so thick that Marian was trapped on the sunporch. Nobody quite knew why, but if there were one bug in a building it would go straight for her, forsaking all others, and bite or sting or fly around and around her head. It was impossible for her to concentrate on what she was doing, either shelling peas or reading *Cosmopolitan* and laughing at it. Sometimes a heavy fly would land on the crown of her head where the hair parted and exposed her scalp — they were attracted by the natural oil — and she would shiver with repulsion. She might pass the morning swatting and spraying, then sit all afternoon out on the screened sundeck, listening to the radio or reading or watching spring activity on the water.

Just before dusk a pair of blue herons would make two or three passes down the lake; often they flew back north with visible fish flopping in their mouths. The loons wouldn't make their appearance until the herons had nested successfully; there might be some rivalry between them or some element of ecological stress. Do herons eat loons?

Purple martins eat mosquitoes, she remembered. Two years ago the boys had cleared away a lot of piled-up brush at the back of the property, near the parking spaces, and had laid down an expanse of sod for a picnic ground. Now there was thick grass, a big picnic table and a string of Japanese lanterns in the shagged beeches where nothing but huge split rocks, chipmunks and juniper mulch had been. She still couldn't go out there till August or September: she'd get bitten to death and it was no fun.

The boys had built a birdhouse for purple martins, (widely reputed to keep down mosquitoes) from a design on the vacation page

9

of one of the Saturday papers. They did not reproduce the shape of the entryways correctly; flocks of birds who were plainly not purple martins had promptly moved in to stay. There may have been one or two purple martins in the crowd, but the mosquito count continued unnaturally high. They had had a wet runoff and a wet early spring. One could do nothing about the black flies.

So Marian waited on the sunporch for the later summer and felt pleased at the immensely wide and high view of the lake and the shore which the snugly-screened windows allowed. In the old days at her grandparents' cottage at Beelzebub Lake the screens had been made of wire mesh which rusted, broke, and left dangerous needlepoints projecting around the holes. Wear-and-tear corrupted old-fashioned screening; the new nylon net was an enormous improvement. The filaments of the mesh were extremely fine but also extremely strong; they conceded nothing to wind and weather, wore for years without corrosion or breakage and interfered only minimally with the view. If they were looked through, they blurred and ran together so that instead of an impression of criss-crossing lines, a vague sense of some impalpable invisible substance ran across the eyes' surface, something like the onset of glaucoma but not so menacing.

The sundeck projected forward from the cottage on tall stilts and there was about six feet of storage space underneath, open in front and gradually closing at the sides where the rocks on which the building stood humped up gradually under the flooring. There were old rowboats stored under there, a lot of plastic sheeting (used to seal the porch windows in the fall) and a sketchy collection of garden tools. Marian's gang didn't make a fetish of gardening at the lake. Now that they had a picnic lawn out back, they were satisfied to share it with martins and swallows and an occasional much-admired pileated woodpecker.

When the cool August nights killed the bugs, Marian would start to go out, but the first two months of summer were hard time; this marshy swampy spring had sentenced her to sixty days. She would know when her incarceration was approaching its end by the phases of the summer light, the gradual progress of June and July to that point about the beginning of August when the mid-afternoon sun would dip low enough in the west to flood the porch with shine and heat and the gleam of the individual ripples as they came onshore brilliantly white, iridescent like oil paint fresh from the tube, thick and creamy.

There was shade and coolness on the porch for several hours and an even lemon colour washed around and through the field of vision. The sun was back behind the cottage at this time of year until very late in the day; the shady dark green of the evergreens was sunk all day in lemon glow. In this genial harmony it was possible to pick out individual birds, identify them, almost name them as pets. She would sit there watching the antics of various tumbling, flipping creatures, slowly realising that they too had their daily routines, like hers and those of the larger birds, especially that masterful quartet of crows who woke her every morning with their bellowed threats at enemies far down the lake.

The small birds were more rigorous in their patterns of instinctual behaviour, their cautious short flyways, their choice of favourite trees, their aerobatics. It became clear that the orchestration and the melodies of their songs changed from one hour to the next around the clock: waking sounds, assertions of territorial right, feeding and mating calls, warnings, shouts of mere fun, information about food, signals to rest. All this was a musical score.

Marian came to be able to tell the time of day by the mingled harmonies of the birdcalls and the radio which sat close to her tuned to CBC-FM until it was time for the Expos' game that could barely be reached on a signal fading in and out.

Birdcalls, broadcasts, ballgames. How alliterative, she thought, how naturally-formed. Flight. Some of the birds kept doing something in front of her, winding around five particular evergreens, two tamaracks, a spruce and two dead pines which still stood up stiffly with spiny bare branches twigged in smaller and smaller points towards invisible tips. Sometimes a bird would stand at the very end of a branch, poised airily on a filament of support so dry and stiff and thin that it would seem balanced over nothing. Then the bird might make a sudden stab at its toes and curve in rapid flight down from the branch directly towards the face of the cottage. Marian would stiffen involuntarily, but no bump of small body against plywood siding ever shocked her. Those aerial swings and rushes, ending somewhere under her feet, finally brought her to realise that at least one bird was up to something under the porch.

She began to take a close interest in what was going on, would arrive at her watching post after a late breakfast about the time that CBC's "Mostly Music" came on the air. She associated the theme music, and the names of the program's announcer, Bartley MacMillan, and its producer, Roma Angus, with the nesting activities of two specific birds whom she christened Bartley and Roma. Unusual, slightly phantasmagoric names for swallows. They were certainly swallows, but to which sub-group they belonged she could not say. There were the usual bird books in the cottage (rainy day reading for idle inquirers), but even the superb Peterson line drawings could not finally make clear to her whether Bartley and Roma were barn swallows or cliff swallows. They didn't seem to have quite the right shape to their tails for barn swallows. An extra bar of grey around their bodies above the wings didn't seem correct for cliff swallows. She concluded that they must be barn and/or cliff swallows, Roma and Bartley.

Sometimes she fancied that she could hear the movement of their wings underneath her feet; the notion disturbed her. If there were to be birds underfoot, what might dwell in the skies? They kept flying right at the cottage, coming hard, dipping and vanishing at the last moment. They were up to something. The radio hummed and burbled. The 1:00 P.M. news came on, followed by the familiar theme and brisk loving voice of Bob Kerr from Vancouver with the broadcast of classical music. He sounded so friendly and likeable that Marian plucked up her spirits, rose from her chair and sounded the back bedrooms in search of children. Only Ruth, her daughter, was in the house. Busy in the bathroom applying an experimental coat of make-up, Ruth was about thirteen.

"How come we never go down under the cottage like we used to?" said Marian. Ruth burst out laughing. "We could get up some kind of game with lumps of coal or something."

These were bits of dialogue quoted from James Thurber, familiar to everybody in the family and particularly loved by Ruth, a Thurber enthusiast from infancy. She looked over her shoulder at her mother, nodded once, then turned back and squinted at the mirror. "I'll come in a minute." Her eyelid flickered. "Damn."

"Language!" said Marian mildly. Both giggled. Ruth wiped a trace of mascara from her lashes and turned to face her mother.

Her *maquillage* was elaborate and bizarre. Bright plumage. Unrestrained.

Marian said, "Did you know that the swallows are nesting under the porch?"

"Everybody knows that but you, Mumma. They've been going in and out for days. You should see them circling around in there."

"Have you found the nest?"

"No, I haven't looked. Do you think we should disturb it?"

"We won't disturb it, darling, we'll just have a little peek. We've had them nesting before, you know. Maybe you won't remember. It must be ten years ago. Before we screened in the porch."

"I remember," said Ruth, though she was uncertain about it.

"You would have been just a tiny girl at the time."

To this observation, Ruth would make no rejoinder. The mother and daughter strolled around to the front of the building and underneath the open face of the porch. They were now in sunny shade, out of the direct line of the sun, right below the picnic table on the deck. A piece of music came to an end and the comfortable voice of the broadcaster explained the peculiarities of the record, its loved and special place in his huge — monstrous — collection.

The charming, friendly voice, the warmth without glare, the half-light, the absence of insects, the presence of Ruth. Marian felt so well that she almost felt sick.

"Here it is," said Ruth. "In under the floorboards, tucked up on the beam. I think they may be trying to hide it."

"You and your premonitions," said Marian, and they giggled again very quietly. The nest was cleverly concealed in a corner formed by two main supporting beams roofed in by the plywood flooring of the sundeck. Only an informed seeker or one of the swallows could have spotted it because the sunlight could never get in there at an angle acute enough to illuminate the crossbeams. It was a small nest, about the circumference of a softball, delicately and precisely put together with pine twigs and juniper needles. Dried now to a russet brown, the juniper shone in shadow.

There were four eggs in the nest, each the size of a green grape, but very different in hue, a pale grey or grey-blue found in expensive stoneware, neither polished nor shiny, chalky. Ruth pointed at them with a forefinger. Careful not to touch.

"Yes, four," she muttered.

"We'd better get out of here," said Marian. "They'll be wanting to get back on the nest."

And pat on cue, like the poor cat 'i the adage, a bird hurtled into the crawl space beside them like a projectile, whizzing past Marian's ear and out through the narrow opening at the side of the cottage with extraordinary speed. Marian stood up in shocked amazement and bumped her head noisily and painfully on the firm plywood.

"Fuck!"

Ruth said, "Language!"

The presence of the nest explained the perpetual comings and goings of Roma and Bartley, perhaps of their friends and relations too. It didn't seem possible to Marian that two small birds could give so readily the impression of a crowd. It wasn't that they were noisy; rather, they were around all the time, circling and diving, peeling off in echelon or sitting motionless in front of her at ten yards' remove on bare spiny twigs or hidden in thick pine boughs. Their speed, their surety, their swift instincts confounded her and caused a terrible commitment to their survival to rise up in her breast. Nothing must happen to them but good, she resolved, and she was desperately, bitterly, dashed to learn from one of her sons that the baby swallows had all died.

"Ohhh, no, don't tell me . . .," she said.

"I saw the broken shells, Mum. Maybe I shouldn't have said."

Neil could recognise the signs of his mother's genuine sorrow. He took a spoonful of Captain Crunch and shivered; the cream was chilled and the morning fresh. "Why not go and see for yourself?" he said, not unkindly. "I might have been wrong."

"How are the mosquitoes?" she said morosely.

"It's cool. It's cool." So she went.

The fascination of the process, the cycle, pulled her under and into the shade. The nest was visible, but only just, at this hour. There were — oh, damn it — half-shells and little bits of broken shell lying here and there on the rocks just below the nest. She picked up a half-shell and stuck it on the end of the little finger of her right hand. It looked like a terribly smart cloche hat of the 1920s, such a chic colour too! She wiggled the finger then forced herself to peer into the dim light trying to see what lay in the nest.

She was able to make out what looked like a pile of slimy mucous, a kind of muddle of bones and half-formed feathers and semi-liquid greyish matter without vital form. The look of the mess almost made her gag. She withdrew her head and started back outside. A swallow — possibly Bartley — passed her as she left, heading gracefully towards the nest with something hanging from his beak. This detail didn't light up in her head for several days, well on towards the beginning of July. Those slithery glistening minute exposed tendons, that liquid, the failure of generation. She strove to put the matter from her mind.

One Sunday afternoon she received better news. She was monitoring a double-header from Pittsburgh for Neil, Ruth, Daisy and John who were down at the water. She caught sight of Ruth climbing slowly from the dockside and called down to her, "Pirates leading by two runs in the third on Parker's double, Moreno and Foli scoring."

Ruth turned to relay the news to the beach and Marian sat down and let herself relax in the sun. Insects buzzed outside the mesh. Broadcasters exchanged rhythmic dialogue. Crowd noises in the background. Impressive recurrences of between-innings commercials. Sleep in the heat.

"Mumma Mumma Mumma, they're not dead," shouted Ruth from somewhere underfoot, "they're not dead at all, they're sitting in the nest; oh, they look so funny, come down and look. Hey Mumma!"

Marian roused herself. A huge powerboat passed in front of the cottage, the discharge of its spark plugs causing a rasping buzz on the radio like the roar of a power saw.

"Come on, Mumma," urged Ruth, "down by the nest."

There was thrilling vitality and certainty in the child's call. Marian's shoulders were covered in a fine light sweat. She trembled, blinked, then trotted out the side door and around to the front of the building where Ruthie beckoned to her from the crawl space. She was crouched beside the nest making a lot of noise, while Roma and Bartley buzzed around her angrily, trying to drive her off.

"You're frightening the mother," said Marian.

"I know, I know, I know, but you've got to come and see them this one time; they're so funny with their little heads all in a row."

This description charmed Marian. She decided that one quick

examination would not be traumatic. She inclined her head and climbed in under the flooring and there, sure enough, the four nestlings sat piled up on top of one another with very little room — none — to move about.

They were an absurd sight, feathers forming thickly, heads almost circular, all in profile. They had minute, whitish-yellow bills which opened and shut avidly and they were all, without doubt, very much alive. They bore a farcical resemblance, in their insistence on remaining strictly in profile, to much mediaeval religious art whether in mosaic, fresco, or painting. Marian was reminded of dozens of groups of saints, viewed in right profile and superimposed one upon the other, with geometrically regular round haloes piled up like gilt coins on a dark plate. Some Biblical incident was insistently recalled, most likely from Ottonian representation in gospel book or fresco. All at once she had it: in the way the pulsing bodies were heaped together, in the pattern of unblinking eyes, working mouths, perfectly round little skulls, the small birds evoked the attitudes of the apostles rocked about in the stern of the fishing boat when Christ stilled the waves. There was the same awareness that something unexpected was about to take place. The same profoundly human confusion.

Bartley and Roma screamed in busy anger. Ruth and Marian withdrew. The radio hooted in excitement. Somebody had just got the go-ahead run. . .

Coke adds life, Coca-Cola adds life . . .

Maybe Bartley and Roma were feeding the kids on Coke. The nestlings got bigger and bigger and their home bulged. Once or twice in ensuing weeks, Marian surprised one of the parents in the act of shoring up the side of the nest, working fresh twigs into a space which threatened nestling-fallout. The grown swallow was perched nervously on the crossbeam, pecking away at shreds of twisted woody stuff, working it into the crevices, making everything tight. Under here, rain was not a problem.

How clever of them, thought Marian, then she remembered that the action was, after all, dictated purely by instinct. The birds could be conceded no moral credit for their sense of parental responsibility. They were always around the nest now, feeding the next generation with bits of matter almost invisibly small. Marian never saw any worms, but was able to identify the act of feeding. The parents would post themselves beside the nest with their backs to her. They would make that funny unmistakeable dip of the shoulders. Competitive pipings from the young, almost inaudible. Should be on film, Marian thought. Disney would make a killing with this. She never actually witnessed the passing of food from mouth to mouth.

The small birds grew and survived, crowded and hampered in their movements as they were. How would they learn to fly, Marian wondered. How would they ever find room to move their wings; how could they see at all? What could they hear, how receive instruction in the difficult art of self-powered flight?

By mid-July crisis impended; there was no more room in the nest. In a day or so they would start falling out. The nest was balanced over bare, flinty, ancient rock. A fall would make mush of infant bones. She worried, knowing that this was absurd, that the species would perpetuate itself with losses according to statistical norms. A couple of the young would fail to negotiate first flight, but so what? We all have to take our chances. It made her laugh to imagine that the classical music, the commercials and the baseball broadcasts would form part of the inherited natural sound patterns heard and instinctually assimilated by the next generation of barn and/or cliff swallows. Maybe the Coca-Cola jingle would turn up in their territorial calls next summer. Fusion of art and nature.

On Saturday, 19 July, she was lurking near the nest, thinking she might anticipate some infant attempt at flight, catch the creature if the attempt should go badly. She might retrieve some squeaking Icarus before he hit rock, a basket catch like those the outfielders kept making in National League play as described in the summer-long sequence of Expo broadcasts going on in the swallows' sky. In a bird's mind, the account of the game would seem like the voice of God, superior to the visible order, coming from elsewhere. Something given, a part of pure life.

She moved over to stand looking at the infants. They were fully formed, she thought, all set to go. Above her on the porch came one of those irregular broadcast interruptions and the game faded away into a distant blur of competing signals from thousands of

miles off. Invisible influences crossed in the upper air. She turned
her head to look out from under and then she heard the strange
sound.

A swift-running rushing breathy sound, blurring, whistling, like
being kissed by the angels, whispering, running past her hair.

When she looked back, the nest was empty.

There was nothing on the rocks.

She began to sniffle, then repressed the impulse.

Now there would be six particular swallows to be picked out of
the circling crowd. She wondered if she would be able to recognise
them. Could she draw them home by familiar sound? Would the
voice of Bob Kerr call them to himself? It seemed a better than
fifty-fifty wager. Afternoons on the sunporch lengthened; she
began to struggle with binoculars, trying to focus directly on the
branches close to the cottage. It ought to be possible to get a look
at one of the birds in tight closeup, almost as though perched on
the end of the glasses. They were too quick for her. Every time
she got one of them into focus it would dart away. She would
swing the glasses to try and follow the flight but the milky and
confusing impressions caused by the nylon screening made her
blink and lose track of the motion.

Eventually Marian's nature studies began to decline in interest.
The glasses were more an impediment to observation than anything. She would catch herself mumbling, I could see perfectly
well if it weren't for these damn glasses. The annoying element
of the situation, which she recognised as fundamentally comic,
was that the life of the birds grew more fascinating and complex
just as she began to be bored with it because of her natural incapac-
ity. This paradoxical relation struck her as exceedingly lifelike. She
let the glasses alone after that, content to enjoy the weather.

It was almost aggressively warm and sunny on the sunporch in
the August afternoons. The illumination that flooded the space
reached an unmixed golden tone which it retained very late. It
was hot and sweaty, not just in a light perspiration but in big
drops which stood out on the forehead, arms, and neck and ran
down inside bathing suits. Marian felt she could almost swim,
certainly slither around, in this home-style sauna. She would put
her head down on her arms and sit there, wet, hot, solitary and
happy.

She kept hearing wings, wings, and the ballgame on the radio and new recordings of ancient instruments playing the infant symphonies of Mozart. Birds all over. Sitting on pine branches right outside, closer. Very close as though listening to baby Mozart or the game fading and returning. Swimming in the heat and the gold light. She moved her head idly, turning a cheek down into her bent elbow and feeling the wet in the hair on the back of her neck, warm sweat on her shoulder blades. Pipings. Soft calls. She lifted her head from her arms and opened and shut her eyes, trying to clear them in the blurring sunshine. The birds clustered just outside, listening to the game in their own space.

Marian whispered, "They're all around me." She glanced to the right and caught a glimpse of a young swallow motionless in the corner of her eye. Directly in front of her hovered a plump little dark silhouette, changing size in the wash of intense gold and blue. She blinked and looked again from left to right, picking them out one after another looking in at her and listening, leaning, tiny bright eyes gleaming in at her through the net.

August Nights

The banner

"WHAT'LL WE PAINT ON IT; what can you do with a name like Orlando Saint-James?"

"Could we put, 'Don't make Orlando Furioso?' "

"I don't understand you, Treesha. What does that mean?"

I said, "It's the name of some poem. And don't call me 'Treesha.' You know perfectly well what my name is."

"Patsy," said Sally. She spilled a little tin of silver paint.

"Not Patsy."

"Patty? Little Peppermint Patty?"

"You know my name."

She wiped silver paint on her T-shirt which made the cotton stiff. It stood out over her nipples. "You're such a straight arrow," she said, "you must have a sour pickle up your asshole."

"Maybe I do and maybe I don't."

"'Patricia,' for God's sakes!"

"At least I don't rub my thighs with Coppertone. At least I don't wear shorts that look like they're painted on my butt. I don't wear a skirt on the Métro and change in the toilet during BP."

Sally can't keep her mind on anything. "What about 'Ollie's Dollies'?" she said, surprising me. I thought it was cute.

"Let me think about it. What kind of cartoon would go with it?"

"You could draw us like a team of ball-girls."

"Listen Sally," I said, "we don't want to make ourselves into a pair of Baseball Annies. I bet you they're already talking about you in the bullpen."

She said, "That's why I wear shorts. I don't want them looking up my skirt any more than you do, Treesha. Why can't I call you that anyway? When Cookie Money asked about you, I told him you were called Treesha and he thought that was wonderful."

"When was that?"

"After the first game of the Pirates' doubleheader when he came out to loosen up before starting in the nightcap. I told him you said he should be starting every day."

"What did he say?"

"He said, 'I don't tell Hammacher how to manage the club and he don't tell me how to play second base.'"

"No, I mean what did he say about me?"

"He said, 'Treesha, Treesha, Treemonisha, she must be one foxy sister.'"

"Well I be dog!" I said. I felt pleased. "Cookie Money can call me anything he likes. He gets the job done in the field and at the plate."

"Orlando says Cookie sometimes doesn't execute."

"Ballplayers shouldn't knock each other," I said.

"They're just young guys away from home, Treesha, with the same desires as the guys in the office."

"One foxy sister?"

"That's what he say, girl."

"When we finish this, let's make one for Cookie," I said.

"Hokey-cokey."

"He'd be easy to come up with: 'Money talks.' 'We're in the Money.'"

"Money is the root of boll weevils."

"Take your Money out in Cookies."

"Keep it clean, soul sister," said Sally, "let's finish this banner. Who'll carry the banner? Sister Sarah will carry the banner."

"Hard-hearted Hannah, the vamp of Savannah, can carry the banner," I said, pulling the sheet straight out on the floor of my bedroom. There was just enough space for it between the bed and the vanity. It was an old sheet, pale pink, queen size, without any holes. I took a narrow brush and began to draw in two chicks in ball-girl costumes like the ones those girls in Philly wear, Mary-Sue and that other one. Mary-Sue got married early this season but then she was back on the third-base foul line right after. I wonder what her husband thinks about it. She gets on TV all the time and I have to admit she has great legs. Better than mine but not as great as Sally's. Sally Slither! That's what the guys on the team call her. You can see them looking up from the track or the bullpen or the players' field entrance whenever we're up beside the foul pole in right.

"Hey Slither, Sally Slither, hey look this way."

She pretends not to notice. Gene Frumkin, the long man in the bullpen, keeps passing up notes on the end of a stick. She throws them away every time, just crumples them up and flips them back onto the warning track. She showed me one. All it said was, "Phone number???"

"Who does he think he is?"

"He has a three-year contract," I said.

"He can be gone, just like that, if he doesn't produce," Sally said. "He's only the tenth man on the staff."

"It could be worse," I said. "He could be the tenth man on the Jays' staff."

"That's a bad ball club," we said simultaneously.

"Imagine DH-ing with the Jays," Sally said.

"Would you go out with the DH on the Jays?"

She had to think it over. "He'd be old and slow but able to hit with power. No, I don't think I could bring myself to do that. Who is it this year? It used to be Solaita."

"Solaita only hit against righthanders and, anyway, he's now in Samoa or Japan or somewhere."

I waited and Sally started to giggle and we said together, "Well, that's what happens when you can't hit the curve ball."

"That applies to everything in life," I said.

I brushed in the drawings of us as ball-girls, trying to make the likenesses as close as possible. I gave us very short shorts and I made the figure of Sally longer and taller than mine. I'm not obese or anything, I'm just not as tall as she is. I drew us in team jackets with the logo very carefully lined-in, and I gave Sally the number *100%* on the sleeves of her jacket; you could read it easily. I put Cookie Money's number on my jacket just for fun, a big number *44*. I made our faces really recognisable. I'm a taffy-blond and Sally has long shiny bronze-coloured hair down to her hips almost. Of course, she doesn't wear it out loose in the bleachers or even in the 300-level seats over the bullpen where we usually sit. It would blow all around if she didn't loop it up under her baseball cap.

"They look just like us," she said, looking at what I'd done. "Now paint in Ollie's head and shoulders just above us and in between. Make it good."

That's not as easy as it sounds. Ollie keeps growing a little bit of fuzz low down on his cheeks and under his chin. When it gets hairy and gross, he shaves it off; then he'll go with a moustache for a few weeks. He's very unpredictable. I gave him a clean shave in the picture and when it was finished anybody would have identified it as *"Orlando Saint-James, National League All-Star Right Fielder, 1977, 1978, 1980, GO OLLIE GO"* (which was how I lettered it). Above that, in huge blue letters I put *"OLLIE'S DOLLIES"* with wiggly speed-lines leading down to the cartoons of Sally and me. Stretched out on the floor, it looked cool.

When we got it to the stadium we took it out to Section 345 where we usually sit. The ushers know us and they mostly let us do things that ordinary fans couldn't get away with. We got to our seats around six-fifteen in time to watch the Cubbies' infield practice. They had another fifteen minutes to go which gave us plenty of time. Sally had a big staple gun, one of those industrial appliances which can fasten anything to anything. I think she borrowed it from her father's workbench. It's a tool you have to be careful with. If you drove a staple into yourself, would it ever hurt! We draped the banner over the railing just above the bullpen and the players' field entrance. I held the edge of the material rolled over the bar and Sally stapled it into place, tacking it in lightly at first until we had it attached along the whole width of the sheet. We let it flop down so that it was hanging below us against the base of the stands. It began to curl lazily and blow around in the breeze; we could see that it needed to be stapled along the bottom edge. Some of the Cubbie outfielders started looking over at us and laughing. The old punk of an usher wouldn't let us climb down onto the field even though Sally could have done it easily.

The Cubs went on hollering at us, "Slither, Slither, hey Slither, hey Sally, come on down and pin it up."

I think we're pretty well-known around the league. I noticed the camera crew looking over our way so I started jumping up and down and waving my arms. It was the middle of August and very warm. I started to sweat. The TV guys focussed on us and I could see our image on the monitor. I knew they'd try to get a shot of us during the telecast. It's something you get used to, especially when you're with Sally. By now the outfielders were standing right below us at the edge of the track. Some of the things they said were pretty crude but most of them were nice.

"Who's the little blonde?"

"Hey hey hey Sally Slither, how's your big buddy Ollie?"

"Who's the greatest right-fielder since Ruth?"

"Winfield?"

Sally gave the finger to the guy who said that.

"Parker?"

"Clemente?"

"Clemente's dead," I yelled at them just as Cookie Money came onto the field; he was carrying three gloves — Cookie's the best utility man in OB — which meant he might be figuring on playing tonight. He looked up at us and smiled. Cookie's never going to get 500 at-bats in a season but he's been around long enough to get in his four years for the pension and he can play almost anywhere, outfield, infield, even catch a little. He had the outsized catcher's mitt with him — he'd be catching Angel-spit Busby's knuckleball during the warmup. He put his three gloves carefully on the bench in the bullpen enclosure beside the telephone and came over and looked right up into Section 345.

"Hello, Treesha," he said.

"Hello."

"You girls need a little help? Here, let me tack that thing down for you before it blow away in the cool breeze."

"It isn't that cool," I said. I was wet under my arms and my hair would be going stringy.

"Throw me down your stapler," he said.

Sally looked down at him and leaned over as far as she could. An usher came down the steps and held her around the waist. Two of the TV crew aimed hand-held cameras at us. One of them said, "Let them check this out in the booth."

"Catch," said Sally.

She dropped the gun. Cookie made a funny little basket-catch, letting the gun drop almost to the track and scooping it out of the dirt at the last minute.

"The great hands," he said to himself. He stretched the sheet taut over a kind of plywood frame around the dugout roof where he could easily staple it to the wood.

"Don't let it get out of line," said Sally loudly.

The Cubs were strolling away towards their dugout. One of them turned around and said, "Hey Money, you setting things up for the big man?"

We could see the banner spread out straight and tight on the TV monitor. It looked sensational. *OLLIE'S DOLLIES.* We were sure they'd shoot it during the telecast.

At 7:12 P.M. Ollie came on the field down by the umpires' entrance behind home plate. He must have been doing some interviews in the press room because he usually comes out from the dugout just before game time. He's had this thing with the nerve in the back of his leg and a wrist problem so he can't work out as hard as he'd like. He tells Sally a lot of things about his physical condition, ever since she visited him in the hospital when he had the fracture. I guess he was in the hospital for six weeks and all his folks live in L.A. Ollie isn't married. He's really just a big kid. He can't be more than a year or two older than Sally and I.

He sauntered out behind first base and did some leg-stretching exercises, bending one knee and then the other, stretching the hamstring away out on one leg and bending the other knee deep. He did three wind sprints and then went into the dugout. He didn't seem to notice the sign but Cookie, who was chasing wandering knuckleballs, looked up at us and winked.

"He saw it all right, ladies. Don't worry your heads none about that."

Once the game got started Ollie kept looking over at the banner and grinning. In the fifth inning he made a spectacular catch against the fence to end a Cubbies' rally. We were going crazy in the stands and he looked up at us and tipped his cap. I'm sure they saw it on the network. Late in the game he went after a long foul ball, out in the corner past the bullpen; he must have spotted us running over to watch the catch. The ball landed in some unoccupied bleachers' seats out-of-play and rebounded onto the field, but you couldn't see that from home plate. He flipped the ball back into the stands right in front of us, real sneaky, at the same time signalling it was out of reach. I got to the ball first. I've still got it. I copied his signature onto it from the official team guide in blue ballpoint.

It was obvious that he'd be player-of-the-game which meant that we wouldn't get to see him later because he'd be on the post-game show and wouldn't get his shower till too late. We kept shouting at him through the late innings.

"Ollie, we've got a CAKE, A CAKE FOR FRIDAY," I yelled, right off the end of my tongue or the top of my head or somewhere. He started laughing and then the game was over.

The cake

We knew it was his birthday but we didn't know for sure how old he was until I checked him in the *Baseball Encyclopaedia* and it turned out he was only a year older than us, turning twenty-four. He'd been with the club since he was barely twenty when they brought him up for a look in September, and all through the next four seasons. He was selected as an All-Star in his first full season when he was twenty-one and again the next year. Then he missed a year when he had injuries and trouble with Hammacher; the club claimed he was a disciplinary problem. That was all just contract-jockeying; they were trying to intimidate his agent. Last winter he signed his new contract, another three-year deal, but this time worth three million dollars. Right away he got selected for the All-Star game again. Ollie can't handle anger, his own or the club's, and he hates to fight. I know what his problem is, and I feel I understand what he's going through better than anybody. He's really only a boy. He's practically world-famous. He's making all this money. He has groupies and Baseball Annies hanging onto him whenever he goes on the road. He misses his Mom and family. Just because he can run, throw, hit, hit with power and judge the right-field wall in the stadium perfectly, everybody wants him to behave like a third-base coach or somebody like that, a manager's best buddy. Everybody knows they gave him Cookie Money for a roommate to quiet him down because Cookie is the sweetest, quietest guy on the club, not old, not a veteran, but not a threat either.

I mixed up this really disgusting icing for Ollie's cake, a blend of vegetable colouring, gelatine for stiffener and whipped cream chilled together for twenty-four hours before we iced the cake. I mixed it in the team colours in three bowls and whipped plenty of icing sugar and vanilla into it. When I say it was disgusting I mean you could hardly keep yourself from pigging out on it. It was stiff and sweet and creamy, sexy as anything. The cake was easy. We just baked three big white layers in different-sized tins. On Friday afternoon I took off from work sick and went home and plastered the icing between the three layers. I used mostly white icing to go between but I swirled in some of the red and the blue to give a marble effect. I pressed the three layers down, one on top of the other. The icing bulged out around the sides. I swirled some around my ring finger and licked it off and it was really weird gunk. You could eat it with a knife and fork.

I had to wait till Sally came over before I iced the top and sides because I'd promised her she could do some. She got to my place around four-thirty, dressed to kill. I could see she had big plans for the evening, a single game with the Cardinals beginning at 7:35 P.M. Plenty of time to do the cake and the candles and the writing on top. Of course, Sally had to get undressed before she went near the bowls of icing. She was wearing bikini-briefs and no bra. I'll bet it's the first time anybody ever iced a birthday cake for an outfielder while topless.

"If I get this stuff on my shorts I'll never get it off."

"You're not wearing your shorts, Sally."

"That's why I took them off, dingaling," she said, licking her fingers. She kept smearing the sides of the cake with the tips of her fingers like a first-grader in finger-painting class.

"Don't mess up the cake," I said. She had topping on her legs and her panties.

"I know what I'm doing," she said. She kept building up layers of different-coloured icing until the top of the cake looked like a pennant or a swatch of bunting, all striped. We had some big fat candles and there was room on the cake for two dozen of them, which gives you an idea of the size. When she'd done what she thought was enough, she went into the bathroom and cleaned herself off. I think she took a shower but I'm not sure. I was too busy putting on the writing with a bag of blue icing and a decorating nozzle:

HAPPY TWENTY-FOURTH BIRTHDAY OLLIE
FROM SLITHER AND TREESHA

I put Sally's name first because she knows Ollie a bit better than I do even though I was the first one to actually get to talk to him one night in the roller rink near the players' parking area. We call it the roller rink because it's a big smooth space built up between several connecting ramps which go up to the 700 level and down past the 200 level to the indoor parking spaces for VIPs where some of the players disappear after the games if they're not going home on the Métro. That's where Sally and I met Ollie one night in 1979 just before he had his injury problem. Afterwards she started slithering into the hospital to talk to him while the rest of the team was on the road. During the off-season he used to call her up about once a month from L.A., just to talk.

"I can *talk* to you," he'd say, according to Sally. I never heard him say anything like that. He mostly says things a few words at a time like, "Do you dig?" or "Whoo-eee."

We stuck the cake in the refrigerator while we finished getting dressed to give it a chance to chill and to keep it out of the way; it was over two feet tall. I had to slide a couple of racks out of the bottom compartment to make room for it. It was in the fridge for over an hour and when we took it out the icing was set solid. We got it into a big cardboard carton and down the elevator and onto the Métro. It was heavy so we took turns carrying it while the other one went in front to keep the passengers from bumping into it.

Crossing town, we began to experience technical difficulties. We couldn't find a place to sit down until we passed the Berri-de Montigny station. It was terribly smelly and hot in the car because of the crowd. By the time we reached the stadium, the icing was starting to run. I took the box from Sally and made her walk along in front of me. Boy, that thing was heavy. I could smell the sugar in the heat. It wasn't any cooler when we got up into the stadium and went out to our seats; it looked like we might be getting into one of those late-August heat waves.

The lights were already turned on when we got to Section 345 and there was a heavy haze hanging over the building, a smog-effect. We ripped the top off the carton as soon as we reached our seats; sure enough the icing was beginning to drip and sag. I was afraid that it might go liquid on us and drip down all over the seats, which would have made a terrible mess, but it just clung to the edges and sides of the top layer like rubber festoons.

It was crowded in the stadium; there were no empty seats near us. We sat the cake down on one of the pair that belonged to us and inserted the ticket stub in the icing where the usher could check the seat number. We took turns sitting in the other seat; when one of us had to stand she could lean over the railing to talk to the guys in the bullpen. Cookie was down there and Gene Frumkin and some others we knew. We told them to tell Orlando about the cake so that he could look up and see it. By the top of the third inning he'd spotted it and he waved to us. I was sitting beside it just then and I got my arms under it and held it up high where he could see it. When I lifted it up in front of my face, my arms pulled my T-shirt up out of my jeans, leaving my stomach bare. Some real cretin stuck his finger in my belly-button and wiggled it around. I nearly dropped the cake on the man in front of me, a sour old Pepsi who was complaining about icing on his collar.

He certainly wasn't the one who'd tickled my stomach; there wasn't any way I could identify the person who'd done it. This made me feel frightened but there was nobody I could tell about it. I tried to say something to Sally when we went to the ladies' room but she was on such a high I couldn't get anything across to her.

"Honestly Sally, he stuck his finger right in here. I could feel the fingernail and he scratched me."

"They're just a bunch of old farts from the east end. Forget about it. Nobody will dare lay a finger on you."

"But that's exactly what he did and I didn't like it. It scared me."

"Baby, that's one of the risks you have to take. Come on, let's go back and shake our cake."

A crowd of men had formed around the cake when we got back to our seats, looking like they wouldn't mind a slice of it, but we just pushed our way through them and grabbed it. It was the fifth-inning break and the grounds' crew was out raking the basepaths during the stop in the action. Orlando saw us come down to the railing with the cake; he gave a big smile and trotted over from right field to call up to us from the warning track.

"Lower it down," he said. I had to hold on to Sally's bum while she leaned way over, balancing the cake between her arms.

The announcer said, *"C'est aujourd'hui le vingt-quatrième anniversaire du voltigeur de droit Orlando 'Ollie' Saint-James."*

The crowd gave us a standing ovation; dozens of them took pictures. Ollie stuck his finger in the icing, then in his mouth. He smiled up at us.

"It's cool," he said. "I like that. Be around the parking lot after the game, the 'B' lot. We'll take the cake home and have a ball."

There was a big laugh and a cheer when I hauled Sally up in my arms. She nearly over-balanced once but we managed to get back to our places to watch the rest of the game. We won without coming to bat in the bottom of the ninth.

The crowd took its time getting out of the park; it was more than twenty minutes before we could get down to the players' parking lot. Most of the fans who hung around after the game seemed to be over by the front of the building between the beer garden and the Métro entrance. Hardly any of them came back where the cars were. It's surprising how many of the players take the Métro home. It's easy and convenient and quick and most of them look pretty ordinary away from the field. Frumkin looks like a used-car salesman. He's got a wife somewhere but you'd never know it to see him in action. A real punker.

Angel-spit Busby looks impossible. If you didn't know him for sure, you wouldn't believe he existed.

We waited in a shadowy corner where the ramps come down at two different angles to a flat space broken up by a row of cast concrete pillars which support the upper levels. This would have been waste space only somebody thought to use it for a small parking lot where about fifty cars fit between pillars. I don't much like to hang around here because there are plenty of dark spaces behind the uprights where somebody could come out and make a grab at you. I think we may be the only girls who know about the place or maybe the only ones smart enough to figure on running into one of the stars in the dark.

Ollie brings his car to the stadium once or twice during a home stand when he plans to go out somewhere after a game. Tonight he took a fairly long time to get dressed. It got very quiet in the shadows under the ramps. There's a door in the cement wall that only seems to open from inside. I've tried the handle often. It leads to a corridor directly to the home team's clubhouse. You can't open it from outside unless you know how. A couple of players came out and drove away in their cars and then Hammacher, the manager. He looked over and spotted us lurking there and he scowled. All of a sudden he said, "Don't fill Ollie up with that shit, Slither." We didn't know he knew anything about either of us. We stood there with our mouths open while he drove off. He honked softly twice and winked at us as he drove past us and down the ramp.

A few minutes after that, Ollie came out and picked us up. It was like a dream. He kept staring at the cake and licking his lips. "A cake for me. Man, you so *nice!* We gonna eat the whole thing."

We got in his car and balanced the cake on the back seat. He drove us down the ramp and out under the huge fluorescent-light standards by the entrance. His car was an enormous purple boat, I swear to God, purple or mauve or fuchsia. It glittered and sparkled under the orange lights.

Ollie and Cookie share an apartment together just below Sherbrooke in a highrise on Guy. You drive into the building up a lane running in from Saint-Mathieu. When we came to the end of the lane, while the garage doors were opening automatically with a rumbling whir, Ollie put the car in park and Sally slithered over right beside him. She was just about sitting on his lap. They looked at me without saying a word. I opened the door on the right side and got out. Then the big fuchsia barge rolled in through the door. That was the last I saw of the cake.

I wandered through to Guy along the walkway beside the building. It was past midnight. I don't like walking alone at that time of night but the lights are so bright there and the Friday-night crowds so thick that I didn't feel too frightened. I crossed Guy and went and sat on a bench in the parkette at the corner of de Maisonneuve. I might have been sitting there for an hour when I suddenly realised that a man was standing beside the bench looking down at me.

"Don't you have a home to go to, Treesha?" he said. It was Cookie Money. I think he'd just come out of the Métro station across the street. A utility infielder-outfielder, wouldn't you know?

I said, "Certainly I have a home and anyway why aren't you in bed? You've got a day game tomorrow."

"Uh-uh, re-scheduled twi-night doubleheader. I don't think I can go upstairs yet anyhow."

"Oh Cookie, I'll make a banner and a cake for you."

He said, "I don't need no banner."

The roller rink

In September they were only in town at Labour Day and the week after. Then they had to travel all around the N.L. East to play the other contenders and work off seven doubleheaders from postponements that had piled up over the summer. We hardly got to see them the first week of the month. Two short series with the Mets and the Buccos and the weather turned cold. Sally wouldn't talk about anything but her night with Orlando Saint-James. Nothing happened. Amazing! That's all. Nothing happened.

"He ate it all?"

"He was going to eat the candles but I hid them."

"You're kidding!"

"He loved his cake, Treesha, every tiny crumb."

"And nothing . . . ?"

"Not a thing," she said smugly, "he thinks I'm still in my teens." She put her arm up beside her cheek and squinted along it, admiring the peach fuzz on her skin. I could have slapped her. "We sat and talked till two-thirty. He says it's the hardest thing about the season, trying to unwind."

"You helped him unwind?"

"When I left he was so wound down that he went to sleep on the divan in the front room."

"Full of icing?"

"Hammacher isn't going to like that," Sally said. "He's a mean man. He isn't playing Cookie. Ollie says Cookie is dying to play. He carries those three gloves around with him and he has a bat in his hands in the dugout all the time but Hammacher only uses him to pinch-hit against southpaws. I don't think that's fair, do you?"

"You look after Ollie and I'll look after Cookie."

"Do you think he liked you, Treesha? What did you do?"

"We sat in the park and waited till it was time for him to go in."

"Till three o'clock?"

"It was way past that."

"And the Métro shut and the busses not running. What did you do? How did you get home?"

"Cookie got me a cab."

"He paid for it?"

"Yes," I said.

"What about tonight?"

I said, "I'll come all right, but it's going to be cold in right field."

"Then bring your roller skates and keep warm."

We weren't going to see the guys again until the final days of the season when the divisional championship would be settled. It would probably be decided while the club was on the road. When Ollie and Cookie came home everything would be changed. So the final night of the Pirates' series we brought our roller skates to the stadium in over-the-shoulder bags and put them on during the pre-game announcements. We started skating all over the corridors behind the 300-level seats. There was hardly anybody in the park; the attendance always drops off in the second week of September. Especially for mid-week games. There might have been 10,000 people which looks like nothing in the stadium. We kept ourselves cheerful and warm on skates. We had boots in the team colours; my wheels were bright red and hers were blue. We had little short white skirts. We looked like backup singers in a disco act.

The hardest part was skating up the ramps towards the upper levels. We had to bust our buns to make the climb and could only do it by skating from one side of the ramp to the other instead of sailing straight up. Coming down was something else. We had a big crowd watching us by the start of the fourth inning. The team was losing; half the guys in our section came back inside out of the wind to watch us skate. We got them started cheering and betting while we were digging for the top of the ramp.

"My money's on the little red wheels; who's taking the blue ones?"

Sally took my hand when we turned and started down. We knew without talking about it what we were going to do. We started at the 700 level and whooshed down, cutting to one side and then the other like we'd been doing it all our lives. Coming off the first ramp we joined both hands and whirled around and around. Then we pushed off down the next ramp, first on one leg, then on the other. When we came to the very bottom, we started to scamper around the parking area, chasing each other in and out between the concrete pillars. There were chilly fans lined up along the ramps clapping their hands and cheering. We finished up by skidding to a stop, hips together and arms in the air. And then we bowed. Nobody watching the game action. The ushers were laughing right along with the rest of the guys and the team won their game and left in a hurry to catch their charter to Philadelphia.

They had a bad two weeks on the road. The only good thing about that trip was that Cookie got to play in most of the games; his bat got hot and Hammacher decided to overlook his defensive deficiencies at second base to keep him in the batting order. He was collecting a couple of hits in every game. It started to seem like he might wind up with as many as 250 at-bats on the year; that would give him some leverage at contract time. Cookie has always been able to hit but he isn't a power hitter so he isn't a good bet as a DH in the American League. If he had just a bit more power he'd almost be a star. But there it is. You have to learn to accept your natural limitations.

The whole of the last six days of the season we skated our little rear ends off. Honest to God, I lost seven pounds zipping and zapping up and down the ramps and the passageways but we couldn't get the guys to notice us. Cookie wasn't in the bullpen for the last games. He sat in the dugout next to Hammacher, clutching a bat, or he was in the field. I know he isn't a great second baseman. I realise that. Once he went after a short fly ball that Ollie should have taken. They collided and Cookie hurt his shoulder. We missed the accident. We were in under the stands skating around and teasing the guys when we heard the roar and then the silence. When we skated back outside Cookie was just getting up, still hanging on to the ball. When he trotted back to his position, the crowd gave him the biggest cheer he ever got in his major-league career. On the very next play he booted a ground ball.

On the last day they still had a chance to tie for the lead if they could get to Carlton. Hah! Who gets to Carlton in that situation? Hammacher went with the percentages the whole afternoon; he didn't start Cookie. They got locked in a one-run ball game and couldn't do a thing at the plate. Ollie looked at a called third strike for the final out of the game and the season.

It was awful. Neither of us cried. We picked up our over-the-shoulder bags and pushed through the crowds. The fans made way for us but didn't say anything or lay any bets. We skated in circles for hours and they all went away. At last Ollie and Cookie came out of the sealed door for the fuchsia Cadillac and didn't even look at us as we twirled around them. Cookie said to Ollie, "Damn, I sure the man gonna start me today. I sure!"

They got in the car and drove to sunny California.

Every Piece Different

For John Metcalf

HE MUST HAVE HAD A GOOD MORNING she thought as she sauntered into the house about 2:45, rather late for lunch. He was lounging beside the dining-room table with an afternoon paper and one or two pieces of opened mail in front of him. He evidently heard her come in, but made scarcely any acknowledgement of her arrival. A bad sign, she decided, automatically preparing herself to humour him and immediately remembering that she had stopped humouring him and begun to reply to his bitching with her own complaints about a decade ago. They were now completely familiar with one another's litany of troubles. There seemed no profit in rehearsing them. What his tilted head and defensively-poised, lifted, moving shoulder expressed (apart from possible apprehension of the increasing deafness of late middle age) wasn't exactly bitterness nor resigned acceptance of defeat. She knew to the last almost invisible nuance of attitude how expressive of his mental state the disposition of his body could be. She had known nobody else who conferred by the tangle of their arms and legs around the limbs of their chair the same peculiar state of tensed anxiety, a holding oneself in against the sudden impulse to cry out in awareness of frustration and the onset of despair.

A few people can't get their bodies right, can never place them in a relaxed attitude which fits the space they're in. Herself a painter, painfully aware of the dictates of form in space, something of a master of colour and composition, inclining these days to the pursuit of the sculptor's resources, she felt a constant physical disturbance amounting almost to an itch — an unscratchable itch — at the sight of his discomfort. His head was turned three-quar-

36

ters away from her, she could see his hair and the trim hairline at the back of the neck. She cut his hair for him and was partially responsible for the neatness of that hairline but the small fine dark-brown hair which grew from the back of his crown down along the neck — the last place on the skull which hadn't gone quite grey — was the product of his body chemistry, intermittent resistance to the process of aging.

Cutting his hair she often stood back as the longer strands fell away from the top of the head and admired the tight, close, almost furry texture of the neck hair, the symmetrical curve of the hairline behind the ear, down the moving neck muscles and across below the other ear. She used that hairline and the pictorial convention she had evolved to suggest the texture of his hair, in many of her works, the features of the face almost never. She found the shape of the back of his head more interesting than the face.

In the rear three-quarter view she could see the right ear and below it the beginnings of new beard. He had not shaved for three days, usually went unshaven for about that time before deciding once again that growing a beard was a dirty, oily process which he could not sustain. He would shave tomorrow, she knew, for any beard he allowed to mature would come out quite white. She could see the right cheek and just the tip of the nose. His skin was still remarkably smooth, even under the three days' growth, lined beside the eyes and when he smiled, deeply-lined across the cheeks. In repose his cheek seemed that of a much younger man; stillness gave his face the youthfulness observable in sleeping folk; animation aged him. There was a criss-crossing of veins in the skin of the nose, unusual, difficult to account for in a man so abstemious.

"Anything in the mail?"

"A medal-dealer's catalogue for the boys, duplicates of transcripts for a fellowship application and a magazine about horses for the girls. Two announcements of openings for you. A small cheque for me and an appeal for funds from my alma mater, what a hope!"

"Have you ever given them anything?"

"Not a thin dime," he declared with deep satisfaction. "Let them show some awareness of what I've done. Then we'll see."

"You've spoken there. Haven't you given talks there?"

"Always privately, in the context of some small seminar or informal evening study group or at an information session for graduates."

"Surely that must count."

"Count, count. Well I suppose it means something but the invitations always come from some personal friend; they have no institutional authority or *cachet*."

She laughed. "You must be the last person in the world able to invoke institutional authority with a clear conscience. How many times have I listened to you on the subject of the public institutions? The forsworn, damnable, vicious, corrupt, decadent public institutions, the CBC, the banks. Always with righteousness on your side, I will admit."

"I must refuse to be bound by small consistencies."

"No doubt, no doubt, but institutional certification can mean nothing to you. It means nothing — less than nothing — to me."

"Get off it," he said with great force. "In this country we are all bound by institutional authority. We are all in the hands of the funding bodies and the government commissions and the arts' councils and the prison visitors."

"The John Howard Society?"

"The people who come to painters' studios for the Art Bank. The officials of organisations charged with making representations to the Secretary of State. Folks who sit on boards and hold hearings and circulate minutes. I don't see how it is, but we have more personal freedom here and less public freedom, than in any other place in the world. I feel so hedged-in."

He got up and started to walk around the dining-room table. Then he stopped beside the stereo turntable, lifted the plastic cover and removed the disc which lay below it. He held it up at an angle to the light and squinted at the grooves. "It's amazing how the sunlight shows up the dust; this record is filthy. Ah, but what the hell, I've had it twenty years and there isn't a scratch on it."

She said, "It was mine before we got married; it was one of six."

"God, so it was! An *Allegro* record. Kaplan, Mayes and Bodky. The *Concerts Royaux* of Couperin. You know, it doesn't sound bad. And, it's closer to thirty years than twenty."

"It *is* thirty years."

"We needn't insist on the exact length of time. Do you remember how exciting the early days of LP were, all those new labels nobody had ever heard of? *Colosseum, Period, Cetra-Soria, Haydn Society, Oiseau-lyre, Westminster?* How we imagined we'd discover vast regions of new music major labels had never bothered to record because they thought there was no audience for it?"

"I remember," she said, "and I also remember how the new labels all rushed out and recorded Vivaldi until we had Vivaldi coming out of our belly buttons."

"It's true," he said, "and what in the end did we discover from all of that? Have we added anything permanent to the repertoire, any composer, any work?"

"Telemann?"

"Piffle. Telemann is piffle. And an awful lot of Vivaldi is piffle too, if it comes to that."

"Berwald?"

"Try again."

"Scheidt," she exclaimed.

"Very funny, very funny. The fact is, RCA and Columbia and Decca knew what was worth recording long before the LP revolution occurred. Time winnows things out, discards Scheidt and Schütz, retains Haydn."

"You used to like Schütz."

"I got tired of inserting the umlauts," he said. "There comes a time in your life when you can't be bothered inserting umlauts with a ballpoint because you don't have them on your typewriter. It's bad enough being conscientious about the accents in French."

"Which is acute and which is grave?"

"Acute is the long open sound and grave is the middle glide. And then, what to do about the cedilla?"

"What is life," she demanded uneasily, "without cedillas?"

"Mispronounced. Hard instead of soft. Life is hard enough without omitting the cedilla in any language including the Scandinavian."

"Grumble, grumble, grumble."

"Well, so would you in my place."

"I believe I hear the telephone," she said, glad of the interruption. "Did you go and turn the bell down again?"

"As far as it would go," he said. "You're right. It is ringing. I wonder who it is. Are you expecting a call?"

"Stop clowning and answer it."

He left the dining room, whistling softly as he passed through the kitchen towards the studio at the rear of the building. The telephone emitted three further chastened appeals; she heard the click as the receiver was lifted, then the ensuing speeches and silences which formed the near side of the dialogue. Soon it became clear who was at the other end.

"Hello? Yes, it's me. Oh, hi, where are you? Are you in the city? Oh. Oh. Well it's an excellent connection. Sometimes I can hardly understand calls from Toronto these days: The service gets worse and worse and the rates go up and up. Goddamn monopoly! What? What? No. I haven't heard anything. I'm not sure I want to. It hasn't appeared yet, at least I haven't seen it nor heard any reaction to it. I know they intend to run it because some young woman called me from their office; she was an excellent editor too. She'd caught everything that was questionable. She made me clear every item up. He had a mistake in my date of birth. Nobody cares about my date of birth but she wanted to get it right. 1930. What? Come on, how old do you think I am anyway? No, seriously, I was born in 1930. It's on the record. Sure it is. What makes you think that? You're kidding. You have got to be kidding. I don't have any more liver spots than the next man . . . mind you, the next man happens to be a hopeless alcoholic . . . I should say in about a week. The November issue, but they never get it out before the month on the cover, not like your ordinary sensible magazine. Never mind, it's free advertising; everybody in the trade who reads anything — and there can't be all that many — reads it. Librarians, retail outlets, an occasional literate salesman. They have good reviews. Yes. Yes, that's right. No, I saw it in the magazine; I never got it. Are you certain you put it in the mail? Well, it wouldn't be the first time, would it? What sort of clipping service are you using? They don't send me half of what appears. I've only had about a dozen of them . . . or do they originate from your office? Oh, it's the office, is it? Well, why haven't I seen more? I don't object to seeing the bum ones but I don't think there have been any bum ones this time. Not that they make the least bit of difference. It's space, that's all. What? No, I don't think so. Do you know, I don't think I've ever had somebody come up to me and say that they'd bought a book of mine because they'd read

a good review of it. I can't recall an instance. I suppose it's better
to have good ones than bad ones. It makes you feel a little better
but it doesn't seem to make the least difference to sales . . . what?
Am I what? Interested? Well, I guess I'm interested, but let me
see first if I can make a guess. Let's see . . . the book came out
the end of August, right? Figuring in the advance orders as the
August sale and figuring in sales for September and October . . . what? Figure till the middle of October? All right, let's
see, the advance orders and seven weeks of sales. How many did
you manufacture in the first printing? Twenty-five hundred? That
seems about right. Okay, then, okay. Yeah. The problem is to get
through that first printing quickly. Did you sell any to the colleges?
How many? Only 141? Gosh!"

She knew he'd been hoping to sell a great many copies of the
new book to departments of English. That didn't sound like many.

"Well, 141. What's that, about five adoptions? Four? Uh-huh.
Remember Larry Holtzman wanted to use it but we didn't have
it ready for his deadline; maybe he can order it for next year. All
right, that gives us 141 college sales. Not too many. And you had
a few advance orders, didn't you? Say orders for 300 copies? Gives
us around 450 right there and seven weeks sales since. I'd guess
you've sold around 1000 copies so far? A thousand would feel
mighty nice. After all, I'm selling to the poetry audience, not the
mass market."

Selling to the audience for *poetry* she thought sorrowfully.

"What? Say again! Eight hundred? What, all together? Advance
sales, college sales and the trade too? In seven weeks? Boyoboy!
No, it isn't quite what I'd expected . . . not quite."

He was silent while the voice from Toronto rattled clearly in the
receiver.

"Uh-huh, uh-huh, yes, I see that. I do see that. But look, didn't
you say you'd placed 250 with the Canada Council? I thought so.
Doesn't that put us over the thousand mark? A thousand and a
bit more; that's only up to mid-October. It's a whole month since
then; there may be other sales to report. There must have been
re-orders. You said so yourself, the re-orders were starting to come
in. So look at it this way, counting in the Canada Council you've
managed to sell about 500 books a month for the first two months.
That's a pretty good sale. Maybe word-of-mouth will boost it,

coming up to Christmas. We've got two major pieces of publicity still to appear. Suppose you can sustain that average — five hundred copies a month — till mid-December, wouldn't that bring us pretty close to 2000 copies for the first season? Wouldn't that be good enough? Supposing we do that from late August to Christmas, there's almost always additional sales in the following season down through April. If we can get up to around 1800, say, let's be conservative and estimate 1800 in the first season, we'll have done all right. Don't feel disappointed. What? Oh sure, I was a little taken aback when you mentioned the figure because it doesn't sound very large. It's a familiar figure. It's about what the other ones did before I came to you. Fifteen to 1800 the first season and 400 to around 750 the following eight months or so for a total of, say, 2500 maximum in the original trade edition and a trickle for several years afterwards. If the publisher manufactures 2500 to begin with, which seems to be the right figure, he faces an agonising decision about a year after the book comes out . . . and so will you."

The squawks in the receiver grew vigourous and emphatic.

"Oh, you will, eh? Can I take that for granted? Can I build on that. Is it a guarantee?"

Squawk, squawk, squawk, squawk.

"And the what? And after that you'll keep it in print indefinitely? I can count on that! All right, let's figure it this way: for any book of mine, you can expect to sell an original printing of 2500 copies in about a year from publication. By the following August you'll be right at the end of the first printing and you'll have to decide how many more to manufacture. Now listen to this: I believe a steady modest sales effort will keep my books moving almost indefinitely at the rate of around 400 a year, especially if we make a big effort to get them into schools. If your second printing is 1200 copies, you should be out of it in another three years. After that you do a third printing and so on. What? Say again! Not current publishing practice? Of course it isn't current publishing practice but you're going to have to do it all the same or we'll lose our national memory. You see, I'm the national memory."

Always ready with an aphorism she thought. What would he be if he didn't have that resource? The sounds from the receiver grew fluid, supple and unresisting, as if their source had been persuaded away from disappointment.

"Don't be disheartened, Victor. Never let yourself get down on the product. It's a good product. The best there is. Sure. Sure you are. And remember that if you keep the book in print for ten years you'll have sold four printings and you'll be somewhere around the 6000 copy mark and then, my friend, the second market will start to kick in, the colleges and high schools and departments of continuing education. Before you know it you'll have a title that's become a classic. I tell you, Victor, and I'd quit if I didn't believe this, you can get every one of my books over 10,000 copies if you can afford to wait. That's the problem you've got to lick: how to keep your operational costs within the limits of a tight budget and your price around $6.95 tops. Any higher and you're into the bottle of gin, two movie tickets, pizza for two, competition. That's competition most books can't face. If you can keep your price competitive with an LP or a dozen cans of beer, you can move the article. Don't forget that you've got to pay forty percent of the retail price to the bookstore and ten percent to me, so you get to keep half of the $6.95. You've got to produce the book, circulate it, advertise it and run your office and warehouse all out of $3.47½. Can you do it? Sure you can. Get in there and sell. What? Starve to death? Yeah, probably. But nobody said it was going to be easy, did they? By the way, I completed another anthology sale this morning, there's an extra $300 for you and $300 for me. We're going to make it, Victor, I'll keep writing them and you keep selling them and before you know it — in about twenty years — you'll have a dozen books on your backlist that have sold 10,000 copies each. At least, I believe you will. I believe that with every fibre of my being, Victor. Almost every fibre. Some of my fibres are a little stretched these days but, on the whole, I've kept the faith. So, okay now, don't be disappointed, all right? All right. All right. Same to you."

There came the soft sound of the receiver being replaced in its cradle. Then there was a long silence. She didn't care to move. She made no sound. She could visualise all too clearly what he was doing. He'd be standing beside the telephone table looking out at the bedraggled and overgrown garden. He'd be running his right hand through his hair. His face would have that expression on it . . .

He whistled a few bars of "Maxwell's Silver Hammer" inaccurately and in incorrect tempo. She shuddered as he came into the room. He looked about the same as always, almost the same. He'd been a thin man all his life with a long thin neck and no meat on his bones. He'd been able to manoeuvre between chairs and tables and hatstands without knocking them about too noisily while he was thin. Now he was beginning to get thicker through the middle, quite a bit thicker, and she could see what he would look like at seventy: awkward, ill-coordinated, bewildered by the routine givens of spatial existence.

"Victor had some sales figures for me," he said superfluously.

"Oh, yes?"

"I need a hit book," he said inconsequentially. "Boy, do I need a hit book! Something to break out of this ring."

"Do you want to know what your trouble is?" she demanded. "Do you really want to know what your trouble is?"

"If I could find out, I'd change it. I'm reaching the same readers all the time."

"You're making every piece different."

"Isn't that a good thing to do? It used to say that on boxes of chocolates when I was a tad."

"Stop that," she said. "You do that every time I want to talk to you. You make every story different from the last one. Every novel. You keep undercutting people; you never tell the same story twice."

"Well sure," he said, "that's how to do it. You don't paint the same picture over and over."

"In a way I do," she said. "They're all laid out about the same. They have the same palette. You can recognise them as mine."

"Everybody can recognise a story as mine. I've got a distinctive style, same as you."

"Aha, yes, but your style is to be a chameleon. The writing is always exact but the subjects are so dissimilar. You keep turning up in different places and different lexical domains — excuse the language — and the audience has to re-learn all the assumptions every time they start a new piece. You unsettle them; they don't know where they are. Take Scott Fitzgerald for example; he just wrote the same novel five times. An isolated romantic illusionary commences life on terms which life simply can't meet. He expects more charity and truth from others than they can yield. He is destroyed in the ensuing process. The extent of the destruction widens as Fitzgerald gets older but the story is the same. But you, you simpleton, you've never told the same story twice."

"Hm."

"Look at those titles," she said. "They put people off."

"Why?"

"They never know whether to laugh or not."

There was a silence, one of those lengthening points of quiet deeply-significant in a TV drama. In the dining room in real life it just seemed clumsy and inexpressive, awkward.

About once a decade she caught her husband in a momentary state of complete defenselessness in which his habitual optimism, energy, sense of future goods on their way stood revealed as purely and simply a stratagem, a professional device designed to conceal fear and exhaustion. She never cared to witness these moments and wondered from time to time how often they occurred when there was nobody around to witness them. There was his constant day-to-day bitching to put up with, evade and dismiss; they both understood that it was comic in intention and superficial in nature, registration of fleeting annoyance: a muddled press notice perfectly — exquisitely — contrary to fact, a request for information that couldn't be given because it didn't exist or because the matter on which it might be founded had never existed or occurred. Misinformation was endemic in this business: skewness, airy falsehood, permanent conditions of credence given where fact was not.

She didn't mind these conditions of work and neither did he. She understood. He could work around squalid misrepresentation but the problem of an audience, that was the problem to solve. It couldn't be solved. When this aspect of the actual gripped him, really made itself clear, he would sit in the dining room's afternoon light in the big window and his face would open and simplify its expression; then she could spy on his mind and it always froze her, left her chilled for days. It was another man she saw. It was like looking down into a swirling boiling vortex of disheartened misery, the state of being the lost must suffer. Usually the window closed in the following instant and another ten years might go by without such a revelation. More than once a decade would be more than enough.

"The population of Canada has just passed 24 million," he said, "and when I was a boy it was around 11 million. I remember well the autumn of 1943 or 1944 when Grace Campbell brought out a book called *Thorn Apple Tree.* My mother was working part-time in a bookstore that Christmas and she used to go on and on about *Thorn Apple Tree* and what a best seller it was. A best seller, mind you. One day I happened to ask my mother how many copies the book would sell. She said she didn't know for sure but would try to find out. Next evening when she came home she told me that such a book, whose title was on everybody's lips, might sell 5000 copies in Canada, few or none elsewhere.

Five thousand copies, I said to myself, that's pretty mingy. That's tiny! Why, *Gone With the Wind* or *Anthony Adverse,* great best sellers in the States, would sell in the hundreds of thousands, perhaps in the millions. So I decided that selling books in this country was pretty bush-league. That was in 1943 or 1944, it makes no difference.

Now, forty years later, I'm lucky if I can sell 2500 copies of a book in its first year. Do you realise what the percentage is? That's just over one one-hundredth the population of the country. Point-zero-one. That's what I'm going to call my autobiography. *Point-Zero-One.* Make the dickens of a title, won't it? One of those titles where they won't know whether to laugh or not. I read an announcement in the paper last night about the new James Michener fiction book. That's what the paper called it, *the new James Michener fiction book.* The first printing of the paperback is going to be 450,000. I'm so much better a writer than James Michener that we aren't the same kind of being, writerwise. What do you make of that? I used to hope that my audience would build over the years. 'Every great artist must first create the taste by which he is to be enjoyed.' I was ready to take that on. I thought that I'd sell a thousand copies of my first book — and I did — and that I'd carry those readers along with me and get more with each new book. But it hasn't worked out that way. When I got to around 2500, the buildup stopped and I can't get past that number and pretty soon they'll begin to die off.

Dell to the right of them
Seal to the left of them
Into the valley of death
Rode the two thousand.

We're all getting older together, my readers and me, those few hundred decent women in tweed skirts and good woollen jumpers who went to university with my mother and my aunts, the sixty-five college teachers, the hundred librarians, the thousand high-school kids of the 1960s. And who will replace them? I've spent my life learning how to make these beautiful objects and nobody wants them and I can't do anything else and I can't stop making them. Like what old Sam has the fellow say at the end of his book with his face and his whole body pressed down in the shit, really in the shit: I can't go on, I can't go on, I'll go on."

Cute Containers

For Neil and Kathy Vipond

FROM WHERE THEY WERE SITTING you could look right across the street at Love Handles, the sex boutique, and beside that the Angel Gabriel Nursing Home. This seemed a type or abstract of the structure of human life to Max Strathey who had had two scotches, normally his limit. He divined that there ought to be some sort of shop nearby along Yorkville that sold infants' and children's wear and turned to ask Chickie about it. She had no children of record but was a kind woman, he felt, who would know about infant care. He squinted at her under the glare.

There was a flashing electric sign above the shop next to the sidewalk café where they sat. It threw pink, green, yellow and blue tints over the tables and the sidewalk and gave Allen and Chickie the look of mocking clowns. Max reviewed the crudely-symbolist notion that the clown-figure is a primary all-embracing expression of the quality of existence and rejected it as bullshit. The clown means less than meets the eye, he decided. He remembered the trite fact that every clown designs his own makeup which no other will willingly duplicate. Bozo, he thought tiredly, Jojo, Banjo, Boffo and Bimbo, each with the white pancake, the putty nose, the hectic cheeks and those weird fucking lines across their eyelids. Sad. Deeply pretentious. Apt at almost any time to break into mime-play. He gagged. Bugger clowns, he thought.

Chickie winked at him suddenly and wriggled her shapely nose. "A diaper service has a depôt down the street, upstairs over the Betty Parsons North Gallery. And you can bankrupt yourself buying children's woollens at Swallows and Amazons. That's on this side over by Avenue Road. I didn't know you had children."

Max realised that he had spoken aloud unawares. "What did I say?"

Allen Cochrane removed his nose and some of the rest of his face from a big snifter. He chuckled stertorously. Stertorously, thought Max, stertorously. What's he on about then?

"You revealed nothing," said Allen. He cleared his throat and spat copiously towards the nearby gutter, sending his phlegm precisely between the bars of a sewer grating; it was a first-rate shot of its kind. A young woman walking past turned and smiled at Allen with deep approval. "Missed me," she said.

"Get along wid yez," said Allen and the woman turned, came to their table, and started to rub her knuckles roughly over the top of the bushy Cochrane scalp. It must have hurt, Max thought, but Allen made no move to seize the woman's wrist.

"I spit upon you," he said vigorously as she rapped his skull smartly with either fist.

Chickie said glumly, "You can't injure Al Cochrane by hitting him on the head."

"Oho, oho, nutbuster alert!" said Allen.

"Hit him again, Alice, but harder," said Chickie.

Ignoring the two women as best he might, laughing as if mightily tickled, Allen said to Max, "You were mumbling to yourself about sex and death and then you mentioned something about birth and kiddies — that there ought to be something for children along Yorkville to complete the set."

"I said this out loud?"

"It was just a random thought, Max; somebody else had it first. The fellow who runs Swallows and Amazons must be into very big bucks. You can't find anything in there under $300 and that's for a little girl's sweater."

Alice sat on Allen's lap. "Don't you do anything but sit here?" she said, her voice heavy with invitation.

"Sometimes I sit on the other side," said Allen.

Quite a long time later the electric sign above them clicked abruptly off and the vibrating stripes of colour disappeared, rendering the clown metaphor unviable. Its parameters lacked functors, Max thought. He could hear the neon-tubing of the sign sizzling and pinging and cooling; otherwise, the street was quiet as they rose, Alice and Allen and Chickie and Max, (it sounded like the title of some horrid movie) and wandered off along Hazelton past darkened galleries, the Marlborough-Godard and the Electric Gallery where three moderately-ingenious artifacts, left to burn the whole night, turned themselves on and off. Almost meaning something. One was an animated metal mobile of abstract shapes suggestive of insects and butterflies with very small pinprick eyes of electric light. Another was an arrangement of hundreds of flashlight bulbs screwed into a board which appeared to illuminate them randomly. You watched and watched and eventually acquired the impression that the lights might be spelling out urgent messages in a code based on an unknown tongue, Tamil or possibly Finno-Ugric.

The third object was unimportant, a videocassette montage of bits of Mandrell Sisters shows endlessly repeating itself without a soundtrack.

After that they were in the parlour of the Cochranes' house on Berryman, formerly on the fringe of Yorkville, now at the centre of the post-Yorkville real-estate boom. Worth a quarter of a million dollars if a cent but unpurchaseable. There were only four houses like it in the city; two others were on Berryman; the other was on Scollard. These tiny cottages, storey-and-a-half constructions of great antiquity built no later than the 1870s, later stuccoed, then sided with Insul-Brick and finally with aluminum siding in the late 1970s, "these desirable residences."

The floors pitched and fell. If you dropped a ball-bearing and watched it roll, the irregularity of its path would give you vertigo, while remaining susceptible of complex mathematical statement, perhaps an isobaric graph indicating the topological relationship of all points at the same level. Max understood he was mildly-intoxicated when this thought came to him. He only conceived matters in these terms at a particular stage of excess which would shortly be succeeded by feelings of intense but unfocussed sexual longing. Somebody had given him a beer, then another and soon he felt distention in the lower bladder and the penis. He rose and walked carefully across the uneven flooring towards the hall staircase. Statuesque brief cutoffs revealing bronzed thighs which reflected the dim light, Chickie took him by the hand and led him to the first step.

"First door to the left as you come up," she got out.

The staircase creaked alarmingly, bannister railing shook, risers were not all the same height. Could that be? Termites? Dry rot? Wide bare patches where ancient wallpaper had been stripped away revealing cracks in the plastering as aesthetically pleasing as the wallows of the parlour floor.

The house was twisted from inside its own system of stressing with the workings of a century of habitation in the way an old wooden skiff will show partings and gaps in its seams from the complex curving workings of various waves: a hollow chop, ground swell, breakers, a long roll. Every boat works in all directions at once: seams leak. The house must be swaying every which way all the time, he thought. His nose almost against the bare plaster, his eyes followed a long crack from the point where the top stair met the wall to a further point where, inside the outer wall, an ancient stud had begun to bow outwards in progressively more acute need of buttress. This crack made Max think of the great rivers of central Asia winding their way across Siberia: the Lena, the Yenisei, most of all the Ob.

"Can you find it?" said a far-off voice.

He groped his way into the bathroom, couldn't locate the light switch, then fainting with the need to empty his bladder almost chose to aim for the bowl in the dark — invariably an ill-starred venture for the Stratheys of this world — and at last thought of feeling around outside the door and hit a small projection with twitching fingers. As he reeled facing the bowl, the blowup over the tank came into focus: an aquatic scene with men in drooping moustaches and two-piece bathing suits, the trunks fitted out with belts, belt-loops, buckles, the modest singlets lettered LIFEGUARD or BBCC or ICC. Women in bathing caps like nursemaids' headgear of the Edwardian age lolled in elegant punts. A boy of about twelve leaned into the frame and stuck his tongue out at the camera with joyous verve. It was a poster made from an illustration for some newspaper series called "Canadian Yesterdays" or "When Granny was a Girl."

Further elements in the bathroom recalled the recesses of heritage: a bathtub with claw feet, the split brown wooden toilet seat, the taps on the basin with their four-spoked nubby grip, a general air of never having been modified since installation about 1913, perhaps the date of the blown-up newspaper photo. There might be some connection. The original privy for the house still stood against the rickety backyard fence, a conversation piece often written up in Saturday supplements. Max identified the locale of the poster as he zipped himself up. Centre Island in "the old days."

He scanned the picture more carefully and noticed how closely the man in the ICC singlet holding erect a double-bladed paddle resembled Chickie Cochrane. Her grandfather, he remembered, had been a paddler of Olympics calibre, Ebbie Aldershot, member of the locally-famous Aldershot clan, for four generations summer residents at Ward's and Centre, permanently attached in wintertime to some municipal service. Was it the office of the Clerk of Works?

Max remembered Chickie Cochrane as Chickie Aldershot almost from the dawn of his life, aged seven or eight, when she had gone barefoot around the Davenport and Avenue Road district like the local princess. She might have been eighteen at that period. He had a feeling that this house was hers, inheritance from immemorial Aldershot or perhaps just her grandfather. The paddler in the poster was unquestionably Ebbie Aldershot. He had played hockey too (not at the Olympics level) sometime after the first war. It would be a good idea to leave the light on so as not to fall downstairs.

He only stumbled once, on the bottom step, where a strip of metal bordering an ancient heating-outlet sprang loose to try and trip him. He cannoned through the drapes and into Allen who was beginning a funny story in the middle of the room. They disentangled one another, then occupied opposite ends of the rug as Allen, a raconteur not easily deterred at 2:00 A.M., began again.

". . . there's this med student has an exam next morning in gynecology . . . is that right? Or is it obstetrics? Stop me if you've heard this. Anyway, gynecology and/or obstetrics . . . obstetrics, what the hell. Women's plumbing. But he doesn't know beans about it from a scientific point of view. Though like most medical students he has a firm grip on the realities of the matter. There are times when pure science must yield to the expertise of the clinician, right?"

Alice said, "You're pissed, Allen."

"Spoken like a lady. So anyway he goes out the night before and gets pissed as a newt. Tanked. Boiled. And the next day in the exam room he can't remember a thing. The first question on the paper sends him up the wall: 'Give five reasons why mother's milk is better for baby than cow's milk.' So he sits and stares at the paper for awhile, just not ticking over at all. The other candidates are all scribbling away at the rate of knots. He feels deeply excluded. He has to do something. Finally he licks his pencil and writes down, 'In reply to your question as to why mother's milk is better for baby than cow's milk, would only say . . .' The effort exhausts him. His eyes bulge ominously; he gasps for breath but finally inspiration strikes and he scribbles down very fast: 'One, It's cleaner. Two, It's fresher. Three, It's more natural.' Another long interval for thought then he gets an idea and writes: 'Four, The cats can't get at it.' Now he really is at the end of his rope, mind totally blank until he gets one last flash, seizes his pencil and writes down: 'Five, It comes in such cute containers.'"

Max had never heard the joke before. It immediately called up multiplex images, the first unaccountably that of a fat orange-black-white-striped cat; in fact, one of those nearly marmalade cats lying in the attitude of a lover upon a woman's bared bosom. He considered this image. It pleased him. The room rang with his laughter and he noted with satisfaction that Alice and Chickie had joined in.

"Cute containers," chortled Allen.

"Round little ones," said Alice.

"Melons."

"Tennis balls."

"Ping-pong balls."

The room seemed dominated by the delightful image of well-formed female breasts not necessarily in the phase of lactation. Round. Firm. White. Maybe black. Alice and Chickie seemed undisturbed by fears of masculine aggression; they appeared to enjoy the joke as much as the guys.

"If I were in the packaging business, I'd have to think about getting into that kind of carton; I'd have to talk to my design staff about the concept," said Max. He closed his eyes momentarily.

"Cute," said Chickie proudly, surveying herself. She was a woman with a most beautifully-formed physical presence. Alice, marginally less opulent in physique, showed correspondingly less enthusiasm for the quality of Allen's humour but didn't reject it out of hand.

Could it be, Max asked himself, could it be that the insecurely-rooted and essentially media-oriented North American feminism of the 1960s and 1970s had exhausted itself? Tits, he thought, jugs. Probably the most attractive form of packaging in existence. Why did everybody like them so much? No ready explanation of the phenomenon occurred to him. He was falling asleep and had to be shaken awake and bodily dismissed from the house towards morning by Allen and Chickie. It wasn't clear where Alice had gone; she certainly didn't go home with Max. Cute containers, he kept thinking, all the rest of the weekend, sometimes bursting into delighted chuckles.

It was a joke you really couldn't get away with these days, hopelessly *vieux jeu,* even ethically inadmissible in the eyes of many. One didn't make jokes about women and women's bodies in polite circles nowadays — unless you were Allen Cochrane — any more than one stood aside to let women through doorways first or rose to allow them to seat themselves in rush-hour subway traffic. Chivalry was dead, with it the sex joke and there was certainly a connection. At the same time it remained true that most human males retained their fascination with woman's anatomy; enlightenment with respect to the politics of sex had not banished the sexual attraction which continued comic rather than tragic in its motivation of mankind. Is a lovely being a funny being? Do we laugh about tits and bums because we find them so good? Is it a mistake to take all sex jokes as sadistic?

Max was a man deeply-menaced by the nature of woman. He saw that in his guilty relish of the phrase "cute containers" there was an indefensible blend of escapism, anxiety, even hatred, together with a most powerful capacity to imagine the delightful roundness and whiteness and softness, the rosy nipple, velvety skin. When you bite the nipple — not too hard — why do they like it? Do they like it? When he got to this point in his thinking he always sat up straight and looked around at the other people in the office for fear that his penis must be showing. It seemed a dirty trick on men that mere imagining could so arouse the humble flesh but it was the case. "Fact: the sum of what is the case." Wittgenstein. The swollen penis was the fact. Max always thought of Chickie Cochrane at this stage.

Going in and out of the shop of S. Bone, the Butcher, or the

Careful Hand Laundry near the corner of Davenport and Avenue Road, or hanging around the variety store by the bus stop, or throwing a Frisbee with Allen in Ramsden Park, or just lying on the grass looking great, Chickie had been the vessel of attitudes and feelings that twenty years had made surpassingly remote. He remembered watching her as she followed Allen across the park and up North View Terrace or Pears Avenue on some Sunday afternoon long in the past and it was as Allen's squaw that he imagined her, precisely his squaw.

She was a tall girl with shining black hair and skin always bronzed by the sun; her face flushed from running after tennis balls or softballs or Frisbees; the bronze and red tones mixing below her eyes gave her exactly the skin colour of some Hollywood version of the Indian maiden or possibly spouse of young brave absent on warlike excursion against the pacific Hurons. He always saw her as a Mississauga or Caughnawaga girl.

She was nothing of the sort: She was of English extraction, an Aldershot from the home counties, one of whose ancestors had probably taken the name of a town notorious for the comings and goings of military personnel in default of legitimate surname. She was no Indian maiden, no squaw, but she had that look. She always walked a couple of paces behind Allen, very springily, her gait almost bouncing, well up on the balls of her feet with a long stride that made you imagine her treading forest mosses, walking tirelessly all day and all night on some migration accomplished in company with husband and, positively, papoose.

He would shake with alarm when the image of the birchbark over-the-shoulders knapsack with matching baby swam into his mind. This whole body of reflection was illegitimate. He shouldn't allow himself to go on this way, trifling with taboos to which he subscribed very earnestly. Papooses, squaws, peoples' bums. Shocking! He thought of calling up Alice but couldn't remember her last name.

How young Chickie had seemed to bounce, to float with the long, strongly-muscled bronze legs, bare above mid-thigh with fringe of denim ringing firm flesh. Everybody who watched her in the park had considered her the most feckless, unemployable, almost shiftless young woman in the parish ready to come to no good. The cluster of sexual nuance was palpable; you could almost reach over and part it like a curtain of velour, to gaze in at the high cheekbones, rozy bronze flush, parted lips, slumbrous eyes.

"Al Cochrane's little squaw." He had once heard a woman describe Chickie in those words as the happy pair, now husband and wife, drew near the Gibson Avenue tennis courts displaying exhilaratingly their total lack of visible means of support. Max thought of brassières, thought again of Allen's joke, wished heavily that he could see Chickie again as she was at twenty or thirty. He would take forty.

Neither had ever seemed to toil, spin, take thought of the morrow. Allen was the more culpable idler of the two; you would never be able to find out what Al Cochrane did for a living. His drinking was, of course, a matter of public record and concern. Allen Cochrane would have to do something one of these days, he really would, about his drinking. Or it would catch up with him. Sometime. Already, they said, the skin around his nose was growing veined and sweaty. Max couldn't see it. Allen had retained his infectious charm, his athlete's physique, his vigour long after his behaviour ought to have stripped him of these desirable qualities. He was a tall man with curly light brown hair the colour of maple fudge, with shiny white teeth and the ruddiness which gave rise to rumours about his alcohol intake. How ask such a person what he earned?

The Cochranes owned their house, for starters, and the house was the joke of the century according to most Cochrane-watchers. It had begun existence as practically a shithouse. Some primaeval Aldershot had made his way to Toronto in the 1870s and gotten some sort of job working for the city at a time when most of the Annex was open meadow. This ancestral Aldershot had lived into the twentieth century and by dint of frugality and economy had managed to build the ramshackle cottage which had survived into the tail-end of the present age. When the Aldershots had finally put in a bathroom, about the time of the first World War, they had simply thrown a wagonload of loam over the pit under the privy, never troubling to clean it out, so that it bubbled with shit for years afterwards; in wet weather it emitted an evil smell until decomposition was complete and a clump of wild tomatoes grew up around the privy and along the back fence.

Like Allen and Chickie, Max was a child of the district, born two blocks away from Davenport and Avenue Road near enough to the Joy gas station to treat it as one of the landmarks of the neighbourhood in childish games played along the sidewalks in the early sixties. Some lunatic designer of service stations back before the war had treated the Joy station in the manner of a residence for elves or gnomes. It had a gabled roof with heavy imitation slate shingles, a pointed turret over the entrance to the office and a general air of the thirteenth century. A service station in a fairytale, made of gingerbread, a witch's gas station. Many times in late evenings Max had hidden himself behind the Joy station to spy on Allen and Chickie as they sauntered hand-in-hand down Hazelton towards Berryman to say a protracted goodnight. More than once he watched as the courting couple drew closer and closer together on the porch steps until you couldn't see moonlight between them. Up the driveway behind their clutching forms leaned the dark shadow of the old privy, slanting imperceptibly further and further off true as it began to acquire the status of a hallowed antique, an historic edifice, something that ought to be protected by Heritage Canada.

In the 1920s an affront to the whole neighbourhood because of its smell and the lowered tone it imparted to manners there, the crazy wooden structure was now getting to be an integral part of our history, a link to valued life styles of the previous century. In the full flood of the 1980s, with a new century coming ever more distinctly into sight, Max saw that ordure and earth were transmuting themselves miraculously before his eyes into historian's gold. He could barely remember the malicious gossip of old Hazelton Avenue ladies who considered the Aldershots trash because of their stinky house. Farm labour. Poor whites. Almost like Indians. That isn't an exaggeration, he thought. There were plenty of people around when I was a little boy who thought that Chickie's folks were poor whites because they lived in a smelly little house with imitation brick siding next to an outside toilet. When you went inside their house — which you never would — you would smell unwashed bedclothes; you'd expect to trip over broken flooring.

Nineteenth century, twentieth, twenty-first. My life is being pulled all out of shape by length of time, he thought. In the year 2000 — menacing apocalyptic phrase — Max would only be forty-five. His life would last well into the next epoch. Even Chickie and Allen would likely live on into the third millennium, enriched by their inheritance of valuable antiques, wavy floorboards, the look of the shiftless unemployable annexed to riches, buried treasure made of dung, traditional affiliation with municipal administration, a complex network of mortgages which adjusted themselves to one another in an incredible relationship as provider of investment capital.

A man who passes his life in apparent idleness, his days on the boulevards, his nights at his club or favourite watering-hole may be either an elegant playboy and *bon viveur* or he may be a shiftless bum. There is no middle ground. And as extremes so often seem to meet, why shouldn't a shiftless bum be transmuted by the untraceable alchemy of interest rates and real-estate values into a man-about-town, as if Jeeter Lester had suddenly been metamorphosed into Bertie Wooster, a transformation far from inconceivable? It seemed to be happening all around us, for if Allen Cochrane, who had never done a stroke of work in his life that anybody knew about could turn into the most-admired man in Yorkville precisely because of his capacity for idleness, *while still young enough to enjoy it* — that was the important, even the psychologically crucial element — then true leisure might become possible for the citizens of Toronto. Not the palsied and crabbed leisure of those who owned their own homes after twenty-five years of desperate mortgage-reduction to find themselves preoccupied with the shrinking power of the fixed income, nor the suicidal inertia of the half-dead denizens of Allan Gardens, but the unearnable elegance of true uselessness, the lily of the field.

Max felt angry as he followed out this chain of reflection. He knew the Cochranes must have some means of paying their way; they were not deadbeats; people liked to have them around. They had never asked him for the smallest loan. Indeed, he had been their guest, after nights in the gardens of Yorkville, far more frequently than their host. He had never been their host, in the sense of inviting them into his home, something he was unable to contemplate. His home had shrunk to the proportions of a tiny disagreeable apartment in a Hillcrest highrise. He never went there except to take off his shoes and socks and drop for eight hours into fatigued and often-interrupted sleep. He couldn't afford the place either, even though he was in the most expansive professional field of the day.

There was a balcony and an impressive view of the north end of the city, for which he paid all that rent. The actual living space was claustrophobic and indefensibly expensive. He could not allow Chickie and Allen to inspect the poverty of his living quarters. He paid $850 a month for a hovel and they owned one of the most famous houses in the city, an actual Berryman Street cottage. This perception intensified his rage. He felt as if history, conceived as a personal pursuer, the president of the immortals, were out to get him. He, Max Strathey, almost a rich young man, had been selected by the Furies as an example of the poverty of wealth. He slept in a prison cell in solitary confinement. His bedroom smelled of dirty socks and infrequently-changed sheets. He didn't have a cleaning woman. (Who can afford a cleaning woman?) He no longer owned a car. You could not justify owning a car in these days of energy crisis and travel by subway. He walked back and forth to the Rosedale subway station twice daily with the dumb inarticulate resentment of a serf in a nineteenth-century Russian novel at the mercy of a master whom he never sees and cannot comprehend. You could no longer find cotton broadcloth in Stollery's and he seemed to have a mild polyester allergy. Wool. What was wool? Max began a round of phone calls to downtown associates to check on the Cochranes' employment records. Finally he got hold of a securities salesman at Ames who claimed to be managing the Cochranes' portfolio.

"It isn't what we'd call real money, but with care it might be coddled into something quite respectable."

Max fought off an impulse to grind his teeth and scream.

"What are you telling me?" he said. "They are virtually indigent, penniless. Let me put it more simply. They have no money."

The securities salesman cleared his throat. "I'm afraid that's not exactly true, Max."

"No?"

"Not exactly, no. You see, Allen has borrowed heavily against the house at different times. They own it free and clear. Chickie got it from her father about fifteen years ago and they've kept on raising money on it in a leapfrog pattern. They took small loans at the end of the 1960s when the house didn't seem to be worth very much. It's practically falling down."

"I nearly fell out of it the other night."

"Right. From a structural point of view it's a bad investment, but look at the location! The location alone is worth a couple of hundred thousand. If it were a pile of rubble it would still be worth six figures. As the value keeps jumping, Allen keeps borrowing. He pays off loans made against the earlier book value with new loans as his credit improves along with the rise in real-estate prices. Then he invests the difference for quick growth. Look at it this way, the difference between what that place was worth ten years ago and what it's worth now — and therefore the difference between loans available against it at different times, is enough to keep two people in comfort without doing anything but manage their money. In some investment situations I can get twenty-two percent for Allen on money that he only paid twelve percent to borrow . . . Max . . . are you still there?"

Max's deskmates at Datatronics had never seen him so disturbed; he couldn't sit still; he couldn't eat; he fiddled with the phone book trying to recall Alice's surname, the girl with whom he and the Cochranes had passed last Friday night and Saturday morning. Lesser? Leesor? Leeson? Reasoner? It was something like that. Puns rolled around in his imagination just beyond the fringe of attention. He was sure he had the right rhythm; it was a three-syllable name like Reasoner with the stress on the first syllable. Farringdon. Wolverine. No, not Wolverine. Cavalry. Calvary. Caverly. On his way for bitter coffee he tripped over a waste-paper basket and they were afraid he'd hurt himself but he just leaned against a desk and muttered, "Beazley. Bensonhurst. Sealyham."

"Are you all right, Max?"

"Of course, I'm all right! Do I look like there's something the matter with me?" This tart inquiry elicited no reply. He left the office early and darted uptown to Noodles, ingested a disgusting *quiche*, then began to prowl west along Yorkville and, of course, spotted the young woman immediately: Alice Tennant.

"Hey," he said, "come on over and sit with me." He thought she might massage his head with her knuckles but this was apparently a gesture reserved for intimates. She sat at his table and stared at him.

"Are you the guy I met with Chickie and Al the other night?" she said.

Max nodded.

"Isn't that a darling house?" she said. "And what possibilities. Naturally you'd have to shore up that bulge in the bearing wall, and you'd have to replace about eight planks in the porch flooring. Damp rot, you know, and there are the usual rats."

"Rats?"

"They come up the main drain and into the cellar but they're no problem really; you simply have to cap the drain with a grille."

"Are you some kind of real-estate saleswoman?"

"Salesperson. Yes. The sills are shot but who has to know?"

She gave a careful analysis of property values in the various residential districts of the inner-city core: the Annex, Rosedale, Moore Park, Leaside, Cabbagetown, Parkdale. Then she began to range farther afield. When she reached Mississauga some bitter association made Max scowl and the change in his appearance frightened her obscurely.

"Did I say something wrong?"

He just sat and stared at her like a turtle, his eyes glassy. The woman got up uneasily and strode away. There are plenty of nuts around here, she thought, I better not mess with this one.

He just sat and stared. *Love Handles* said the big sign across the street; he wondered for the first time what that meant. He'd always taken the sign for granted before. Love Handles?

He felt a tough resistant network growing up around him as though he were penned inside the trunk of a big old tree with hard springy branches forming, circling around him at eye-level and higher up the trunk. Leaves overhead, the organism hardening around his body like bark, character, character.

I've Got Troubles of My Own

FROM FIRST TO LAST SHE NEVER SAW THEM. Entertaining angels unawares, she thought, gritting her teeth, giggling. She didn't know a thing about the law of landlord and tenant but she knew that she had to have somebody living in the house to carry the running expenses, immediately, before the mortgage charges and the cost of oil and the wear and tear on her Toyota, driving back and forth three times a week between Kingston and Sweet's Corners, ate up all her earnings, leaving her without enough pay for her apartment and to feed Freda and herself. I asked for it, she remembered, single-parent status, an old country house up Highway 15. And I got it. Pray that you never get the thing you want most; it will bankrupt you. This shining flawless shard of cynicism galled her, enforcing its accuracy as she thought of it. Take what comes that you don't much want; take that. Forget wishes!

Well shit, it was easy to get there; that was the lure. She could slide out of the *Whig-Standard* offices most days by late afternoon on any of a wide selection of pretexts; then she would collect Freda from the day-care centre on Division Street, go out 401 to the Highway 15 exit and be in Sweet's Corners in forty minutes tops. She had pictured herself going into Freda's room at 7:00 A.M. in the stillness of winter, unbroken snowcrust gleaming in the last starshine and first light, waves of hot air billowing from the register next to the child's bed, familiar drafts around her slippered feet as she crossed the wide planking of the floor. An old farmhouse. A country retreat. Single-parent status. You brave brave girl, how can you ever manage? (Who was the father anyway?) You're so self-sacrificing. (She does everything for that child, who would have guessed?) Oh how gallant you are, how much the new woman.

From old lady to new woman in a single leap. She wasn't sure who the father was; it could have been somebody on the paper; it could have been a man in a bookstore; it was probably a zoologist at Queen's. There seemed no point in sharing the baby around so she took it all for herself and was, she thought, the first or second (actually she was the seventh) woman in Kingston to give birth while unmarried, in a public hospital, without using an assumed identity. She had imagined herself "bearing the shame" or "facing up to her disgrace" but there wasn't any shame or disgrace. People applauded. Brave girl. Gallant new woman. Freda was now four and getting to be a problem; there were difficulties with the milk-products enzymes; her spit-ups dissolved pantyhose.

The two of them would have their breakfast next to the kitchen range, would eye the old dry sink and the dim form of the unworkable pump beside it. The first extra expense — in itself almost ruinous — had been the digging of a new well on the other side of the house, the installation of the uncloggable foot-valve and an adequate electric pump. When she remembered what that had cost, she always thought of S.J. Perelman's definition. "A farm is an irregular patch of nettles bounded by short-term notes, containing a fool and his wife who didn't know enough to stay in the city."

The sentence, while not entirely applicable to her own situation, nevertheless possessed a considerable element of truth. At least she had not gotten lumbered with the land from the farm; that had been sold away from "the old Kelsey place" a dozen years before to a neighbouring farmer who now claimed an inalienable right-of-way across her front lawn. She only found this out much later, when the question of re-sale surfaced; nobody said anything about it when title passed to her. There was no irregular patch of nettles but there were plenty of short-term notes which grew harder and harder to meet.

She used to get demand-note loans from the Royal Bank branch near the office at a preferred-client rate; when she bought the house she'd been able to raise a quick $1000 at any time by this means, paying twelve percent for the use of the money and repaying the loan in ninety days. At that rate and on those liberal terms, the bank manager assumed — arrogated to himself or was allowed by her — she never quite knew which — a father-figure status which was probably psychologically inadmissible. He treated her like a little girl who had been bad and now stood before him drawing her toe across the carpet and hanging her head; then he would pat her on the cheek, pass the note across the desk for her to sign, dismiss her with a paternal nod. He did not look like her father, a man with entirely different paternal characteristics; the only fatherly attitude the two men shared was their refusal to admit alarm, disappointment, resentment, any of the traditional emotions at her free-form pregnancy.

Her bank manager had once patted her distended stomach in a comradely way as he leaned across his desk and proffered a promissory note. This gesture had offended her right to the sources of her being. But what could she do? She took the note and signed beside the pencilled X. She needed the money for the foot-valve and the black plastic piping and the new sink and toilet. She had ninety days to pay him back for that pat on the tummy and she had only one resource, her other father-figure, her real father who sent her in turn to *his* father, an old man still deeply involved in the family furniture business, factory, warehouse, retail sales outlet, in Napanee. This old man, whom she hated and feared, said a few forthright things about bastards and gave her $1000 which she accepted with a mixture of reluctance and eager relief. She would never have gone near her grandfather, she assured herself, if he weren't still living in the elegant family home on the bluff which overlooks the river just where it widens and enters the bay, the most superb house in Napanee. And that's saying a lot.

She wanted to live like that. Everybody knows that nobody lives like that anymore but she was going to try. She wanted a house like her grandfather's, filled with the kind of furniture that his factory hadn't turned out since well before she was born. If that old man could stride around those wide verandas kicking porch furniture out of the way while he complained about other peoples' morals, then she was equally entitled to wide verandas and a view. At least her grandfather was decent enough to insult her straight out; her father only looked his reproaches; the sleek manager of the Royal branch near the office just patted her and approved. Fuck them!

After the new well, the rise in oil prices. She never got to inhabit the house for a full winter; there was always something in the city that kept her on the go: a war among the theatrical companies in town, each clamouring for her support and space in her column on the local scene or a secret council hearing on the location of the new sewage farm. She spent days on that assignment, finally winkling a sheaf of most-secret memoranda out of the mayor's secretary who had just had an abortion and admired her for walking around with her navel out to here. It turned out that raw waste would have to be trucked to Belleville for treatment and disposal at inadmissible cost to the taxpayers until a new disposal plant could be put onstream four years in the future. This revelation almost cost the mayor his chair and she got a raise at the *Whig.*

God, the house, the house. She had to pay to heat it for three winters in which she almost never went there. It just sat on its tiny knoll up above the road next door to the Anglican church and drank up heating oil like Freda swallowed expensive formula. She had to have a tenant!

But who? Where find one she could trust to look after her plants, to devote time to the continual attention the house demanded: pointing, weatherstripping, adjusting the thermostat night and morning, keeping an eye on the sump pump, seeing there was oil in the tank, laying more insulation batts in the attic, watching out for traces of water damage through the roof. God, the house!

She called Babs Cornford at the local Century-21 agency and begged for her help. Babs had sold her the old Kelsey house in the first place and continued to send her a booklet each month containing mouth-watering photographs and loving descriptions of other old country houses in case she felt like trading up.

"No possible way, Babs. I'm a single woman. I only have one income. A pretty small income."

"You're unionised, right?"

"I'm what? Oh right, sure, I'm in the guild, but that doesn't make me a rich lady."

"I don't have any union going for me," said Babs. "Anything I have coming in, it's because I got out and hustled for it."

This did not sound like the old Babs Cornford who had been kissing her bum before the closing date.

"Is something wrong?" she asked.

"Wrong, wrong, wrong. I just lost a sale I thought I had locked up. These things happen." Babs started to weep, explosively, chokingly, at the same time reading from her list of properties.

"There's a place on the road in to Chaffee's Locks that you'd just adore (*sob, sob*) and you could move right in for the equity on your present home. Let's see, your down payment was what, $10,000?" Sniffles and gasps from Century-21.

"I put $20,000 into it, Babs. You should know that better than anybody and I'm not in the market. I want you to get me a tenant."

But there was no money for the agent in a search for a tenant.

"All I get is the first month's rent . . . what were you thinking of asking?"

"Just enough to pay the mortgage, the insurance, the oil and the taxes until I can afford to live in it."

"When would that be?"

"I don't know, maybe two years, maybe three." Maybe never, she thought. "Say $300 a month. That would just barely cover it and it's a low rent."

"Could you slip me a little extra if I get somebody good? Three hundred would just pay for my gas and phone."

"Why should I pay for your phone?"

"Give me two months' rent and I'll find you some good people."

"I guess I've got no choice." Dear Jesus, let some big story break, a six-alarm fire, a sex scandal at the university, anything for some overtime.

There wasn't much response to the ads for a tenant. The kind of people who were looking for low rents were definitely not the same crowd who admired mid-nineteenth-century brick farmhouses. Prospective tenants had one thing in common: low income. They were mostly retired couples from the surrounding villages who thought $300 rather a high rent. A barber and his wife who was in a wheelchair; an old man who had sold his hardware store too long ago and now had a poverty-line income; folks like that.

"Really, Babs, I can't let chronic losers into the house. I might never be able to get rid of them when I'm ready to move in."

"Back to square one," said Ms. Cornford pensively.

And then she unearthed the Megarrys, Tom and Lila. "These are real folks," she claimed on the phone. "All they need is a bit of a helping hand to get themselves back on their feet."

The phrase made little waves of apprehension shiver her spine.

"But have they got any money?"

"They can pay the rent, if that's what you mean, if you would be willing to shave your price just a little bit."

"How little?"

"They could manage $250."

"For an eight-room house with a new well, new pump, new sump pump? You're joking."

"These are the best prospects I've been able to locate. Tom is getting compensation regularly."

"What?"

"His workman's compensation."

"You mean he's not working?"

"Not right at this moment."

"When does he expect to start working? He has worked now and then, I suppose. He's managed to get himself onto the welfare rolls."

"Welfare isn't the same thing as compensation. He suffered an injury on the job so he collects a monthly payment from the board."

"How much?"

"He says around a thousand a month. We could easily check on that."

"How can he pay the rent I'm asking on $1000 a month?"

"That's why he's asking you to drop it fifty bucks." This reply had a savage logic which was compelling.

"You feel he can pay $250?"

"Cross my heart."

"What sort of injury?"

"Injury? Oh, Mr. Megarry, yes. He was hoisting a truck engine out of its bed when the block and tackle let go. He took all the weight of the engine in his arms and back. Tore the muscles right out of his lower back," said Babs. She repeated the last phrase with gloomy relish. "Tore them right the hell out of there." It was clear she was quoting somebody.

"Have they got any family?"

"Two of the sweetest little girls you ever saw."

"Hmmmmm."

"I've got the first month's rent here, in cash, and a cheque for the December rent. After that they'll simply remit cheques to you. We won't give them a lease. I know you don't want a lease. We'll write up a month-to-month tenancy agreement and get her to sign it."

"Her?"

"The wife, Lila. She signs the cheques."

"Why?"

"No doubt they have their reasons."

"And you're certain they can make it?"

"As certain as I've ever been about anything."

"Okay then. I'll draft a tenancy agreement and give it to you tomorrow and you can get them to sign it. Do I get any of the first two months' rent?"

"No, that stays with me. But I'm paid-in-full and you can enjoy your rental income without further payments to your realtor and good luck!"

"Oh, stop it, Babs. You better tell them I want my cheque for the January rent on or before the first of the month and no fooling. Maybe they'd better give me a series of post-dated cheques through the end of May."

"And why not?" said Babs.

The new tenants were to move in just after the first of November which left a single fall weekend free for country amusements. She bundled Freda into the back seat of the Toyota under a pile of sleeping-bags and a hot-plate and took the child to spend a restorative weekend with her — perhaps the last for many years — on their property. There were some good moments. When she'd bought the place, very little land had come with it, about two acres. What there was lay well back from the road with cart-tracks of her neighbour's right-of-way running across it to the south towards his fields and woodlot. There was a tacit agreement that she could use his fields for walking or cross-country skiing in return for the regular passage — questionably legal — up the track past her place with a wagonload of fodder or hay or horse dung. This neighbour used to cut her grass from time to time, often when she was staying in the house. A sunburned man with a striped locomotive-engineer's cap and underneath it a bold look. He made her grass look pretty good using a big power-cutter and he let her wander around his own acreage with complete freedom. She had an inkling he knew all about her single-parent status, which was in certain ways more and more a prestige symbol or a species of invitation.

She took Freda out on the Saturday afternoon for a brisk walk across the back fields and along the edge of the woodlot which lay several hundred yards back from the road running along behind the Anglican cemetery and the shining little church. They bumbled around back there until Freda grew tired and began to beg to be carried; as she was almost five and a chunky little ms she made quite an armful. It seemed wise to take the shortest way back.

They struck out towards the little cemetery and came to an almost invisible fence which had formerly marked off consecrated ground. It had been down for some years and was extremely rusty though not barbed. You could just barely make it out; two or three old headstones lay there on their backs entangled in the growth of wildflowers and weeds. Some of these stones gave birthdates in the mid-eighteenth-century for those whom they commemorated. She hadn't realised people born that long ago had lived out the balance of their lives to die in Sweet's Corners in the 1830s and 1840s.

The Anglican pastor, Mr. Marjoribanks, stood some distance away in the middle of the cemetery, his head bent in an awkward and unfamiliar attitude. She saw with relief he was wearing ordinary clothes; once before she'd met him outside the church when he'd been wearing a clerical collar above a dark-grey shirt, an aspect of dress she found repellent. She set Freda down — there was protest at this — and walked over to greet Mr. Marjoribanks, hoping uneasily that he wouldn't bless her or do anything silly. But he only looked up and smiled vaguely. He obviously had no idea who she was.

"I am your neighbour," she said, then wondered if the simple words suggested parody of some Biblical utterance. "From the house next door."

"Mrs . . . Mrs?"

"Mzzzzzzz," she said sturdily.

She realised that he didn't even suspect what *Ms* stood for and decided not to follow up on identification. Let him think what he liked. He probably figured she was Mrs. Mzzzzzzz.

"I own the house next door, the old Kelsey place."

The minister extended his hand and she clutched at it. The palm was firm and dry with a faintly powdery texture; there were many liver spots on the back. He looked to be about seventy-five, as old as her grandfather. Was she always going to be surrounded by old lawgivers?

"I knew the Kelseys well," said Mr. Marjoribanks. "Baptists, most of them, otherwise well-behaved."

She wished he hadn't introduced shop-talk. Another minute and she would be interviewing him for a page in the weekend magazine:

Aging clergyman mourns decline of faith.

Exquisite temple unattended.

What shall we do with our tax-free church buildings?

Pictures of the interior of Saint John the Divine, Anglican, Sweet's Corners. It was a very handsome building, paintwork shining white, pews deeply reflective of fifty coats of varnish, elegant tower, some indifferent glass.

He walked her around the interior, made small talk about local notables lying in the churchyard. One of them had been in the provincial cabinet a century ago; another had lived to be a hundred and ten. She had to get out of here, she saw, or be sick. Already Freda was dribbling something that smelled bitterly of sour skim milk. As she passed out towards the front porch she gave the minister her news.

"I've rented the place to a young family, the Megarrys. Perhaps they may become members of your . . . flock." She felt pride and amusement at remembering the technical term.

"But they may not be Anglicans," said Mr. Marjoribanks.

"I don't suppose anybody insists on doctrinal purity any more. Or do they?" she corrected herself, seeing a look of pain on the man's face. There might be a story in this, she thought, for a small old audience.

"We try not to force our attentions on anyone to whom they may be unwelcome," said Mr. Marjoribanks. "Good-bye, Mrs. . . Mrs. . . I hope we meet again soon." He had picked up on her lack of a married name. The hell with that anyway!

The Megarrys moved in on the Monday and for some time she heard nothing more about the house. Around the second week in December an envelope arrived at her apartment with a series of post-dated cheques in it, drawn on a branch in Lyndhurst, dated January through May. She examined the handwriting on the cheques inscribed in defective ballpoint, a pale almost untraceable mauve. Whoever wrote them had pressed down hard on the pen when writing the signature; some of the other writing, including the amount on the face of the January and March cheques, was hard to make out. The numbers were generally clear enough. "Lila Megarry," said three of the cheques. The other two were signed "Mrs. L. Megarry."

She wondered if there were any specific reason for this. It was the handwriting of somebody who had been taught to write in primary school but had not done much with it afterwards. The letters were childishly formed; at the same time they had a faded elegance like the handwriting one might expect to find on packets of correspondence found in Victorian chests. All the cheques were dated on the first of the month.

She deposited the first one directly after New Year's, intending to pay a couple of important bills with it, but it came back from Lyndhurst under a cloud. She studied the "refused payment" stamp on the back of the wrinkled slip of paper — it was the first time she had ever been given a rubber cheque — and wondered if there were anything she could do with it. An indecent phrase suggested itself; she dismissed it immediately. She rang up the offending bank in Lyndhurst and asked to speak to the accountant, a Miss Belvedere, who assured her that there could be no harm in re-submitting the cheque for payment later in the month.

"It might just get through," she said.

"Might?"

"A proportion of them do."

"When should I try again?"

"Whenever the utterer of the cheque is likely to receive payments. I don't think there's much point in depositing it more than once more; after a couple of refusals a lineup has formed."

"I see."

She did not like the sound of this one little bit. She would have to do without something while those people (they were assuming the aspect of *those people!*) lived in her house for a full month rent-free. In an agony of frustration she crumpled the worthless cheque into a ball and flushed it down the toilet. At ten o'clock in the morning on the first day of February she was standing at the door of the bank in Lyndhurst, first in a small lineup, every member of which, she felt certain, held a cheque signed "Lila Megarry." She shoved the February cheque through the window of the first teller she saw and a *mauvais quart d'heure* ensued.

"The account can't quite cover this."

"How do you mean?"

"I can't tell you that."

"Can't tell me what? All I want is to cash the cheque."

"I'm not allowed to tell you anything that would reveal the customer's balance."

"You've already let me know that it's under two-fifty. What we have to determine is how far under. I mean, is it close?"

The teller screwed her head around on her neck very uneasily. "It's fairly close."

"Within ten dollars?"

"Not quite that close. Almost."

"Then cash the cheque and give them a ten-dollar overdraft."

"I don't think Mr. Ellenbeck will hold still for that."

"Could I talk to him?"

"I'll see." She went away again and as there were only two tellers working the lineup began to lengthen out. There were mutinous grumblings from other customers. In a few minutes the manager came to the counter and asked her to join him at a point somewhat removed from the cages. Bloody bank managers control our lives, she thought.

"They're short again," he said dolefully. "I nursed them through the last three months and now this."

"I didn't get my rent for January," she said, feeling close to tears. "I lost $250 I was counting on." She blinked, staring at the manager. "I have problems. I've got a little girl. I can't afford to have my house sitting empty. Couldn't you pay the cheque and subtract the OD from their next deposit?"

"I might do it for you, but don't, for God's sake, let it get around. I can't do it for everybody. I suppose they do have to have a roof over their heads. And a little food."

"Are there many others?"

"The Bell and Hydro, that's about it. God knows how they're heating the place. Is there any wood on the property?"

"There are trees."

"They won't fell the trees because they couldn't burn them for six months. Or maybe they won't think of that. You might take a look as you drive past."

"Cut my trees?"

"I'll pay this cheque through at its face value," said Mr. Ellenbeck, "but I don't know how long I can go on doing it. I hear he's having trouble getting his compensation. You have to have some sort of income after all, don't you?"

He led her back to the teller and oversaw payment. She just snatched at the money and ran without thanking him; it was her money; it was coming to her. She drove out the sideroad towards Highway 15, past Saint John the Divine, Anglican, and her place. It did rather look as if a couple of the trees at the back were missing. A clothesline hung very slack between the house and a nearby sumach; there were tiny faded dresses hanging on the line like things in a horrible Shirley Temple movie. She sped on, gained the highway, retreated to Kingston and went in to work in the afternoon; her grippe had miraculously cleared off, she said, and she couldn't bear to be away from work a whole day. And they believed her, even sympathised with her. Megarry didn't sign his own cheques, she saw clearly, because the fucker couldn't write. An illiterate. I've saddled myself with an illiterate and his brood, back-country hicks. She shook with an unidentifiable emotion of great intensity.

The March cheque sneaked through. At the same time however rumblings of discontent began to reach her in the form of phone calls from the Bell and the Hydro. Was she in any way connected to the Megarrys by blood? Would she make herself responsible for accounts left unpaid by them? There was a strong, if tacit, suggestion in both inquiries that she would have the dickens of a time getting the phone and the power turned back on once her tenants finally quit.

"You mean I'd have to pay for them?"

"Certainly," said the nasty voice of Bell Accounts. "You could scarcely expect us to restore service unless previous billings were met."

"How much do they owe?"

"They haven't actually paid us anything since installation but you can put your mind at rest; they aren't making a lot of long-distance calls. It's mainly a matter of service charges on three instruments."

"Three?"

"They've got three coloured phones and jacks all over the house. They're like beads and trinkets to them, you know."

"Them?"

"Mr. Megarry is part-Indian."

"I won't pay!"

"You'd be wise to think about getting them out."

Though it was late March, and the weather about as horrid as it could possibly be, wild wind, deep snow, deadly cold, she made up her mind on the spot. "I'll throw them so fucking far out they'll bounce; I won't put any backspin on them either. Do I make myself clear?"

"I think you'd be doing the right thing," said Bell Accounts.

"Bet your ass!"

This was when she began to learn the law of landlord and tenant, to realise that the drift of legal interpretation over the past decade has favoured the tenant. If you wanted to hurl somebody out, you had to show that no lease existed, that one month's notice was mutually-recognised as the intrument of termination, that the tenant clearly undertook to vacate at such a time and was thus responsible for the payment of utilities and fuel bills incurred by him. You had to be able to *show* this. Just to claim it was so would not satisfy a rental board. There might be hearings. This made her quail. She had so often acted the part of the crusading investigative reporter ready to crucify an elected official, reveal the nervous shrinking egotism of an actor or director, the fumbling negligence of a school administrator. She had been fearless in uncovering injustice in fairly high places. Now she was cast in the role of landlord and it appeared that Lila Megarry was pregnant again; that placed her in the position of putting a penniless member of a persecuted minority — positively one of the Dene Nation — on the street with his pregnant wife and their infant family and nowhere to go. Oh, terrific!

She would not swerve from righteousness. She was entitled to rent. January rent had not been paid. April rent had not been paid. When that cheque came back, there was little to be gained from it but the bank's notation in the characteristic green stamp-pad ink on the reverse of refusal to pay. In the sheriff's office, that notification on the worthless cheque stood for something, perhaps almost everything.

The Sheriff of Leeds County, a mild and quiet elderly man, wore no tin star, carried no six-guns, resembled a lawyer or your dentist. He fingered the bad cheques and her lawyer's letter and the unpaid Bell and Hydro bills which had mysteriously come into his possession.

"No problem," said the mild sheriff. "You've got enough here to hang him. I'll issue notice to quit this afternoon and after he gets it he has till the end of May to leave. If he isn't out of there by the thirty-first, my men will put his furniture on the roadway. Show me again exactly where the building is located."

"Don't let them hurt my house plants," she said. "It's right next door to the church of Saint John the Divine, Anglican."

"Right next door to Mr. Marjoribank's church?"

He pronounced the name "Marshbanks."

"Is that how you pronounce it?"

"What?"

"Marjoribanks."

Some slight confusion ensued.

"Never seen it written down, I don't believe. Always called him Marshbanks. Everybody does," said the sheriff.

"I see. My house is next door to the house of God," she said, yielding to some imp of perversity.

"We'll take care of you," said the sheriff. She had a hunch he knew she worked for the *Whig* and had something he wanted to hide. Almost everybody does.

So the Megarrys were overmatched; they didn't hang around to be evicted, just vanished in the night, sometime during the final week of May. Her lawyer phoned the glad tidings on the twenty-eighth of the month, advising her to get right out to the place and start the cleanup.

"Cleanup?"

"The Sheriff says the place is a mess. If you want to rent it or get rid of it, you're going to have to clean up after them."

Driving out from Kingston she predicted dirt and found shit, all different kinds. Mouse shit. Rat shit. Dog shit. Cat shit. Human shit. Shit shit. Smeared and strewn around piled-up green plastic bags in which reposed the detritus of a terrible winter: newspapers, cooking grease, diapers, sanitary napkins, tampons, broken dishes, countless bodies of insects, dead rats, live rats, ashes and clots of other unspeakable substances whose textures repelled her.

She had to clean it all up. She couldn't show the place to anybody — what would they think? How banish the stench? She hired a trucker for the last Sunday in May and together with him and his helper she carted three truckloads of tenant shit to the dump where it was burned.

Then, late in the afternoon, trembling with exhaustion, she determined with fanatic resolution to hose down and sweep out the summer kitchen where the mound of ordure had been stacked. It would take weeks for the odours to disperse. As she played a powerful jet of water over the walls and floor of the infirm frame structure, she saw Mr. Marjoribanks standing not far off, just across the property line. She turned the hose off and walked over to say hello, hoping inwardly for comfort and encouragement.

"You wouldn't believe what I've trucked out of there," she said as she drew near. "Filth! But I don't think they'll bother you any more."

"They weren't any bother."

"They weren't?"

"No, they'd had a very hard time. Mr. Megarry was a cripple and there were interruptions with his compensation money. They were expecting another child and they had nothing."

"I can't help any of that," she said. "I've got to think of myself. I'm not your mean landlord, I'm a person with problems too. I've got a little girl. I work for a living. I have to get income from my house. I can't provide anybody with free rent. Nobody's entitled to a free ride through life. I'm not listening, I tell you. I'm not listening, do you hear?"

Evolving Bud

THE LANDING. What a grand place it was for the youngsters back in 1975 or 1976 when there was something for them to do over there, a place to go where they could enjoy themselves and stay out of grief. Around the clock from May to September you could hear the sound of outboard motors, seventy-five horse, ninety, a hundred-and-fifteen, speeding up the long reach from Wide Water or Bonteen Bay, racing for the three docks at the landing: the public dock which in those days was sinking lower and lower in the water; the gas pump beside the big store; then, to port the smaller wharves for the other grocery stores and marine suppliers with competing Esso, Texaco and Fina gas pumps and services. Each dock had its own clientèle. The smallest dock, Minto's Marina, handled Fina products, fishing equipment, groceries, Coleman stoves and lanterns for the old-timers, folks with island cottages who only came in once a week to buy supplies; they came from really remote parts of the lake where there were no Hydro lines and a summer place might look exactly as it did in 1875. You saw a certain number of codgers around Minto's — Billie and the boys never went there — who still hung on as professional guides for Americans at the hotel, half-submerged flotsam from the era of the balky Evinrude two-and-a-half with lures and flies stuck in their hatbands and crazed looks acquired during epic trolling for a legendary thirty-three-pound pike in the cold isolate reaches: Rummer's Reach, Slick's Bay, Palmyra Cove where, they said, the lake might be five hundred feet deep.

The middle store, Hanlon's Groceries and Variety, was where the comfortable middle-aged cottagers went for the papers, gas and oil mixed in the correct proportions for their big engines, paperbacks and memberships in the Cottagers' Protective Association.

The largest store at the public dock was the trading-post for the summer children and their local rivals in love. The summer children seemed to be mostly girls like Billie, fourteen, fifteen, with a talent for water-skiing and huge insatiable engines you don't see anymore. It seems so long ago and it's only a decade; those sunburnt girls are all married; they have sailboats and conserve energy; they have one child with another on the way. Their brothers work for data-processing suppliers or are doing graduate degrees at some business school. Or they write speeches for some middle-level politician.

At that time the rivalry between the seasonal boys and the descendants of the codgers was an engaging thing to see. For a mile up and down Landing Road lean heavily tanned lads with cutoff jeans bleached to the faintest cottony-blue trailed the girls from the large runabouts and tried to get an arm around them: these boys had the local names; Minto, Slick, Shuckerly. They went over to Athens by Landing Road to the high school through the fall and winter; their fathers worked in construction or farmed or sold each other real estate or did all of those things. These old families had been taking their living one way or another from the lake and the summer people for a century. The hotel still bore traces of the elegance of the nineties. There were faded striped awnings over the verandas from June through Labour Day; you could buy your fishing licence at the desk beneath wall plaques of stuffed muskies and pickerel and try to read the fading print on notices about the Ontario Fish and Game Regulations thumbtacked to the wall in the thirties.

The year Billie was fifteen some fugitive movie producer used the hotel all summer for interiors. The sagging upstairs corridors with sudden surprising changes of direction, the doors which swung shut unpropelled, the enormous photographs of long dead picnic parties gave the finished film a persuasiveness offered by few of its other aspects. The colour stock wasn't bad.

Americans still came to the hotel and discussed the places to look for the big fellows in measured ignorant speculation. There was a wonderful slow-to-serve, ill-lit dining room next to a bar already showing signs of rowdiness to come. There was a superb anonymous cook. Once or twice a summer a cottaging family might take the twelve-mile drive around the shore on the twisting rocky roads to the Landing to eat fish or steak and justify a vacation. Summers were distinguished by planked pickerel or char-broiled filet.

"That was the year they were making those rhubarb pies. Gollies, but they were laxative in effect!"

"But they sure were tasty!"

"And then the next year everybody was selling blueberries and there were no desserts that didn't turn blue on sight. Blueberry flan. Blueberry shortcake with whipped cream, oh my."

"The fruit cups!"

Billie used to leave the table to stroll down Landing Road to the dock and socialise with the locals while her elders lingered over coffee. She was in her jujube phase at the time, keeping complex statistics on the occurrence of green, yellow, orange, red and black in sackfuls of chewy delights. She would come home long after the rest of the family had driven back to the other side of the lake, squired across Wide Water by some knave in a fibreglass runabout with a hundred horses at his command, a tale of jujube frequencies on her lips, giggling, unworried, our girl.

"Why are the red ones invariably the most frequent?"

"Ah child, these are the romantic secrets that only great age or great wisdom can illuminate."

"And then there are always far fewer green ones than anything else . . . I think the black ones come in second in order of frequency."

"The other mystery, jujubewise, is their shapes. What are they supposed to be?"

"Little black babies," she would gurgle.

"Look, these are lanterns."

"No, silly, they're barrels."

"What's this orange one?"

"Isn't it a peeled orange in sections?"

"So it is; and this is a little bunch of grapes, I think; and this is a banana."

Ah, summer.

Billie would seek her silken couch. The water-skier who had brought her home would nod in embarrassment and withdraw, filling the scented night with the roar of immense power which would gradually fade. Tales of eager teenagers who smashed open the stoutest fibreglass whizzing through Stone Fence Gap in the dark circulated at that time at the Landing like a *chanson de geste,* often built around the distressful image of some overbold youth turning over and over high in the air like a thrown football, flung out of his boat as though from catapult by the shocking abrupt stop. One boy died in this way and a summer or two later a revolving red light was placed in the gap by the authorities. This accomplished little. Spectacular accidents continued. Good old times.

Billie has never been eager to bust her noggin on some spur of limestone issuing from the depths; she would go in slower boats or on the pillions of dirt bikes, never on street bikes without a helmet, one prudent girl. She'd have been sixteen by now and was never really impressed with the high-speed operators though she would accept a boat-ride home from the Landing, a ride on an XL-170 around the Barn or somebody's free games on a Commander America pinball machine. At that time the Barn was in full efflorescence; it had just forsaken heavy metal for disco.

It really was an old barn and not some weatherboard fantasy standing at the top of the hill, up Landing Road for a long long time. Whoever owned it did a smart thing in 1976: They added a lean-to at the north end with a counter and stools and burgers and fries, lined the barn walls with pinball games and installed an enormous coin-operated record player with thunderous amplification; they went from Chicago to Donna Summer in the course of six weeks during the first season of operation. There was a rudimentary stage platform which might, once upon a time, have formed some part of a feed-loft. The planking of the walls showed starlight through a hundred chinks and knotholes but the roof was sound and the hard rain never came on down; the flooring was laid on level ground which would not give or vibrate under press of rock or disco. When you got in there with the speakers giving tongue, the bells of the pinball machines ringing and clanging, the shuffle of kids' feet whispering along the polished pine and the sound of dirt bikes whining around and around out back, it was stereophonic, man.

Billie loved the big bad Barn. They all did, the summer girls and boys and the natives. Families could leave a couple of daughters there at 10:00 P.M. on a Friday or Saturday, secure in the conviction that someone or other would bring the girls safely home in big boats. The whole scene was memorable for the sound of motors — bikes, hundred-horse muscle-outboards — and for voices, that long rippling giggling gurgling and growling blend of girlish laughter and boyish persuasion. Harmless, immemorial, shot with luck, defined by pleasure craft of wondrous variety.

A certain red punt began to incur upon the scene, an undistinguished little boatling of ancient conception and design: flat-bottomed, slab-sided, homemade, handpainted with a five-horse Johnson suspended from a transom deeply marked with roundels punched into the yielding wood by the retaining screws. Probably forty years old and leaked like a son-of-a-bitch; had that peculiarly smelly tang of the wooden skiff left long in stagnant berthing. Late at night on big weekends, after the fibreglass runabouts had holed up for the party, you might hear this low-key pop-pop-popping and it would be the red punt, solitary boatman astern easing the thing along in the dark, heading around Bessborough Point towards an unidentifiable destination up the creek mouth. There were six or eight ancient cottages back in there (which more recent arrivals seldom saw), the property of aborigines who had built up the cottaging tradition early in the century. Their names were visible on hand-lettered signs tacked to trees, arrows pointing up shore roads or across limestone ridges on which no city-dwelling weekender dared risk his muffler. *Gavin and Markell, Leeder, Alguire, Bairstowe, Charland.* Pickups and graders drove up in there.

Very late one Sunday night when the Barn was closed, Billie came home in the red punt, sitting in the bow to trim the graceless hull which had about an inch of freeboard. Well, say six inches. The boat came creeping along the shore without any running lights and drew in under the circle of clarity provided by a Japanese lantern hung on a pine and meant to serve as a leading-light for late visitors. The lantern was orange-coloured and it gave the otherwise ordinary cement platform an air of imaginative chic. Billie hopped out, thanked her escort and came tripping up the stairs waving a paper parasol which somebody had bought for her at the Landing.

"Good night, Bob," she hooted into the shadows at dockside. There were grunts in reply; then the creaking hull disappeared, blocky form in the stern hunched over the motor, one of those antique devices with an exposed flywheel and a hook-on rope. It might have qualified as some sort of marine-museum piece. The boy had likely inherited it from his father, one of the Leeders, Bairstowes, Charlands of longtime local affiliation. The under-powered little motor and the ugly old boat — and the boy — seemed strangely like the creations of an earlier time.

The midnight boatman began to come around to the dock by day; they all did, everybody who ever brought her home. There was this one hockey player, almost a household word, who owned a whole island down Rummer's Reach. He used to take her water-skiing on Wide Water for hours at a time. The hockey player taught Billie to operate his huge boat then did all sorts of acrobatics astern: stood on his head on one ski; criss-crossed the wake; showoff stuff; one great athlete. He was killed two years later in a hang-gliding incident on another lake. There were dozens of American kids (who thought Billie was a Northern princess), costive Montréal anglos with choked accents and the sons of professional men from the river cities twenty miles away. And the locals who never had much of a look-in. And this Bob or whatever, a hard person to know.

Never had much to say for himself and looked like an otter. Might have been fifteen, perhaps a year younger than Billie, not exactly shy, more watchful than anything. He would dive from the rocks into five or six feet of water in a neat flat racing leap. No stomach at all and even at fifteen those ropy knotted muscles hard physical labour confers on certain forms not in themselves beautiful. He swam in a choppy, exceedingly speedy style and would jump off any of the fifty-foot cliffs along the shoreline, always testing the depth of the water first.

There was some confusion about his identity. "Bob? Bob? What Bob?"

"How should I know?"

"What's he doing on our beach then?"

"Swimming, silly, can't anyone?"

"It's a private beach."

"Oh, it is not!"

"It is if you pay attention to politeness. We don't go over and swim at the Mellanby's without being asked."

"That damn Jean Mellanby. What's she got to be so stuck up about?"

"Several million dollars."

"Money means nothing to me," Billie would declare and that was true; it didn't. She never was one to pick and choose among her boyfriends on the basis of their prospects or their parents' investments. And just look at who she finally hooked up with!

Anyway, Bob. Yes. She got this Bob to stay for dinner one evening and nobody could get a word out of him. He sat at a corner of the table with his place-setting sandwiched between Billie and her mother looking up slantwise from under a heavy forehead.

"Is your cottage around here, Bob? Have you always come here for your summers?"

"Did your Dad build that boat for you, Bob?" It looked like rough carpenter's work. "Did he teach you how to make them; are there any others like it on the lake?"

The kid could eat, no question about it. Not like a glutton but steadily, with plenty of wristy follow-through. He had the appetite of a grown man accustomed to physical output. When he'd finished a plateful of Fudgee-Os and Oreos he finally straightened out his neck and held his head up and said to the table at large, "Actually, my name is Bud."

"Bud?"

"Yup."

Billie was flustered. "Bud?"

"He just said so."

"Well, anybody can make a mistake."

After that his name got worked into every sentence. "I think it might rain overnight, isn't that right, Bud?" (This in the accent of the summer visitor consulting local sage.) "Sounds like the wind's getting up a bit, eh, Bud?"

"What about that boat of yours, Bud? Is she going to be okay in these waves?"

"We'll bring her onshore, Bud. No need to let her swamp. Maybe have to dive for your motor, eh, Bud?"

"How about it, Bud?"

"Are you going to be all right, Bud? Do you want us to take you home in our boat? You could come over for yours tomorrow, Bud. What do you say?"

He got his boat home just fine. Probably sidled along the shore and around into the creek mouth without any trouble, probably heard foolish echoes of his name sounding like confused birdcalls in the trees. "Bud Bob Bud Bob Bud Bob."

Everybody felt mighty silly.

He was just one of the Charlands, that's all, a notable local family that used to hold all the land on the east side of the lake from the village down to the highway, eight or nine miles of shoreline and a big stand of back-country brush and abandoned nineteenth-century roads, wonderful cross-country trails and snowmobile runs. About the time Bud Charland came upon the scene, the provincial department of natural resources began buying up much of this land for reforestation. None of the purchases was made by expropriation; in every case a high price was paid. All land that might be useable for recreational purposes was left in the Charlands' hands. From being a poverty-stricken band of back-concession failed farmers, they began to metamorphose into an understated sort of local aristocracy, an old family, people with a century-and-a-half of township affiliations behind them. Billie had no notion of this; neither did anybody else. All the same, Bud Charland's name and his appearances at the Barn, during the short time left to that institution's career, began to have special undertones.

"He's somebody important," Billie said a little suspiciously. She knew nothing about township history. Billie is a city girl. She still has that paper parasol and now claims that Bud Charland gave it to her. Nobody knows for sure if that's true but she enjoys teasing her husband about it. He never gave her a parasol; but he has interesting holdings of his own in Mississauga.

In the second or third summer of its operations, say 1977, the Barn began to be affected by changes in the locality just as the Charlands and the Bairstowes were on the other side of the lake. A special kind of money began to circulate around the Landing, loose money, beer-drinking, dirt-biking money, snowmobiling money. Two snowmobile dealerships opened on Landing Road,

Arctic Cat and John Deere. People began to spend a little wildly at the same time that unemployment and inflation were in flood, confusing issues. How could prices and unemployment be high at the same time? That didn't make sense. Everybody was buying porn mags at $2.50, then $3.95 a copy. Times were hard but exhilarating in an odd way.

When Bud Charland entered the Barn that last summer all the girls wanted to dance with him; after all, if the Charlands had been able to hang around the lake for 150 years, they might be good for a few — maybe many — more.

Bud had nothing to say, naturally, but looked older and even stronger. Swam off Billie's end of the dock at her personal invitation, needing no introduction.

The Landing was less fun than it had been because the recreation money had moved into the hotel and the dining-room clientèle was changing; the chef left. They had a sex show on Friday nights and a country-and-western concert on Saturdays which often blurred into Sunday morning. People started to come from as far away as Elgin. Sectional rivalries, forgotten for a century, now surfaced; there were fist-fights outside the hotel every weekend in the early hours of Saturday and Sunday morning. The rough crowd started to turn up in the Barn around 9:00 P.M. to kill time until the strip shows came on.

It killed the Barn as a place for kids. Some of them sneaked into the hotel bar but most of them simply stopped strolling up Landing Road from the docks: they concentrated more and more on their boats. The government reconstructed the dock and improved the moorings. The price of gas continued to rise.

That year you would see burly OPP types lounging around the lunchcounter in the grocery store. It seemed a very short time since the presence of a policeman at the Landing caused surprised comment. Now they were there frequently, collecting evidence, waiting for something serious to happen. Finally one Friday night towards the end of the summer of 1979 some wise guy burned a stripper on the leg with the tip of his cigar. In the fight which followed, a death occurred. Nobody was ever charged with anything. No arrest was ever made. But the hotel closed soon after. The Barn had shut down the summer before. Outboard motors were shrinking. Dirt bikes were out of vogue. Snowmobiling continued a popular winter sport and cross-country skiing boomed. You supplied your own energy and grew healthy.

The Charland property on the other side of the lake slowly increased in value. As long as the provincial government was determined to buy up scrub bush and reforest it, just so long would lake-country property rise in price. A painful banality.

In the winter of 1979, about the time Bud was getting into his twenties and Billie was receiving her first proposals, the Charland family opened up an old farmhouse back in the woods which had been built, then speedily abandoned, in the late nineteenth century. They didn't paint the exterior although they did put in acceptable heating and some rough furniture and called the finished results Charlands' SnowTrail Clubhouse. They sold memberships and rented skis and marked trails for cross-country and snowmobiling.

The big store at the Landing laid in a stock of snowmobile suits which looked from a distance like mummification, peculiar polyester sarcophagi, garments worn by mediaeval knights on their tombs, completely wraparound, bulky, puffy with heraldic colours and stripes, zig-zags and checkers.

Billie lost all her beauty of form in a snowmobile suit, but gained in the exchange a subtle mystery. She always detested snowmobiling, too darn cold, but would risk a trail-run in pursuit of fashion and dominance. She got out to Charlands' SnowTrail Clubhouse — with immense difficulty — the week after Christmas with her boyfriend two years ago. The holiday developed into one of those comic fiascos that go down so well as half-hour sitcom segments on television.

On the first night they found their reservation was only for a single room. Then Bud Charland stepped into the picture, all taciturn chivalry, the authentic outdoorsman, to arrange another room for the boyfriend.

"Do we really need favours from this Daniel Boone?"

"Angel, he's just trying to be nice and we can't sleep in the same room."

"Who says we can't?"

"Not me." Business of crossing arms and looking demure.

"Who then?"

"I wouldn't want to embarrass the Charlands."

"Bugger the Charlands!"

"You'll feel better after a run up the creek, invigorated." She laughed at the boyfriend, then — as she tells the story — kissed him in a sisterly manner. It was at this moment that Bud appeared in the room to remove some of the excess baggage.

"I'll just carry these down the hall if your *friend* . . . " (Heavy work with lowered forehead and twitching eyebrows.) ". . . if your *friend* will follow me."

"Bud, I'd like you to meet my future husband. Arnold, this is Bud Charland. You know, the Charlands own everything around here for miles, timber rights, the paving company. I don't know what-all."

Your basic townmouse-countrymouse confrontation.

There was a heavy silence which Billie broke by exclaiming, "Bud Charland, that was a chaste, sisterly kiss. I won't have you making a federal case out of it."

She plunked herself down on a brass bed of somewhat studied antiquity and began to cry with a pretty air of distraction. Bud and Arnold grinned at each other like travellers who, upon meeting and going some way together in a desert, eventually recognise a familiar oasis.

They ignored her manoeuvres for the remainder of the week. They went on long snowmobile runs together. From the veranda of the lodge, Billie suffered the indignity of watching the two men zipping round and round on the vast spread of ice in the creek mouth.

On the next-to-last day they made her come ice-fishing. The three of them sat for hours in a tiny smelly shack on a single bench next to a round hole in the ice taking turns dangling a thin filament through the aperture. They had a fire in a cutoff oil drum. A Coleman lantern hung from the roof. There were no windows in the shack, only an ill-fitting door through which hyperborean blasts shrilled. Billie sat clad in her snowmobile suit looking, she says, like a brass rubbing of Princess Mathilde of Anjou, only the exquisite oval of her face showing, the rest armoured by plastic fabric. And Arnold . . . Arnold . . . Arnold all at once hooked the legendary thirty-three pound pike through the hole in the ice. He will never let her forget it!

There are new methods of mounting fish now, which keep them from getting that greyish-greenish look of painted plaster characteristic of displays in the old summer hotels. Maybe they freeze them instantly and cement up the guts. Who knows?

Arnold got that fish out of the back country and up to the city the same day. It was hard. They had to pack their clothes in half-an-hour and carry everything back to the access road in three snowmobile trips over progressively darker trails. The woods were dark and deep but unlovely Billie said later, fraught with visions of collisions. Their car was parked next to the abandoned grocery store of McIntosh Mills; their retreat occupied hours. It was early-winter dark when they finally laid the huge fish on the back seat of Arnold's gas-guzzler and set off for civilisation.

"I won't let the soft flesh of my fish be scarred by decomposition," swore Arnold, moved erratically towards poetry by intensity of emotion. Billie thought that he had stronger feelings about his big fish than about anything they had done together. Her recollections ran back in half-sleep (she was exhausted) to the perfectly round hole in the ice, about the size of a manhole-cover, under the glare of the Coleman radiating the glitter of polished snow crystal and foot-thick ice, shining grey streaked with veins of dead white, underneath the ice floor the living water and the blind fish. She imagined herself as such a fish with blood that would never warm, circulating in super-cooled dark in a medium that flowed with her, swam along her fins. Down through the exact circle of pale yellow like the sun at the frozen end of the world, into her depths dangled a filament so thin as to disappear in the cold swimming dark, traces of living oil (bacon fat?) signalling out along the chilled current to the organs of fish, drawing them to the three-pronged hook. She bit.

"Hey, wake up, baby, hey! Throw newspaper around my pike."

Arnold got his fish to his Mississauga freezer and then to a Toronto taxidermist on the following Monday. The mounted pike, laminated in almost-transparent plastic — just the faintest hint of ocean blue in the laminate, is permanently fastened to the wall of the poolside changing rooms at the place near Brampton where he and Billie live. Three miles away are acres of Arnold's condos.

The family misses Billie but kids grow up and away; if they don't actually inhabit new towns and condominiums they change themselves so that you can hardly tell them for what they used to be. Driving along the hazardous road around the east side of the lake, early this spring, just after the runoff, the family found they had to pick their way carefully over erosion ruts where trickles from the high ground had been powerfully-freshened by torrential rains. Not snow, rain. There hasn't been any snow to speak of in the 1980s and it rains hard in late February.

At one point they were obliged to stop the car, get out and lay some small logs in a particularly deep gully. The Charlands don't permit any blacktopping.

When they got back in the car and inched gingerly across the insubstantial surface they heard a tremendous noise developing near them from back in the bush. It swelled to a roar. Everybody trembled.

From the recesses of Bairstowe/Leeder/Charland territory there burst a muscle-car, a 1973 Dodge Charger hardtop with double-reinforced shocks on the rear wheels tilting the car upwards with peculiar insolence to expose immensely fat dragster tires. Rubber spun and grabbed and dug at the road surface, threw up fine gravel and old clotted crankcase oil in a wide spray. Visions of a flaming chariot.

Bud Charland sat erect behind the wheel sporting enormous sideburns, a long cigar clamped in a corner of his jaw. He waggled the cigar once as the Charger, cherry-coloured with black rally stripes, threw improvised fill behind him. Logs, branches, big stones. An unknown girl sat immediately on his right, no visible daylight between them. Small and dark, she gazed up at him adoringly, rocking sidewise on the seat. The huge tires bit deep, the hardtop lunged away around the next bend and headed for town. Nobody could decide whether the cigar, the girl, the tires, the shocks or the sideburns pissed them off most.

The Blackmailer's Wasted Afternoon

I LEAD A BLAMELESS HUMDRUM LIFE. I was therefore somewhat taken aback this afternoon when the doorbell rang and I heard a shout from the front porch, a man's voice calling me by my nickname. It isn't a nickname everybody knows. I use my real name at the office. My nickname is a special one known only to my wife and a few intimates. My children don't know what it is.

There I was, sitting in the living room in semi-darkness, scratching my left testicle which had been pinched by the crotch of my jockey shorts when I sat down, hitching myself around in the easy chair trying to get comfortable, admiring my parrots. All of a sudden this total stranger called my name. The front windows were open and I could hear footsteps on the porch. I could see somebody out of the far left window but the angle was bad and I couldn't recognise him. I wasn't expecting anybody. The voice was unfamiliar, but not accented or foreign.

The bell rang again, bing-bong, just the once.

"I know you're home: the car's in the driveway," said the man.

I stood up unwillingly, wiggling my torso to free up my scrotum which was still stuck in folds of underwear. The skin stuck to my groin. I lifted my left leg and shook it, then went into the vestibule and opened the door. A stocky sort of fellow was standing just outside, a nondescript man a little shorter than I, wearing a single-breasted two-piece suit, blue with a faint pinstripe which looked like he bought it at Woolco. About a $149.95 suit. He had a small ring notebook in his hand which he flipped shut when he spoke.

"I'm the blackmailer," he said. "Can I come in?"

I thought at first that I'd misheard him. I said, "I'm sorry, I gave at the office on the United Services Plan. Community Chest. I forget what they call it."

But he simply repeated himself, moved a step closer and pronounced my nickname with a rising inflection.

"That's me," I admitted, "but I don't believe we've met, have we?" I didn't like to ask for his name outright. I might have met him somewhere and forgotten him. People hate it when you don't remember them. "I didn't catch the name."

"I didn't throw it," he said, smiling.

I thought, he's got a sense of humour anyway. "What is it you wanted?"

"I'm the blackmailer. I believe it's time we had a little talk. But I don't think that you want to talk to me out here, do you? I mean, with your friends and neighbours mowing their lawns and going by and raking their leaves. You'll want to keep this pretty quiet."

I said, "I don't know what you're talking about. I'm afraid I'll have to ask you to show me some identification. Some credentials. Who are you anyway?"

"Oh, you know me," he said quietly, moving another step closer. "Sure you do, if you just think back. They always do."

"Have you covered both sides of the street?" I said, playing for time.

"I've given the area thorough coverage."

"With what results?"

"Oh now, that would be telling, wouldn't it? And it doesn't concern you, after all. I really think we should go inside."

"You're the blackmailer?" I said finally. I think I'd always known he might show up.

"That's who I am."

"And you're sure it's me you need to talk to? I mean, wouldn't one of the children do, or perhaps my wife?" I felt a little mean when I said this; actually it just slipped out.

"No. You're my assignment for today."

I didn't like the sound of that one bit. "Are you working for some big corporation? Is this sort of a poll?"

He lifted his eyes and stared at me and I took a step backwards. I said, "Won't you come in? I'm sorry there's nobody home but me, but I could fix you a cup of coffee or some soup. Would you like a nice bowl of hot soup?"

"Thanks, I just ate. But we might go into the dining room," he said. He was taking off a pair of toe rubbers. "I'm out in all weathers," he said when he caught me looking at them.

"I guess. In your line of work."

"We need a room with some light in it. I think your dining room would do fine. The living room is very dark." He took a quick turn around the living room as though he'd once lived in the house. "You've got new drapes," he said.

"Yes, she ran those up sometime over the winter."

"Don't the children's photographs look lovely?" he said. "And you've got a fire laid in the fireplace, all ready for the fall."

"Is there something about that you don't like?" I said. I'm not an easy man to anger. I'm basically pretty contented with what I've got. However, I'm not too keen on utter strangers who force their way into your home and then make insinuations about it. "It's hard to get much light in the living room in the afternoon because of the way it faces," I said. "And then there's that big tree on the lawn. That tree belongs to the city. It's just over the property line and they won't allow a householder to lay a finger on it. It needs cutting back. My next-door neighbour is always complaining about it as though it were my fault. I keep telling him to call the city forestry department and ask them to come and prune it but he claims that's up to me. I don't like to get involved with the city. It's enough that taxes are what they are. But you can see that it's hard to brighten this room without using artificial light and I hate to have lights on at 2:30 P.M. As a matter of fact, I like it dark in here in the afternoon. It's restful. I spend a lot of time just sitting here in my recliner . . ."

"We'll go in here," he said.

I followed him into the dining room sun. A big back window looks out on the garden and from where I sit at the head of the table, the sun shines directly in my eyes until about six o'clock.

"Perhaps we ought to sit sidewise on for this interview. Better still, facing," I said. I've been interviewed before so I know how it goes. "I'll sit here and you sit on the other side and that way neither of us will get sun in our eyes."

"No," he said. "I believe I'll sit right here next to you on this chair." He took my chair; I had to sit on my wife's chair, catty-cornered from the head of the table.

"Are you sure you'll be comfortable?" I asked him.

"Quite sure. How about you?"

"I feel relaxed and at home," I said.

"Then I expect we'd better get started," he said. He produced the small ring notebook suddenly, like somebody doing a card trick. I couldn't see where he'd had it hidden. He flipped through it. It was one of those cheap little books with the rings at the top from which you rip out the pages and throw them away once you're finished with them. He removed two or three sheets, crumpled them up and put them somewhere.

"Hmmm," he said, "hmmmmmmmmmm, isn't it true that at the age of ten you always used to steal copies of the *Globe and Mail* from paper boxes so you could read the hockey scores?"

I was flabbergasted. Who keeps track of things like that, for goodness' sake? You can't treasure up a child's minor misbehaviour and bring it against him decades later. We've all done things we're a little ashamed of and wouldn't do as grownups. A child should be judged by how he turns out, not by what he does when he's just learning to behave. I said a lot of this to him and some other things besides. I blustered at him a bit.

"That's all very well," he said, "but have you never stolen a paper since?"

"Stolen? That's a hard word. The paper only costs a dime after all."

"A daily paper costs fifty cents in the corner boxes nowadays. As you perfectly well know. You ought to be ashamed of yourself."

"If I don't happen to have change, I put the money in the next time."

"Always?"

I said, "All right, you make me feel a bit ashamed of myself. But "ashamed" isn't worth a cover-up. Everybody takes a free paper now and then. If you put everybody in jail who takes a paper once in awhile, the cells would be overcrowded."

"That isn't much of a defence."

"Maybe it isn't but it means I have nothing to fear from you."

"Have you never failed to report income on your tax return?"

"I'm sorry to have to tell you that I simply refuse to go into this whole question of taxation. Simply refuse to go into it. Ninety-nine percent of my income comes from salary covered by deductions at source. I pay far too much in taxes."

"No declarable perks? No free secretarial services? No free stationery boosted from office supplies? What about those ballpoint pens in your pocket?"

"I paid for those pens!"

"What about that leaf-green one with the piggy-back refill. Isn't that from office stock?"

"What if it is?"

"Expense-account lunches?"

"All right. What about the money of my own I spend on company business? I take people out to lunch at my own expense quite often."

"The last time was in early 1977," he said.

My mouth dropped open. Then I clamped it shut. Then I said again that I wouldn't discuss the tax question. Everybody in the country agrees we're over-taxed and over-governed.

"You want to write the laws to suit yourself, is that it?"

"I have nothing further to say about it."

We sat and stared at each other for about half a minute. One of my parrots, the green one, rose up with a great flapping of wings and flew over our heads into the living room where he perched on the valance box.

"I think he's trying to tell you something," I said smartly.

"Isn't it true that during sexual intercourse you spend most of your time kissing and embracing your wife's bottom?" he shot back.

"What?"

"I think you heard me correctly."

"I've never been asked such a question in my life. You've got one hell of a nerve, you have, coming into my home on a quiet afternoon and cross-examining me like some sort of commissar. What if somebody had heard you?"

"Your actions can't be very agreeable or satisfying for your partner," he said with what I considered great impertinence. "That's the sort of conduct that causes feminism."

"Keep your voice down," I said, looking around. The green parrot returned to his perch where he sat looking at me accusingly out of his left eye. It's strange the way a parrot's eyes are set in its head: either eye can look directly out of the side of the skull. I wonder whether the two fields of vision coincide and whether they see straight out the side when the other eye is blinking or closed.

"You're not paying attention," he said. "Do you know what I'd call that? I'd have to call it an ugly immature onanism. Pretty ugly!"

"'Pretty ugly' is self-contradictory," I said. I was scoring a point.

"Don't attempt to bandy words with me, sir," he said. "I suggest you invariably leave your partner in a state of dissatisfaction."

"I'm not admitting anything," I said, "and anyway, what if I do? We're not all perfect. In fact if you go by the porn films and the skin books, hardly anybody's perfect. I've never claimed to be a sexual athlete. And no nice woman expects it. I don't care what they say in *Penthouse* or in the feminist press."

"Oh, you don't?" he whispered. His voice now took on undertones of silky menace.

"No, I'm afraid I don't. If you really want to know, I think an awful lot of men spend their lives gazing up at some woman's ass; and yet, the world continues to rotate. We weren't promised sexual bliss when we entered this existence."

"And you're content to be observed in that position?"

I said, "No. I'm not. It's undignified and somewhat obsessive. But, it isn't the sort of thing they take you to jail for. Or to the concentration camps. Ashamed, I can live with. Undignified, I can live with. Those are simply personal foibles. Maybe I have more fun than my wife does, but she isn't going to prosecute or inform on me to the sex-police. At least I don't think she is. I haven't heard anything about it so far. And you can't sue and recover for foibles. Can you imagine Dostoievsky writing a great novel called *Foible and Punishment?* There's nothing in it for you."

"You wouldn't want it talked about."

"Who says so? People talk about these things all the time now. When I was a kid I thought I was the only one who imagined these actions and they seemed very wicked. Now I find everybody's up to the same tricks and a lot of the thrill has gone."

"Shall I list your other kinds of foreplay?"

"Publish it and be damned," I said. "I'd have the whole world on my side. There isn't a soul alive who doesn't get up to some little kink when the lights are out. I don't suppose your own record would bear too close an examination."

"But I'm asking the questions."

"Ask away," I said. I had him on the run.

"Do you think I like doing this?"

"Nobody invited you," I said.

"Not so. You send out signals all the time. You're simply begging for it."

"Are you all finished?"

"I haven't even started!"

This reply made me anxious. "Do your worst," I expostulated. "You haven't got anything on me. I'm clean."

"You're a brute."

"Prove it."

"You're a coarse bullying coward who doesn't scruple to inflict torment on the weak who can't hit back."

"Are you joking?" I said. "I'm notorious for my mild manner. I'm a regular Casper Milquetoast — if you happen to know who he is."

"What about the night of the Webern broadcast?"

"I don't know what you're talking about."

"I think you do," he said and, of course, he was right. I couldn't control my reactions. I felt my face go hot and I felt sick. I didn't care to remember what I'd done. It was rotten and I regretted it bitterly. I think it might be about the nastiest thing I've ever done and I certainly wouldn't want it talked about. I might even pay to hush it up and I could see that he knew this.

"I've got you where I want you," he said. "On the night of Sunday, 15 November, 1964, there was to be a broadcast of the six short pieces for orchestra of Anton Webern. Isn't that so?"

"Yes."

"I thought you'd remember the occasion. The broadcast had been announced some time before, more than once, on the FM network and you were planning to listen to it."

"You have to allow for the circumstances," I said. "It had been raining hard all day; we couldn't get out of the house. The kids sat around in the kitchen whining. They didn't want to go to church; they didn't want to stay inside; they had my wife frantic. It was raw and cold and the landlord wouldn't put the heat up high enough. He said he never adjusted the thermostat before the first of December. It was a day like that, a day everybody runs into often enough. You have to put that into the balance. And I'd heard about the six short pieces by Webern for years; how influential they were; how hard to find on records; how rarely performed. They only last a few minutes, you see. There's hardly anything to them. If you turn your head, you'll miss them. I was really looking forward to hearing them. It was going to redeem the day. At supper with the kids I was hugging myself and thinking, well, after the hullaballoo there'll be the six short pieces on FM. And my wife knew this. She fed the kids a bit early and got the older ones off to the front of the apartment where they couldn't be heard. She put the baby to bed in his crib about half past six and he lay right down. We thought he'd gone off to sleep. Actually, he wasn't a baby; he was close to three and was only sleeping in his crib because he seemed attached to it. We used to leave the sides down to make it look like what they used to call a youth bed. But for some reason we left the sides up that Sunday night and went back into the kitchen where the FM radio was, right next to the baby's bedroom. I don't know why I keep calling him the baby. He must have been close to three. More than two-and-a-half anyway. A strong husky child."

"And seven o'clock came."

"Seven o'clock came and the radio was silent for a moment. Then there were two or three program announcements and finally a voice said, 'We hear now a performance of the six short pieces for orchestra by the modern master, Anton Webern.' He gave some details about the composition and the players. Then came that breathy silence which tells you a tape is about to start. And then my son stood up in his crib and held on to the sides of it and started crying.

"You have to understand about these pieces. They originated a whole contemporary style of writing. They're mostly silence, a few chiming and tinkling noises interrupted by long silences. I don't think they last three minutes. I ran into the bedroom and begged the child to be still; this agitated him. I ran back into the kitchen and I thought I heard a gong but I wasn't sure. He cried louder. I ran back into the bedroom and entreated him with tears in my eyes to hold it for a minute but he cried louder. I scurried into the kitchen. I couldn't hear anything but wails from the bedroom.

"Then the announcer said, 'Those were the six short pieces for orchestra of the modern master, Anton Webern, a leading member of the school of Schönberg. Anton Webern was accidentally shot to death by an American sentry at his home in Germany in 1945. The composer had stepped outside his home in violation of the curfew to smoke a cigarette when a young soldier ordered him to withdraw. Webern apparently failed to hear and the sentry fired on him, killing him instantly. We now hear a work by Elliot Carter in his mature serialist manner.' I turned the radio off."

"Yes."

"He was still crying."

"Yes."

"You know what I did. I don't want to talk about it."

"You went into the child's bedroom and punched him in the face as hard as you could, knocking him down, didn't you?"

"I told you. I don't want to talk about it."

"That's brutality, pure and simple. That's the action of a beast. Afterwards you tried to make a joke of it with your wife who was disgusted and horrified. You said that at least you'd stopped the little angel from crying. Didn't you?"

"You know," I said, "from that day to this I've never heard those pieces on the radio again. More than twenty years."

"You don't put that forward as an excuse?"

"No. I'm simply expressing regret."

"A pretty unbecoming regret."

"They're too short for one side of a disc and they don't really go with anything."

"What did you say?"

"Oh, nothing."

"Brutal, trivial, degraded."

"And totally unacquainted with the six short pieces for orchestra by the modern master, Anton Webern."

"Folly."

"Yes."

"And worse to come. One of these days you'll do something you'll be genuinely sorry for. You'll kill somebody."

"I couldn't kill anybody."

"You were capable of knocking out your own infant son."

"He was lightly-dazed. He got right up."

"He was stunned. You could easily have killed him if you'd hit him in the right place: in the back of the neck; in the solar plexus; on the temple."

"I wouldn't have hit him there."

"In other words, it was a measured calculated blow. You're a potential murderer, that's what you are. Suppose we talk about Mister X for a minute."

"Who is Mister X?"

"There's a young man in your office doing exactly the same work you're supposed to be doing. In fact, you trained him; you taught him the job and he's outstripped you. Isn't that so?"

"The hell he has!"

"You know he has."

"I don't know what you mean!"

"He produces more billings than you do. He sees more clients and they like him better than they like you. Where people used to ask to see you when they came into the office, now they ask for him. The secretaries prefer to take dictation from him. He learned how to use the word processor much quicker than you did."

"Now there you're wrong. I'm a wizard on the word processor. Everybody says so. You'd better take another look at that notebook of yours."

He paused and consulted his notes. "You're right," he said finally. This was extremely disquieting. "You're perfectly correct; you're a better man on the word processor. I have ample testimony to that effect."

The word "testimony" made me very uneasy. I said, "You can make mistakes too, you know."

"Very seldom. And my errors don't lessen your responsibilities. You hate Mister X, don't you?"

"I wouldn't want to see anything happen to him."

"Come off it. Wouldn't you be delighted if he died? Isn't it true that you hate anybody who has a later date of birth doing the same work as you?"

"It isn't that I hate them; it's just that I'm closer to dying than they are."

"Maybe. But you'd be glad to see Mister X eliminated, isn't that so? Suppose you could annihilate him utterly by pressing a secret button or simply by wishing for it, without any likelihood of detection? You'd do it, wouldn't you?"

"I've thought about it."

"You'd do it if you could get away with it, wouldn't you?"

"Yes," I said. "I'd like to liquidate the bastard."

"And what about all those members of the *Parti Québecois?*"

"Them too."

"And Premier Levèsque?"

"More than anybody."

"There you are then. You've got murder in your heart."

I thought this over for a while. "You know, you're right," I said.

"I intend to let everybody know unless you pay me to keep quiet."

We haggled over price. I saw I couldn't risk exposure at my time of life and I started to itch to get my hands on him. He edged away from me nervously two or three times. He mentioned sums beyond my power to raise. I trembled with fear and rage. "A contract to that effect, an income for me for life, security at last."

"Are you insane?" I cried. "You must be insane. I couldn't begin to raise an amount like that. I haven't the resources."

"Then you'll have to find them, won't you?"

It was at this point that I lost control of myself. I leaped up and made a grab for him. I'd have throttled him on the spot but he was much too quick for me. He threw his chair over backwards and got to his feet and ran from the room. I chased him out onto the porch but the exertion and the anxiety were too much for me and I had to sit on the steps puffing. He dashed away up the street. I lost sight of him as he turned the corner. He hasn't come back and I don't think he will. He simply wasted his afternoon, that's all. But I wish I knew where he got all that stuff.

We Outnumber the Dead

BRONSON WAS LAUGHING IN A DREAM. He knew what was happening was terribly funny because it made his chest heave convulsively, throwing the single blanket and the sheet to one side, exposing his damp pajama top. But he wasn't sure what was taking place: there was a shadow over everything and what he felt immediately was the deep pleasure of the laughter. It was a body event. He felt shaky and weak from a confusion of nervous impulse and woke up suddenly still laughing but unable to recall any of the story of the dream. For perhaps a couple of seconds the rhythm of his laughter persisted into wakefulness with the extreme physical delight of relaxed limb and cleared mind which are conferred by response to the truly comic. He wished he could remember what had triggered his mirth but the cue was no longer in his mind. A good way to start the day.

After breakfast he decided to inspect his bird sanctuary, up back of the cottage towards the road. There was a plank walkway through light woods and over a rock shelf which led to the spot where the family car was parked; along this walkway were several vantage points from which small wildlife could be observed: chipmunks in legions, porcupines in trees, raccoons, now and then a fox. Bronson suspected that a few wolves remained concealed somewhere in nearby brush. There were infrequent barkings and howls, usually at night, which seemed to come from recesses in the woods where no domesticated dog would likely roam. In the space of a decade he had twice sighted deer crossing the road in front of his car, once at night, once just before twilight. There might be many more deer in the wooded area on the other side of the road, or there might not. Seventy years ago there had been great herds of the creatures in these forests. From the beginning of the age of cottaging the hunting regulations had been carefully enforced; no excessive depredations of the deer population had been permitted. Where was the herd now? Deeper in the woods? Gone away?

He climbed a short flight of steps and walked slowly along an elevated part of the walk, below which lay some enormous old rocks split into separate chunks perhaps 50,000 years ago, if the worn edges of the cracks and seams were an accurate indicator of the date of the last major rockfall. Bronson amused himself in the summers by reflecting that though the last upheaval sufficiently powerful to toss five-ton rocks around like ping-pong balls had occurred long ages ago there was no reason why another similar disturbance should not occur in our own time. He realised that very great energies and extreme heat must have been in play the last time newly sharded boulders went hurtling about the ears of the living inhabitants of this acreage. What a day that must have been, what a once-in-an-epoch morning and afternoon!

No such natural disaster seemed to impend this morning. The birds were going about their routine flights with precision, elegance and a wholly spurious air of disinterest in Bronson's movements. He had almost got them used to him; he didn't shoot at them or throw things at them. He had rigorously enforced Bronson's Law. *No grandchildren at the cottage before the age of thirty.* His little clump of woods and brush was therefore agreeably tranquil. He hadn't in any true sense made a bird sanctuary; he had simply refrained from doing very much to disturb natural arrangements of tree, bush, rock, rainfall. The only thing he had constructed was the walk; it had taken the birds four or five years to forgive him the intrusion.

Now, however, they ignored him as he stood leaning against the railing, looking carefully around him at certain patches of brush where, he was almost sure, a pair of American bitterns were living. He knew they must be American bitterns because no other bird he could find in his books had legs that colour. He had returned to the cottage yesterday around three-thirty with the papers, two canned soft drinks, a licorice pipe, three chocolate bars, and two frozen Hungry-Man TV dinners in a paper sack. He ran the car into the customary space at roadside and climbed out. He picked up his parcel from the other bucket seat and turned around. There, about thirty feet off on the same side of the road down a gentle slope, stood this nutty-looking bird with its head way back on its neck as though it looked at heaven. The bird had a ham-shaped body and a long neck which quivered in a swallowing motion as Bronson stood and stared. The bird seemed to be trying to ingest a whole fish, perhaps to lodge it in its gullet for regurgitation and consumption at some more formal meal later on.

It was the colour or his — or her — legs that excited Bronson. They were the colour of well-chilled, frozen solid lime popsicles. A clear unmixed smooth lime-green without any chalky or scaly whitish or greyish tone, such a green as is only found in one or two kinds of things, lime popsicles being the first things to come to mind. Where else do you find that colour? On some 1980 Lada automobiles. Russian cars; the colour wasn't used on American makes. Could the lime-green of the Lada be a reflection of profound cultural peculiarities operative near the Urals? You wouldn't see that almost unique shade of green on anything else that Bronson could bring to mind. The bird gave its neck a couple of rhythmic twists and turns, then walked leisurely into the heavy cover of the ditch, and from there down onto Bronson's lot. You could hear the heavy chunky body moving in the brush. There was obviously a mate somewhere around, probably close to the water. A nest perhaps?

Now and then, from this particular vantage point on the little wooden bridge over the rocks, he had spotted birds that were really out of the ordinary: a huge pileated woodpecker, which isn't a bird you're likely to sight from one day to the next! Two summers ago there had been a great wave of nesting partridges (ruffed grouse? pheasants?) with highly visible young passing along the roadside over a stretch of two or three miles. Several times he or Viv had had to stop the car at the side of the road where a female partridge (pheasant? ruffed grouse?) had been standing, eyeing the car, plainly waiting to cross the road in safety. They would sit there without even bothering to turn off the engine and the mother bird would move carefully out of the light cover beside the road, crossing in front of the idling car. And then, like sentries popping out of their boxes, as many as six of her young would follow her, one after another appearing from concealment, forming a line, disappearing onto higher ground in deliberate parade. For some reason this preponderation of grouse (grice?) had never repeated itself.

Not more than a week ago, Bronson had sighted a peregrine falcon, a bird now very rare east of Manitoba. This observation had been deeply pleasurable to him because conservationists had been declaring repeatedly that the peregrine was on the verge of extinction. In the last couple of years the species has made a bit of a comeback; a few pairs have even been encouraged to nest and breed in downtown Montréal, specimens brought into the city as part of a planned experiment. Bronson's sighting had in no way been effected by his efforts; his peregrine had arrived spontaneously.

He thought he heard the sounds of a pair of large creatures moving around in the bushes below him, down the glen towards the lake, and he suddenly remembered what he had been laughing at before he awoke — the look of the bittern's throat as it swallowed the slithering fish. In the dream the fish tail had been clearly visible, flipping back and forth as the bird ingurgitated it. He was sure he could hear them and tried to get a fix on the location of the nest. Crackle, crack, crunch. Splitting and snapping noises. They might come from a pair of nesting bitterns but were just as likely to be sounds from a fat old porcupine who hung around in the trees further down the glen, sometimes regarding the earth and the fruits thereof from fifty feet up — an impregnable fastness, unless somebody were to take a shot at him.

The sounds below were suddenly obscured by another noise, much louder, the engine of a trail bike in third gear coming along the road from the deep woods. This was perfect terrain for trail biking, traversed by nineteenth-century logging roads which had been allowed to revert to wilderness so that a faint parallel pair of ruts, which disappeared on the many bare rock shelves, was all that could be discovered of the original track. In the last three or four summers, trail bikers had multiplied. There seemed to be about half-a-dozen bikes in the neighbourhood, mostly 175s, one or two 70ccs. Kids rode them. At seventeen or eighteen the trail-biking impulse seemed to desert all but the most ardent en-thusiasts. The bike on the road this morning was proceeding at modest speed; you couldn't remain long in top gear on such a trail. There were too many blind curves and short steep rises. Perhaps the experience with the small, low-powered bikes was good for these boys. It would show them that high speed wasn't necessarily the most desirable quality in a powered vehicle. Trail biking was a male sport, Bronson observed. He had seen no woman biker, not even a girlfriend on a pillion. Bikers and birds enacted alike instinctual impulses.

When the bike had passed, he mounted to the road and stared at the whirling cloud of dust left by its wheels. The road surface was very dry and powdery, except where curves had been blacktopped by the property owners' road committee. For most of its course this private road crossed a series of exceedingly hard rock ridges; there was never any question of washout in spring, never any potholes. At the same time, the hard surface was a constant threat to wheel alignment. A summer's driving usually caused pronounced front-end problems (shimmy, shaky tie-rod ends) in passenger cars.

So the cottagers clubbed together and gravelled and graded the roadway twice a year. Even at that, the small amount of traffic was enough after a few weeks to reduce the surfacing to fine greyish dust unless rain came often and hard. This summer there had been scant rain; the ditches and weed growth along the roadsides were coated with grey powder. The passing trail bike had laid down a very distinct treadmark in the dust, which was thick and caked here. The marks caught Bronson's eye and he followed the narrow track along the road for some distance. He was amazed to see how thick the gravel dust was and how tacky, how firmly molded in the outline of the tread. Sherlock Holmes would be able to tell immediately the brand of tire, the size, the sort of nail which had punctured the casing six months before, the material used for repair. Bronson fixed his eyes on the impressions, trying to figure out how much a skilful detective could reasonably infer from these traces.

All at once he was astonished to see a ghostly grey caterpillar moving slowly along the tire tracks, sliding its frame over the neatly squared-off tread marks. Roadway dust gave the creature an other-worldly appearance (it might be the essence or abstract notion of caterpillarhood, a Platonic form sent to make Bronson think). Damned thing ought to be green, he thought. Would all that dust choke it, damage its respiration? Would it have some sort of lungs? It was one of those bugs about four inches long which seem double-ended like a ferryboat. Unless you look at them very carefully you can't tell which is the front end. They expand and contract in the oddest way. Stretched out at full length — perhaps pulled out in torment by some cruel child — such a creature might be six or seven inches long. They have the look, and very much the action, of a self-propelled concertina, if such a thing exists. An accordion played by a ghost. Bronson began to study the specimen before him with close attention. How the hell could it expand itself and then contract in that absurd way? He fancied the strains of minute insectual concertina music which might issue from such writhings. Did it have feet? It must have feet. After some moments he began to be able to conclude that it wasn't backing up; it was headed somewhere, moving forward. The eyes were up at the front underneath the little horns.

He was at best an amateur field naturalist, had no idea of the entomology involved here. Bug. It's a bug, he thought. Is it an insect? He didn't know for sure. Insects come in three sections, right? Do caterpillars come in three sections? Too much dust.

Call it an insect. This insect — or bug — was for some reason staying right in the middle of the trail bike's track; if it were to remain there it might very well be crushed to death by the returning biker. Bronson had often noted that it seemed to be a curious point of honour among the trail bikers around here to make only one track in the thick dirt. That is, they seemed to enjoy superimposing their returning track on that laid down when outward bound. He had often watched some of the younger riders wobbling in low gear along their own trails, trying to superimpose new tire marks immediately over old. To confuse pursuit? No rider would violate the principle of this compulsion merely to preserve the life of a bug.

He found a twig which seemed to be long and strong enough to bear away the caterpillar. For several reasons he was reluctant to pick it up in his bare fingers. Jaws! Bites? They may not bite, but they look alarming in full-face closeup. He might just poke one with a forefinger but he wouldn't pick it up. He slid the long twig under the persisting caterpillar, wishing he knew how to communicate to it that he wanted to safeguard its life. He angled the twig to the right so as to fix the bug in the fork made by a twiglet. He lifted it in the air to the height of perhaps two feet; it fell off, landing in the dust with an inaudible thump. It writhed about a bit, whether in annoyance or mere agony he couldn't tell.

My God, thought Bronson, I've hurt its insides. He was relieved to realise that these contortions were apparently the expression of the caterpillar's struggle to orient itself and resume forward progress. He had got it turned around when he dropped it. The horned head was pointing in the direction from which it had come. Somehow it knew this. Bronson was amazed. How could a thing that small see enough to know that it wanted to go the other way? Surely all it could see were the sides of the tire tread moldings. How large a world of vision could it command? Now it turned itself around, sprawling across the forms of the treads, and moved forward towards whatever goal it had proposed for itself. It reminded Bronson of some of the people who had gone to university with him. It couldn't be allowed to stay there; the returning bike would crush it. He now began to feel a powerful need or wish to assist the caterpillar. There could be no question of finding out where it wanted to go and carrying it there in his pocket, but he might at least remove it from this track of death.

He shoved the twig under the thing and lifted it high in the air to about the height of his own waist. He meant to put it down on the vegetation which abounded at roadside. All at once he felt a shivering motion in the twig and then a snap or click. The caterpillar closed shut up on itself in a snail-like shape as if suffering a seizure or catalepsy. It's died, he thought. I've frightened it to death and I didn't mean to. Disappointed and much in sympathy with the bug's indecipherable goals, he dropped the twig, the caterpillar wound tight around it (apparently in the final rigour) and thought bitterly of the need of the living to league themselves and take up arms against the opposition.

About the year 1972 he had read a number of popular essays in various newspapers and magazines which made great play with population figures and statistical curves tending to either of two conclusions: either the increase in human population was so rapid and so great as to threaten disaster to existing civilisation, or the same phenomenon — the population explosion, as they used to call it — constituted a significant breakthrough in health care, a magnificent victory for humanity. There had been two recurrent headlines, possibly retained in type ready for use whenever one of these somewhat repetitive articles was to appear:

POPULATION RUNAWAY THREATENS PLANET

WE OUTNUMBER THE DEAD

It seemed in the early 1970s that the population explosion, like every other great change in human history, could be given either an optimist's or a pessimist's reading. We were all going to be buried, by the year 2000, under great mounds of humans, some alive, some dead. Or else we were going to share in man's final victory over his mortality and would be able to choose whether or not we might live forever or for an indeterminate time up for grabs.

At this time a statistic surfaced in the popular press which gave credibility to the optimistic reading of human destiny. The huge increase in the numbers of the living (never mind what sort of life they might be leading) meant: THERE ARE MORE PEOPLE ALIVE RIGHT NOW THAN HAVE LIVED AND DIED IN ALL PREVIOUS HISTORY. It seemed in 1972 — how one remembers it — that a count of all those who had died since humans began to exist on the planet (forget about our ancestors) showed that all of the vast imaginable hordes of history, and even pre-history, the vanished civilisations, the cave-painters, the folk who invented the wheel and discovered the uses of fire, all of them together, including the peoples of the classical civilisations, the Middle Ages, the Renaissance, the Enlightenment, the whole kit and kaboodle whom we, uncaring and unthinking, call "the dead," all those underground, or ash, or lodged in urns and mausoleums were taken together no more than a billion in number (what about the legions buried at sea?) whereas we living, thanks to modern medicine and sanitation, were in all as many as two-and-a-half billion. Precisely. There are more people alive today than have existed in all past time.

Bronson had always known, when he encountered the various avatars of this tale at that period, there was something bogus about it. Was it in any way verifiable? He thought not. The statistics put forward were never given any close documented support. How much was known for certain about the population of ancient

Babylon, of Persia or Egypt? Some inferences might be drawn from the amount of land judged to be under cultivation, the presumable annual rainfall at the given epoch, the movement of rivers, clearing of forests, introduction of land-drainage systems, gradual evolution of desert areas. To move from these more or less checkable observations to accurate statements about the number of people alive at a given time in the past could only be rough and ready guesswork.

But suppose it could be done. A large supposition, but just suppose!

Suppose it were true that up until 1 January, 1970, say, the sum of human dead could be put at an accurate total of one billion (or — what the hell — one-and-a-half billion), what would follow from that? If the number of living on that date were TWO-AND-A-HALF billion, if we outnumbered the dead by a billion now vital, what did it mean?

Maybe it meant we were coming out ahead. Winning.

That's what jarred Bronson down to his Adidas. Maybe we've found something out, he would hint to himself. On the whole, if the contest between the living and the dead were to be imagined as a game, like a team contest, some enormous soccer match, he felt a strong prejudice for the side of the living. He wanted to be on the winning side. Now if you could draw a curve which gave a true representation of these population and death-rate figures, showing how the living had caught up with the dead and then outstripped them, and if — further to that — you could introduce into your plotting axioms the growing preponderance of the birth rate over the death rate, you might then be able to argue that for the foreseeable future the numbers of the living would continue to distance those of the dead.

You might get a curve which would predict when practical immortality is going to arrive.

For it was clear that human longevity was progressing to the point where life expectancy would be prolonged almost indefinitely. It wasn't, he thought in bewilderment, that fewer people died. The same number died. Everybody. But they died slower and slower and more of them were born.

At this point in his reasonings Bronson always began to grow confused about his proposed graph. If everybody continued to die, and yet there continued to be more and more people living than had died, what biological conclusion might be drawn from the curve? It could only be that one hell of a lot of people were being born. He always remembered the famous *Believe It or Not* proposal when he reached this stage: "If all the population of China were to march past a given point four abreast at the US Army rate of infantry march, they would never finish passing, though they marched forever." Only so many could march past in a year and in that year more would be born than could complete the march-past evolution.

WE OUTNUMBER THE DEAD

And then, halfway into the decade, a drastic series of economic upheavals shook the entire world, most of them connected with the price of oil and gas. Mass shrinkage of ambition occurred. People lowered their expectations; were prepared to settle for a chicken in every second or third pot, for Chinese marching three abreast or even two or maybe not marching at all. It was ridiculous. I mean, how the hell could you ever get all those Chinese lined up for their march? Where would the women have all those replacement babies? In field hospitals? Robert Ripley had died a long time ago and people didn't care whether they believed anything or not.

In the latter half of the decade, news stories debunking the earlier statistics became common. By 1979 feature editors were eager to run material which showed that, far from beginning to approach the numbers of the dead, humans now alive barely approached twenty percent of the total deceased. Different, downwards-turning curves appeared with these revisionist estimates, often attributed to exactly the same sources as had earlier proposed more optimistic extrapolations: UNESCO, the International Monetary Fund, other entrenched international bodies.

In our own time, right now, Bronson didn't know what to think. He was left with a few modes of feeling which he decided to go with. He felt that recurrent newspaper stories based on long-term statistical records and predictions were probably best ignored. They should be assigned the mental status of myths-in-the-making like those recurrent tales that the earth's climate was growing colder. Or was it warmer? One or the other anyway. Or the conflict between the steady-state and big bang theories. If you can't say anything about something, you should shut up.

He kept his prejudice in favour of the living and gave his interests to birds, fish, whales and dolphins, thinking to count them all on the side of life, the biological victory. This caterpillar's stroke or seizure, sudden yielding, possible heart attack (do caterpillars have hearts?) unnerved him. He looked at the greyed lump where he had let it fall, curled in a clamped hysterical knot among small pieces of gravel, many of which would seem as imposing to the bug twisting between them as the five-ton boulders under the walkway seemed to him. The bits of gravel, pebbles really, split and tossed about by the weight of passing traffic were each about the size of a cocktail onion or a ripe olive, much larger than the caterpillar's head. The creature had lodged between two of them and seemed caught, its rear legs now moving slowly without traction, a tiny distance above solid ground. The poor thing had been coated, layered-over with dust, dropped from a height, trapped between big rocks. It must be thinking that today wasn't its day.

Very deliberately, Bronson removed several of the small pieces of gravel which lay in front of the bug, forming a labyrinthine track which, if followed to its end, would lead to a safe position at the side of the road near vegetation. He arranged some of the gravel carefully beside a deposit of sticky mud left over from the last rainfall. He didn't care to see his friend and ally trapped in a bog. He wished he could spray it somehow to clear its vision and briefly considered pissing on it. He concluded that his urine, in no way poisonous to himself, might prove toxic to other life forms.

As he mulled over this possible tactic, he saw the caterpillar start to move along the track he had prepared. With infinite caution and sharp acuity of sight it inched its way along the winding track, curving and extending its length around the shapes of the little stones. He could form no estimate of its speed. Was there some way he could give further assistance? How far was it going? What was its estimated time of arrival? Was it looking for company? It was being extremely careful, no doubt hoping that no further extraordinary adventures would occur on this trip. In half an hour or so it managed to work its way out of the gravel labyrinth and onto some dusty leaves at the bottom of a roadside sumach. It hauled itself up onto the lowest of the leaves and positioned itself there with a certain air of assurance. The leaf, an inch or two above the ground, bobbed up and down like a little hammock in a faint air current. Bronson got the notion that the insect was resting and thinking about lunch, perhaps. This thought made him realise his own hunger. He looked at his watch. He'd been staring at the caterpillar for two hours.

So he turned and walked back towards his own property, taking his time, considering a light salad and some chicken noodle soup. He started down the steps and then stood motionless halfway down. The returning trail bike. It *was* the same bike. He knew the individual motors of all the bikes in the neighbourhood by their performance characteristics. One of them had a peculiar high whining note in second gear; another clearly stood in need of a piston job; you could smell the contaminated exhaust of a third. This was the same bike as before returning from some cruise into the back country where those abandoned nineteenth-century farm-steads lay open to the sky, walls fallen in, lilac overgrown above hidden foundations. He wanted to hide and shrank back out of the biker's line of vision until the boy had passed. Then he scram-bled up the steps and ran back to where he had left the bug. He was able to identify the leaf on which it had rested. There were new bites out of the leaf, ragged edges, almost invisible. He spotted the caterpillar eleven feet further on its way and gave it a farewell whistle. Bikers have rights too, he remembered, and he started to try to think of what they were.

Moskowitz's Moustache

AT THE BEGINNING OF THE DECADE, a young man of the name of Moskowitz started to appear on the local CBC television station, carrying out the minor chores of a staff news reader at the lowest level: attending the meetings of a parent-teacher's association to report on some adjustment of educational policy; narrating the doleful circumstances of a *règlement de compte* in an east-end bar; sometimes discussing the first snowfall or the earliest crocus on record. He was just one of those aspirants to an anchorman's desk who flitted through network stations across the country, sometimes establishing in viewers an agreeable sense of their being, more often passing quietly out of the profession into another walk of life like superannuated hockey players. Ginger Jackson, Cynthia Grumball, Linda Howe-Perkins have all gone to weather-girls' heaven. Dave Wonderly is a male model in New York and the best of British luck to him. Not a career one would wish on anybody. They are all gone into the world of light, those agreeable folks in their twenties who once upon a time paraded their charm and their teeth and eyes before us.

"And this is Cynthia Grumball for Channel Six in Lachine."

"That's the weather picture for tomorrow and now here's Brian with sports."

"We'll be back after these messages with tonight's top story and the wrap-up."

". . . at the Sexe-si-bon Discorama in Rosemont, this is Mark Moskowitz for Nightbeat."

Difficult to believe that signoff has undone so many.

Moskowitz was less instantly disposable than the others. He stayed with Nightbeat for six months; suddenly he'd been visible

113

for over a year and had survived two changes of set and producer. It was hard to see why he should retain his position, maintain a posture of qualified assurance, while one attractive young woman after another turned in her chalk and blackboard and huskier, more obviously male, on-the-spot reporters quit to go into PR. The Moskowitz magic was elusive and understated. He never got out of line, very rarely introduced sneezes, coughs or apparently inadvertent fluffs and recoveries into his reading of script. He just got the job done, reading his inoffensive signoff simply and clearly. There was never any doubt about his name.

"At the murder scene, this is Mark Moskowitz for Nightbeat."

"Mark Moskowitz here with Fire Chief Sentenne. How do you think it got started, Chief?"

After a while he seemed to be getting disaster assignments as a matter of course. Not major disasters which drew the top news team and occasional network exposure, but minor local disasters which appeared on the third page of *Journal de Montréal:*

TUEE A COUPS DE HACHE ET BRULEE VIVE

HOMME DE POLITIQUE TERRASSE PAR UNE CRISE CARDIAQUE

DISPARITION MYSTERIEUSE D'UNE DANSEUSE NUE A GO-GO

You name it, Moskowitz covered it.

Un homme à tout faire. That was Moskowitz in those days. With all this minor exposure he started to acquire an insidious professionalism, audience recognition. People began to be able to remember who he was from one appearance to the next. Given the immensely resistant character of human attention, it seemed a definite advance for the young broadcaster to have reached the point where, upon hearing some such phrase as, "Now here with the story is Mark Moskowitz in Ville LaSalle," the slumping, grouchy, tired late-night viewer might feel unwilling symptoms of recognition, even faint stirrings of anticipation. He was carving an audience for himself out of the rhinoceros-hide of viewer indifference. Once or twice the authorities tried him out on the six o'clock news but it didn't take. His image seemed incongruous and out-of-place at the dinner hour. Nobody seemed to want to listen to his quiet clear recitals of muted disaster at 6:00 P.M. He only seemed to fit into the few minutes between 11:20 P.M. and the Barney Miller reruns.

What is it about late-night viewing that invites this calm acceptance of accidental blood: the entertaining, mildly titillating aspect of the bomb under the hood in the labour dispute, the body which has evidently been in the water for some days, the eviscerated stripper, the disgraced city councillor? You lie back on your hipbones in a position deliberately chosen for its discomfort; your eyelids sag; you aren't taking all this in. The melancholy recital continues. People escaping in their nightclothes at thirty below. Retrieval of a pet thoroughbred which has been gone three days. Slim hopes of recovery. None. Then the beer commercial and the public-service announcement. Through all this winds the thin-spun thread of mortal life, the voice of Moskowitz seldom striking a disturbing tone. Maybe there's a decent movie on PBS.

What do you call that depression below and between the nostrils framed by the muscles which control the upper lip? There doesn't seem to be any word in the language for that particular place on the body though everybody has one. Some mothers describe it to their children as their guardian angel's thumbprint. You ever hear of that? After Moskowitz had been around for a couple of years, there appeared one night on that place beneath his nose where his guardian angel might have placed his thumb a small black mark or spot, much like the thumbprint of some angel or other celestial resident. It looked like it was made of black shoe polish, a small round faintly shiny smear, the mark priests used to make on the forehead on Ash Wednesday, a thumbprint on a credit-card application or an identity-card for some secret place. One of those little black dints.

It was days or weeks before anybody noticed what was happening. We were in the decline of the age of facial hair, that greatly hirsute time which began in 1965 and has continued almost to our own day. People were just starting to think about getting rid of their headbands, pony tails. Males, that is. Hair distinctly seemed to be receding about the date when Moskowitz installed this greasy thumbprint on his upper lip. Some viewers thought it was merely a lapse in makeup. Authority had decided that the telecaster's features required sharper definition and had thought to create such an effect by judicious shadowing. A more impressive mouth might throw his cheeks and nose into unearned prominence.

But no. It wasn't greasepaint. The darkness in the anonymous hollow persisted, eventually declaring itself as an attenuated cluster of facial hair. You couldn't at that stage define it as any of the receivable kinds of male ornament, hairwise. All the same, there it was. It shone faintly under the revealing studio lighting; not as well in remote situations where natural light obliterated it. Nightclub settings rendered it nearly invisible. Time went on and the angel's black thumbprint became a viable element of the Moskowitz persona; true, there was a certain amount of home-viewer resistance but no outright decline in audience measurable by the available research methods. The thing remained *in situ*; then, after a while, it began to move and mutate.

When no concerted attempt at its removal was mounted by either production staff or audience, the moustache — for this it now declared itself to be — moved outwards on two fronts and after some months had established a disconcerting independent life which began to call into question the substance of its owner's existence. Confusion of identity and ownership began to press on observers of moustache trends. Was the moustache — or moustaches, for there often seemed to be more than one of them in play — genuinely Moskowitz's property? Had he got the thing under adequate control so that its mobility and its ambitions (there is no more accurate word) were functions of his own?

Or had the moustache, or moustaches, turned Moskowitz into a mere appendage of his own lip? Had the moustache, in short, *taken over?* A more familiar statement of this theme, a favourite among lovers of the horror-film genre, is the case of the ventriloquist's dummy who, refusing to accept the status of mere thing, begins to exercise a weird preponderance in relation to the person who supposedly manipulates it. Either the dummy is giving expression to a concealed other side of its master's character or it is, in fact, inhabited by a living spirit stronger and more intelligent than his nominal controller. The dummy refuses to remain stationary upon the ventriloquist's knee. He rises and walks about under his own steam. When put away in his trunk for the night, he continues to chant obscenities and abuse, eyes focussed in an intense and hate-filled stare. He recites embarrassing and disgusting incidents, often purely imaginary, from his master's sexual life. He attempts to exert sexual command off his own bat. Visions of coition between dummies and women begin to haunt us. Or between boy dummies and girl dummies. Or between girl dummies — quaint succubi — and hapless ventriloquists. The story ends in madness, despair, self-destruction; in the final frames, the dummy, his owner dying or dead, either capers about exulting in a radical freedom or he sags over, his face becoming expressionless and his voice silent. Can't have it both ways.

Moskowitz-moustache-watchers tended to read the history of their own malign and hairy preoccupation in terms of the optimistic alternative. When old age and decay should have wasted the broadcaster himself, they felt, his facial appendage might live on, a friend to man. There was more to the hair than there was to him.

And indeed this view seemed appropriate. Proliferation of growth brought the moustache and its wearer into greater prominence. Moskowitz was given a shot at the anchor desk on Nightbeat, at first only on Sunday nights, when customarily there isn't too much hard news to distract the viewer and turn his attention rather towards the sound than the picture. On Sunday night you supposedly enjoy the picture — the innumerable clips from the NFL or the politicians making liars and fools of themselves on free-time political telecasts. Sound isn't important. Nightbeat, produced in a city of relative political insignificance, without an NFL franchise of its own, was often reduced to providing unadulterated visual comedy for the residue of viewers who could still cope, at 11:15 at the tag-end of the weekend, with the effects of the broadcast media. The producers allowed a succession of buffoons to appear on Sunday nights to give the viewers something to giggle at, to induce sweet Sunday night dreams which God knows were desirable. They would display weather girls with pop-eyes, treble chins, huge flapping ears. Sports announcers who were stone deaf (with screaming in their tiny head-sets) and producers trying to feed them correct scores. Newsreaders of unlikely accent and Bulgarian tailoring hove in view, entertained with intense comic effect, passed from sight. They even tried Moskowitz, thinking perhaps that the moustache would prove suitably diverting on silent shrouded Sunday winter evenings. This was not a wise move for the moustache sped at once into a vertiginous and dazzling set of transformations. One Sunday night its form and sources were Groucho-Marxist, oblong, about four inches in length, plainly thick rich pure black greasepaint. Moskowitz seemed suddenly to have acquired a set of matching eyebrows and a suggestive leer which he had never exhibited before. Seismic tremors of mistrust moved sleepy watchers around in their Naugahyde recliners or on the edges of daybeds.

A lot of lights flickered instantly on the studio switchboard. Declarations of rebellion and mistrust from the folks out there. Moskowitz wasn't allowed back on the anchor desk for a month. But then, satisfied that audience suspicion and distaste had been allayed, they put him back on the air. Everything looked kosher as he advanced to the desk from the wings of the rickety set. But when Nightbeat came on the air the moustache all-at-once assumed a sinister Oriental appearance. It shot out to either side of the man's nose for a good three inches either way, heavily-waxed and twisted and shining. At its ends, it suddenly jutted directly downwards in the traditional Sax Rohmer stiletto points. There were muffled gasps all over the studio. In the control room the producer exclaimed bitterly under his breath, "Many men smoke, but Fu Manchu!"

"What did you say, Chief?"

"I said, 'Go to three with the graphic.' Five, four, three . . ."

Out on the floor, Moskowitz was nearly hysterical. "What are you doing?" he demanded. "Am I on? Am I still on?" His hands moved agitatedly over his face. He seemed unconscious of the effect he had produced and perhaps — people whispered to each other — perhaps he had not, in fact, been in any way responsible for the incident.

Long, long was the passage of time before they let him on again. The third visitation was more sinister than those which had gone before. This time Moskowitz was kept under close surveillance from the time he arrived in makeup until he came on the set.

Things were credible in the terms of ordinary life right up until the end. He even looked all right under the titles. But in the first close shot his upper lip and his mouth and his cheeks were invisible behind a vast sheriff's moustache. Not a moustache for a vast sheriff, a vast moustache for a sheriff. You know the kind of thing: intensely black, brushed out full, seeming to spring off the face, launching itself disturbingly forward toward onlookers as though *lunging* at them. A moustache as worn by persons photographed in the act of robbing a train or lynching a road-agent, wearing the tin star or forming a posse. It was massive, floating as though impelled by some hot invisible air current originating from within and behind its substance. After this it was darned lucky for Mark Moskowitz that the producers' and technicians' strike hit the local network offices, rendering programming impossible for close to four months. It didn't seem as though the poor young man could carry on in his profession if his appearance were to continue so unpredictable and so jarring to the eye. As things developed local viewers saw nothing of him for some time.

Everybody took to watching the competing news programming on CTV once CBC went definitively silent and invisible at 11:00 P.M. Many of us consider 11:30 our normal time of retirement, a change of state necessarily to be prepared for by contemplation of television news. The programmer who tries to dictate a change in viewing habits does so at his or her peril; in those days no switch from eleven to ten o'clock impended. The *Journal* was unheard-of. When the eleven o'clock news was blacked out locally on CBC, the already much more popular CTV newscasts simply took over the small segment of late-night audience the competition had managed to attract. Perhaps unconsciously, watchers accustomed to the amateurish *contretemps* which occurred regularly on the publicly owned network expected to find them on the unfamiliar show and were astounded to find that on CTV there were no news readers with unzipped trousers, no faces devoid of makeup glaring from the screen as expressionless masks, no weather girls who collapsed speechless in uncontrollable giggling, no on-camera lacunae caused by the accidental locking of a sports-caster in the lavatory two flights down. There was none of the comic "I'm sorry, I'll read that again" or "We should have that videotape shortly" or "Programming will resume as soon as possible. In the meantime, please stand by" which one encountered routinely on CBC.

It had been kind of exciting to guess what mishap might overtake the local news on a given night. A particular audience favourite had been the swing man who read everything badly, never knew which camera to look at and conducted muttered dialogues with his miniaturised headpiece in the fond belief that nobody could overhear. This man rivalled Moskowitz in the unpredictability and histrionic force of his duels with electronic equipment, but he too disappeared when the strike began and the only alternative was the private network. On CTV, production values (at no time high) were admirably consistent. The local show boasted a pair of weather girls of great beauty, one of them of striking serpentine slenderness. Sports scores were delivered accurately in resounding voices describing (amazingly) the hockey clip onscreen at that moment. This was refreshing. It became possible to make sense of the local news.

A few chronic malcontents went around saying they missed the almost commercial-free atmosphere of the public network. Others mourned the absence from the little screen of favourite performers. Moskowitz was occasionally mentioned in this context. Not often. Then a shocking revelation took place. A middle-aged suburban late-night viewer claimed to have been sitting quietly watching the late local news on Pulse when *tendrils* protruded from out of the side of his twenty-one inch black-and-white Panasonic screen. Wisps. This man had immediately attempted to contact his local channel to report the apparition; he found that the station's switchboard must have closed down for the night. All he got was a busy signal. When he turned back to the screen there seemed to be, for a tense moment, an area of furry opacity all over the picture tube which suddenly clarified itself and faded, leaving the first observer of these singular guest appearances guessing what it was that he had glimpsed.

Two nights later a woman in Pointe-Claire, a veteran insomniac, reported to police that her television was full of moustaches. When a patrol car arrived at her home, the officers found her wandering distractedly on her front lawn, mumbling incoherently about sideburns.

PHANTOM HAIRPIECE TERRIFIES NEWSWATCHERS

LA MOUSTACHE DE L'ANIMATEUR MOSKOWITZ — EXIGE UNE REPONSE FORMIDABLE CHEZ LES TELESPECTATEURS

Nothing like it had been witnessed since the very first attempts at telecasting in Canada when bizarre and shaming on-screen revelations boggled the mind from one second to the next. The roamings of the phantom moustache, or possibly beard, were at once attributed to the true source of the problem, the luckless Moskowitz; but, when print-media journalists attempted to charge him with responsibility, in searching investigative interviews, they couldn't track him down. According to his former landlady, he had left the city some time before.

Viewers of all ages and conditions now reported further sightings of the hair.

A famous psychiatrist commented in various magazines on the phenomenon, citing it as a remarkable instance of mass hypnosis.

There was talk of some sort of exorcism. A sharp debate blew up among clergymen of various faiths. The efficacy of the rite was called into question.

Then, for a time, the moustache lay doggo, gathering power for some unheralded strike.

Moskowitz had simply gone up to Ottawa, clean-shaven and with excellent references. He arrived at a time when political activity in the capital was abnormally vigorous and multiform. It was the epoch of constitutional reform; almost anybody who had ever worked in TV news could find something to do on or near Parliament Hill. Moskowitz's ambiguous celebrity had not preceded him. Though the distance to Ottawa was a scant 120 miles, news travelled slowly in the direction of that city. It is part of the mythology of Canada that nobody in Ottawa ever hears about anything going on in the rest of the country; this is probably quite correct. Mind you, the hiring of personnel who appeared onscreen from the capital was invariably done from Toronto. The national news broadcasts are inevitably centred on the metropolis. In Toronto, even more than in Ottawa, the tales of moustache-contamination circulated around a distant city were dismissed out-of-hand as some further bilingual nonsense, part of a story about social unrest which was essentially dead, of the 1970s, cold, cold, cold. Wow!

So Moskowitz got on staff and began to be sent on trips to Hull and other spots on the fringes of the national capital district: Nepean, Vars, Vankleek Hill, what propagandists like to call the Ouatouais Region. I don't think I've spelled that right; virtually nobody knows how to spell it, French or English. Moskowitz roamed about this swampy desert place making videotapes about civil-service cutbacks, mayoralty candidates at supermarkets, death in Stittsville. Some of these appeared on the air. The whole terrifying cycle began to repeat itself, all because they wouldn't listen, those people in Ottawa, they wouldn't listen. And the ones in Toronto were worse. Uncaring. Ignorant. They let the facial hair out of the darkness again and they haven't any way to control it. The last time we could even tell it was Moskowitz, his eyes, terrified, wildly-rolling beneath huge drops of sweat, were the only elements of his countenance discernible behind a dense zareba of overgrowth. Now when we go to look at *The Journal* — Oh God — what we see — unappeasable and peregrine — is what somebody who doesn't know about the horror might mistake for a tight close shot of the top of Barbara Frum's head. But it isn't that. It isn't that at all. What it is, what it is — Oh, God — is Moskowitz's moustache.

Quicker Coming Back

GRACIE FALCONER WENT ON A WALKING TRIP to the West Country with her live-in lover. Everybody seems to be doing that this year: cliffside jaunts around Cornwall; walks across Dorset uplands on protected footpaths; questionably legal rights-of-way marked in little dotted lines on the Ordnance Survey maps. This is something that trippers wedded to rental vehicles wouldn't have dreamed of doing five years ago. Walking, who walks? Now there are articles in the New York *Times* Travel Section giving accounts of bed-and-breakfasts in remote spots like Chard, Charmouth, Chideock, Butleigh or Street. A century ago the walking tour was a recognised adjunct of polite courtship common also among university men (pale curates or poets) during the Long Vac.

Gracie and Dan didn't make a fetish of walking; they were prepared to use the railway to reach some population centre, Bristol, Bath, Exeter, from which a bus would take them to a more isolated or perhaps just smaller town. There might be a gorge or chasm, cliff, cove, something wild nearby, or a ruin or historical monument, supplying an excuse to pass the night in the locality. The overnight stays justified the walking; nothing relaxes so agreeably as a couple of miles up and down a cliff path, a careful clamber along a hedgerow, one eye on possible rabbit holes and the other on an inquisitive bull or perhaps not a bull, just some harmless cow; but, look, it must be a bull; what's that big thing?

"Gristle."

"It is not. It's its what-do-you-call-it."

"Gracie, you're so dumb. Can't you tell a bull from a cow. If that was a bull you'd know it."

"Oh Danny, it's looking at us." (Embrace. He pats her, fondles

123

secret places, tries to slide his palm under the tight waistband of her shorts.)

The creature hitches its enormous hindquarters backwards and forwards indecisively and takes a few paces in their direction, honks plaintively, lowers its head and hauls an enormous divot of grass and mud out of the hillside, swinging it like some lumpy dead thing between its jaws.

"Oh, Danny."

"It won't hurt us."

"I'm not staying here to find out."

Sex comedy.

They scrambled gasping and giggling along under the hedgerow to a gap in the stiff springy weave of leaf and twig, just greening, and rolled down towards the adjacent roadway, fetching up in a ditch, interlocking her legs and his arms. They took their time about wandering back to their bed-and-breakfast, moving on later in the week to the nearby cathedral town where they stayed in an elaborate hotel, a seventeenth-century wayfarer's inn featuring four-poster canopied beds and full snack service in every room. Here they remained for over a week, doing the appropriate excursions in the country roundabout, caves, castle, enchanted forest, Celtic antiquities of dubious authenticity. Gracie unearthed an ancient coin and a pottery shard which she hid in her luggage, fearing that the authorities might exact restoration of the items as state property according to some obscure regulation. In the hotel near the cathedral she polished the coin which appeared to be of legitimate historical interest and some small value; she thought it was copper or bronze. It shone prettily when buffed up; she rubbed hard with the softest thing she had in the room, a pair of worn panties which imparted an almost new glitter to the metal which retained some of the delicate perfume of the thin fabric.

She glanced up from her polishing and saw that Danny had his eye on her beseechingly. He rolled across the bed and spoke quietly behind her neck; she felt his breath on her skin. She wasn't as tired as she'd thought. "Could we?" "What?" ". . . hard to describe, but let's try it this way . . ."

He explained what he had in mind in halting and inaccurate terms.

Well, she thought, what the heck! It took them some time to

develop a practicable acting-out of Danny's fantasy. In the end it proved full value for money, and they installed the practice in their deck of cards, to be shuffled among other evening possibilities.

Next morning, springy and refreshed, they enjoyed the copious breakfast included *gratis* in the hotel's service and bounded out onto the street in search of the bus station some distance away along the main road. They had already done the cathedral and meant to do it again several times before they left the district. Today was for country walking; but not among bulls and not uphill and down.

They boarded a bus headed south through a series of well-known tourist attractions into what passes in Britain for open country. Sitting on the overstuffed seats, they unfolded the map of the region, following their route with their fingers. They were looking for a day excursion, some place to which they could walk in an hour or two, return at their usual easy pace, then catch the bus back to their base in time — they said to each other laughing — for Evensong.

On the map, near the location of the upcoming village, they noticed the term "Monument". The precise nature of this monument was not indicated but it seemed to be within walking distance, so they alighted in a few minutes at a stop next to a parking lot and one of those lightly-constructed, quaint, countryside imitation shopping-centres which are characteristic of rural England. First making certain that their return bus left this same spot at 3:15 P.M., they proceeded to the southbound road out of town and walked down a long slope, keeping sedulously to the right side of the road so as to face oncoming traffic. Soon they found themselves well out in the middle of carefully-tended countryside near the meeting-point of three counties, terrain with that peculiar confusion-together of local landscapes often found in borderline territory. Off to the southeast, peeping up above a thickly-wooded hillside, was a thick finger-shaped object of some considerable height which, seen from a closer vantage-point, would certainly dominate its surroundings; this must surely be the monument indicated on their map. It had that peculiarity of the sizeable structure set in rising woodland of seemingly receding as one approached it.

It took them not quite two hours to get to the monument, walking steadily, not too quickly, in single file along the side of the road. The monument towered erect atop rising ground in the middle of thick woods. It had a lot of writing on it, commemorating the exploits of some long-forgotten military commander, a native of a nearby hamlet who had risen to high rank, then given up his life on the other side of the world. Names of obscure battles, mottoes of regiments of horse and foot long ago merged in more efficient formations were inscribed on all sides of the 110 foot high column forming the central feature of the edifice.

"It's as big as Nelson's," exclaimed Gracie. She climbed over the bordering iron railings and onto a terrace surrounding the column which she clasped in her arms, attempting to reach around it.

"Nelson who?" demanded Dan.

"Admiral Nelson, the one who asked Hardy to kiss him."

"Oh, one of those?"

"Don't be silly! Nelson was involved with lots of women."

"I don't know about that so much," said Danny. "What about all those cabin boys, nasty little nippers?"

"Let's go back," said Gracie briskly. They turned around and trotted down the incline through the trees and onto the secluded by-road. They could feel pulling in the quadriceps; it's harder to go downhill than to climb if one is not a practised hiker. Gracie, strolling along in the lead, sniffing the sweet grass as she looked over a prospect of farmland, felt that she must increase her pace if they were not to miss the 3:15 bus. She walked more quickly and began to feel that slight soreness, not entirely disagreeable, often induced by copious sweating between the legs. Her thighs grew chafed; in another mile she began to feel less convenient chafings and she grew conscious of Danny's presence behind her.

He liked to watch her from behind; it was his big turn on, the rhythmic movement of her body seen from the rear while walking or running. He often spoke of this with relish. Now he broke a protracted silence as they turned onto the main road back to the village.

"It seems a lot quicker coming back," he said as she began to labour in her pace on the sloping roadway into town. The remark, oddly indicative of a state of feeling which she didn't share, surprised Gracie with its opacity. She realised again that she never knew what Danny was feeling and thinking, never had the faintest idea what the things they did together felt like to him. At this point in their walk she was some few feet above and ahead of him and she grew increasingly conscious of the movement of her humid flesh under her clothes, wetness, nervous impulses more and more overt.

She was certain that if the warmth of the afternoon hung on and the movement of the bus over the inferior paving of the narrow roadway was as marked as it had been on the way down, neither of them would get to Evensong at the famous cathedral. By that time of day they'd be lying on the creaking canopied four-poster entwined in some situation which, as a younger woman, she would not have been able to envisage.

She was now twenty-seven, in most respects a knowledgeable and skilful person; in matters of emotional tone and nuance less adept than in most other activities. She had had two or three female apartment-mates after graduating from university. Their relations had almost always been excessively easygoing and friendly without being specifically homosexual. Gracie found it difficult to bring herself to more than a light simmer about friendship. One or two of her apartment-mates had shown signs of wanting to cuddle with her or climb into her bed but she knew instinctively how to repel these understated and invariably uncon- summated overtures. She liked the look of girls' bodies. She had not had a chance to examine many male bodies but suspected she would like them too. She had certainly never allowed herself to get into a sweat about anybody. At the same time, she was a compliant, good-natured woman who hated to deny a favour.

Then Lise Lapointe moved in, a computer programmer on a major research project in microbiology at the university, an exceed- ingly bright and liberal person who preferred to make love in all conceivable modes with men, women, boys, girls, or babies.

Gracie found Lise in her bed on their third night together, un- clothed, rosy and gleaming from her tub, inviting and unfamiliar. There seemed nothing to be done about this but to undress and grab a quick shower, then to accept a succession of knowledgeable embraces. They passed two hours in this way; afterwards Gracie felt an overwhelming need for food. Lise had many attractive features, usually two of each, but Gracie could take them or leave them. She felt a great world of pleasure was denied her because of her facile and superficial nature. Why did she feel no guilt at these stolen Sapphic adventures? Or shame or overmastering passion? What she remembered feeling was purely physical. Lise was very smooth; here and there were faint prickles where she had shaved but not closely enough. It would be hard to shave close enough in those places without risking raw red skin, less pleasing really than silky hair. Oh, it was all a muddle, she felt petulantly, remembering most of Lise as delightfully cool and sweet-smelling. This memory was mixed together with the image of frozen lasagna sitting on the kitchen counter ready to go into the microwave and, oh dear, she was so hungry.

"You darling! Oh my lover. Oh. Oh."

"Can I do something else? What about that, or this?"

Lise emitted some stagy moans and they dined together in more or less contentment. Gracie was sure there was a missing element and wished she could try a few things with some man. Nothing too offbeat. It was Lise who introduced her to Dan Perrot not very long after the lasagna evening (folded leaves of softening cheese, tomato sauce, stuffing of chopped meat).

Danny may or may not have been a superseded male friend of Lise's left behind when she moved definitely into the search for female bonding. Gracie was never perfectly certain about this. He was like Lise in several ways. He liked to explore, as he said, "on the great sea of the human body." He was a young man from Montréal, working in Toronto for CBC French-language radio. He was not very distinctly (or upon principle) an exponent of the French fact. He liked to have girls in different ways and otherwise to enjoy himself, not a temperament exclusively the possession of any national group.

Danny and Gracie and Lise lived together for longer than might have been predicted without any more conflict than would have been developed in the story line of some sitcom like *Three's Company*. Certain comic *contretemps* occurred: an uneven number of people trying to have a party, often four women and one man.

One of these misdealings resulted in Danny's being left all to himself for most of a weekend, lonely and muttering, while Lise, Gracie and a girl named Ilona tried to establish some sort of amorous sawoff in the larger of the two bedrooms in the apartment. After this unequal contest Lise and Ilona moved into their own place. Danny and Gracie remained in the pleasant two-bedroom midtown apartment with solid walls and substantial doors which kept noise in the building to a minimum and encouraged mildly deviant sexual action, nothing very distinguished. On their own like this, Gracie felt, she and her new partner could tastefully attempt *things.*

Things involving noises: squeals, groans, moans, muffled grunts, the crisp smack of impact harder than a love-tap, softer than an uppercut. Laughter sometimes, very occasionally tears. Panting. The repertoire, in short, of extended sexual inquiry, copiously illustrated in the new cinema and in the paperbacks and skin magazines of which Danny possessed a select library. They would perch together on the edge of the wide bed in the larger of the two bedrooms and study postures and attitudes represented in the richly-coloured illustrations, both of them wondering why the models had such peachy-perfect skin, such formally-correct shapes never found outside the land of photographers' fantasy. How were those girls made up to look like that? What gave them that softly-textured sheen and glow? How were the photography studios lit? They imported special lights, various mirrors and a lot of toys and games; it was all fun; everything they thought of seemed worth doing.

Gracie could faintly remember her mother's conversation on the subject of what was and what wasn't permissible in the field. Mrs. Falconer had deployed a specific vocabulary for sexual criticism. Virtually nothing was licit. The lights had to be off. He never saw you naked. He never saw you on the toilet. You retired to the bathroom fully-dressed; there you removed your clothes and donned a modest flannel nightgown. You did unwisely to rinse out your underclothes and dry them where he could see them. When the bedroom had been darkened, you approached the bed in your flannel swaddlings and slid under the bedclothes while at the same time casting your nightgown from you, a devilishly tricky evolution in total darkness. None of this occurred prior to the marriage ceremony.

Mrs. Falconer had sought to transmit to Gracie the language of sexual assessment which had stood her in good stead in the perpetual marital war, at last reducing the late Mr. Falconer to a qualified serfdom. The single — or at most the small number — of available sexual options, enchanting when contemplated by the male from afar, could only grow stale and withered by custom unless continually refreshed by love; even true love could only with extreme prejudice undertake fifty years of one on top, one underneath, face to face.

It was the unvarying eyeball-to-eyeball contact of their sexual encounters that had chilled her father and mother, Gracie concluded. She had no hard facts to go on, no after-midnight witness as three-year-old of the classical *point de départ* of family romance. But she did possess a close knowledge of her mother's discriminations of response. Her mother called certain acts "unthinkable." There were six of these she could scarcely bring herself to discuss with her daughter. Surely it is a sign of true unthinkability, real incomprehensibility, if a woman of nearly sixty still stammers, blushes prettily, searches for decent words in which to name something which she can, to all intents and purposes, barely bring herself to contemplate?

A somewhat larger group of curious forms of behaviour she labelled "disgusting." Gracie figured her mother had never been able to do anything unthinkable; but she might just — say once or twice in fifty years — have done a few disgusting things, many of which appeared to involve the introduction of a foreign substance, or a foreign body, into lovemaking. There was the trace of a gleam in her mother's eye which hinted at deeply-repressed enjoyment. "That's disgusting," she would bark, or else, "That's revolting." There seemed no clear distinction between the *disgusting* and the *revolting*.

A much larger class of activities simply wasn't "nice." When Mrs. Falconer spoke to Grace about these matters, her back would stiffen and her pretty nose wriggle with distaste. What wasn't nice was less culpable than what was disgusting but, Gracie thought, her mother had perhaps done more disgusting things than things that weren't nice. Her mother had had a kind of heroism in these respects: she could bear with the genuinely revolting; the merely distasteful turned her right off.

And Mr. and Mrs. Falconer had been happily married: nice home, nice dog, nice daughter, everything nice. The mother lived to a great age; the father died somewhat younger, adequately-insured, greatly-mourned by his curling club. He never witnessed the perplexities of Gracie's young womanhood and would certainly have had no sound counsel to proffer, either to herself or to Danny. It amused Gracie to think of her father in relation to Danny; there could not possibly be two men more unlike in their appearance, occupation, their luck in love. She would do anything for Danny, the not-nice, the disgusting, the unthinkable and other kinds of loving that were newer than those. If not newer, plainly unknown and therefore really unthinkable to her parents.

Creams. Pictures. Instruments. Marital aids. Splints for the male. Relaxants for the female. IUDs. Home movies. Pills. Medically-induced miscarriage. Gracie liked the unthinkable best, then the not-nice, thirdly the disgusting with the permissible bringing up the rear. And she could think of things her mother would not have begun to imagine. There was nothing she and Danny did together in the privacy of their apartment, or with another couple, or with one other woman or man that caused her to draw the line. She bought it all.

And her appetite grew by what it fed on. Occasionally when a girl she had heard some tedious moralist or other exclaim that pleasure would not last, that those who indulged themselves too often in some delight would suffer its loss by way of boredom and utter disillusionment. She found that this was not so. The more she did it, the more she liked it. She loved watching herself in the mirrors on the ceiling and the walls and at floor-level. She loved having a few other folks along for the ride. The one thing she really didn't much like was a big crowd; she didn't function well in a group larger than four. She and Danny used to pore over instruction booklets, wondering if this could be a sign of some deeply buried problem which might surface later in life, causing one or other of the mid-life crises or loss-of-identity neuroses familiar in the lives of their bosses and other old people. Probably not. Probably she just didn't like crowds. Some do; some don't.

Her mother had had that arbitrary and witless system of judgment. You could do this; you couldn't do that; you *certainly* couldn't do the other thing. Gracie couldn't discover any foundation for these discriminations. She would do whatever Danny asked for; he asked for some pretty surprising things. Some of them made her wonder how he managed to think of them. It isn't just anybody who can invent a new variation. She knew this very well because she had read everything there is to read on the subject and had once or twice been troubled by the suspicion that the sexual repertoire had much narrower boundaries than most people suspect. If you go right out to the edge of the field instead of standing in the very middle like some fat ruminant, you find that there are fences out there in the blue, even though you are unaware of them at first. The really nice thing about Danny Perrot was his untiring search for something novel, some closer approach to the distant fences.

When they did country walking, she seemed always to take the foremost position as she had done this afternoon. She slogged up the last bit of hill coming towards the bus-stop feeling her buttocks rubbing most cruelly together. Was she leading him on? Was Danny foredoomed a follower?

If you were going to do S & M stuff, who was the *S* and who was the *M?* Or were you both a bit of each? You could be on top or underneath or side by side, but what else was there? She realised that solo flight wouldn't do; obviously two were required for S & M. A sadist is somebody who's sweet to masochists and vice-versa. "There's our bus," she squeaked.

It was 3:15 when they clambered aboard the vehicle and seated themselves down at the back. Gracie set herself down most gingerly on the overstuffed seat-cushions. The swaying of the vehicle caused them both to slide from side to side as curves were rounded. She felt Danny's eyes upon her and didn't have to guess at what he would say when he got her off by herself.

"The hell with Evensong," he said as the bus slowed to a halt near the celebrated west front of the old church. "Come on, I'll buy you a cream tea."

They were both crazy about West Country thick cream. They crossed the narrow, curving main street and entered an up-market tearoom which they had visited before. The proprietress, a terrible bandit, seated them at once and took their order; this solicitude was invariably justified by a huge overcharge but the scones were convincing and the jams varied. The thick cream was the best they had found in the West Country.

As they left the tearoom feeling bloated, they bought a large take-out container of the cream. They might get up to almost any amusement with a lubricant like that; it would function equally well as an edible or cleansing cream. Five minutes after they got up to the room, the big container of cream was half empty. Stimulated by its extraordinary richness and super-smooth lustre and texture, they achieved a first sexual peak in a very short time, a summit on which they were able to rest for a considerable while. When they brought themselves down, they lay together in a state of the most delightful exhaustion for forty-five minutes. Gracie began to sense a series of highly coloured pictures flashing on her inner screen.

"We should have bought some jam," she murmured drowsily.

"We can do better than jam," Danny whispered. He started to talk about new postures, describing something he claimed he had just invented.

He was lying. She could always tell when he was outlining a project to which he had given deep thought. She knew exactly what he wanted; in such a procedure jam would definitely be superfluous. As he talked, his shaking voice outlining his notions, Gracie felt herself increasingly aroused. What he wanted was quite unlike anything she had heard of or imagined; she wasn't sure about doing it but it was a hell of an idea. Imagine that. Imagine having him there. Imagine him being that crazy about her. Ooooohhhhhhhh, think of that. Getting near the fence.

Her mother used to rule things out. "Walter, you're the absolute limit." Gracie could hear the voice. "Walter, you're the end." Mr. Falconer had said nothing.

Can we do that? Can I manage that? Can I get on? Can I balance like that? Will it hurt? Will I hurt him? How did he ever dream this up? I guess I have to move over there like this, yes like this. Ooooohhhhhhhhhh that tickles ooooohhhhhhhh. A sequence of sounds she had never heard before. She made herself comfortable in the strange posture and began to move slowly backwards and forwards, side to side, with a rotary action, all ways. She felt herself pulled down tighter and tighter. Quicker coming back, who had said that? Where had she heard that today; was it something to do with Nelson's column? In the position in which they had settled Danny was unable to make a sound but all of him was visible and she had never seen him come back as quick as this, huge, red and purple, a spring. She could see his eyes and feel him clutch her and move. His eyes were enormously rounded, needful, imploring. Somehow she had acquired a slave. Her father, she thought dreamily, had been often disobliged but never corrupted. "Corrupt," why do I think "corrupt?"

Bees, Flies and Chickens

BRONSON, SILLY ASS, finished building his sailboat at the unluckiest possible moment. This happened on the Monday morning of a week long committed to Viv, Gary and Irene — the last week before Labour Day — for a day at the Exhibition in Toronto and a more extended stay at the Freer farm somewhere north of Orangeville, a scene allegedly ringed by beauty spots. There remained nothing to be done on the morning of departure but to carry the completed hull and fittings of the boat down to the dock where all might lie safely in repose until their return on the following Sunday evening. They might get one day's sailing out of it in this opening season of the boat's long life, or they might simply have to carry it back up to the cottage and stow it away for the winter on Labour Day. Given Bronson's temperament and habitual fortunes, the second alternative seemed more likely. The hull of the sailboat — by no means feather light — shone with five or six coats of meticulously-applied expensive marine paint and as many applications of varnish of such quality that it might have been some product of Coco Chanel priced at several dollars an ounce.

Working the hull down over the rocks with Gary towards the wooden platform on which it would rest during the week of their absence, Viv and Irene standing by anxiously to furnish whatever aid they might, Bronson felt his wrists and fingers growing nerveless and flaccid. There came a protracted scratching noise and the family shuddered as a single soul. When the hull was safely stowed, they examined the paintwork with feverish attention, at last locating a fine long scar or cicatrice abaft the starboard bilge keel.

Two hours were spent with the lightest of delicate sandpaper

135

and a little jar of touch-up paint. Bronson would allow neither children nor spouse near the wound. He dripped thick, uncut, International Ocean Green into the thin pit in the manner of one of the great colourists: Bonnard, Matisse, Lorenzo Lotto, perhaps Seurat. There was an element of *pointillisme* in method of application of the paint.

It was during this episode, they all afterwards agreed, that their subsequent excursion began its swift degeneration into farcical fantastic dream. Bronson in particular felt that the entire structure of their group consciousness had been altered by the fated wounding of the hull, the incident of the immediate repair. The dripping clotting viscosity of the superb paint made him think of Keats's line, "Thou watchest the last oozings hours by hours." This reference, in default of the clear argument of the poem, had always suggested to Bronson the slow escape of arterial blood from the body of somebody who was just finishing up bleeding to death. The last blood would ooze from the lipped cut in precisely this slow way. But he, Bronson, was introducing new blood, new ocean green; complexities of allusion grew muddled in his head.

"We've got to get on the road," declaimed Vivianne.

"Just coming, just coming."

He rinsed out his brush, twisted tight the lid on the jar of touch-up paint and joined the others in the waiting sedan. They sped away into dream country. The boat slumbered tranquilly on the dock for five days of intense aridity as Ontario sweltered under a blanket of infernal heat. No rain. Far fantasies.

In Toronto, safely arrived after certain misadventures on the expressway, missed "Right Lane Must Exit" signs, perplexities connected with the translation of miles into kilometres, indecision about approaches to service roads, they stayed over Monday and Tuesday nights with Elaine Freer, longtime associate of Vivianne Bronson in her maiden years as Vivie, the dream-girl of Rosedale. The two girls had attended the same private academy, retaining joint memories of the absurdity of the undertaking; they had suffered together through terrible embarrassments at fifteen when obliged by the school's stern regimen to wear close-fitting black tights under the briefest of uniform skirts, a requirement of which some bad girls had taken illegitimate advantage.

For Vivianne and Elaine the dress-code had served only as a

source for acute adolescent self-absorption of a kind from which they felt themselves mercifully released by maturity, modest womanhood. Elaine Freer was the sole child of a senior military officer of the period of World War II. Her mother had died long ago in some obscure accident to a military aircraft in which she and the General were being transported to a new posting in occupied Germany. That was in the late 1940s. Elaine had not married. She had lived alone for a number of years on the Freer farm near Georgian Bay in a thinly inhabited region of the province and had more recently acted as her long-retired father's chatelaine in their Toronto house. In the last few years General Freer had not been at all well and was now "in for tests."

On Tuesday morning Irene and Gary set out for the Exhibition, each clutching fistfuls of money saved during winter months of painful expectation and rigorous economy. They loved the CNE in their late teens as they had loved it in infancy: the Midway, the Pure Foods Building and especially that spacious edifice whose name nobody remembers (just down from the Dufferin Gate to your right as you proceed towards the Bandshell where exhibits of all kinds without discrimination as to specific field of utility are displayed, a kind of Aladdin's Cave of small new products). Here one might find rug merchants, vendors of unusual plant foods and seeds, traders in exotic wooden furniture and rattan, strange hobby booths or booths for strange hobbies. There were extensive displays of military and naval models (haunted by Gary Bronson during those few instants before his purse was exhausted) and pyramids of pet supplies, ant eggs, sunflower seeds. At a bird-lover's booth, Irene was entranced by great fans of ostrich plumes and peacock feathers, lustrous dark purples and semi-transparent featherings of light through scarlet and green. And there were chanting parrots, lories, conures, African Greys and the lowering great blue and gold Macaws. She bought a spread of peacock feathers, intending to present some to their hostess in the huge old house on Chestnut Park Road. Elaine shrieked with alarm when she saw them, forgetting for an instant the duties of the chatelaine.

"Oh, bad luck," she quavered, "dark peacock feathers mean a death, a death."

She was genuinely stirred by the incident, a curious psycholog-

ical frailty which powerfully impressed Irene. Gary, fingers dripping adhesive, eyes screwed in mystic concentration as he applied
one tiny structural component to another in the hope of producing
an authentic Sherman for a Desert War Diorama, refused to pass
comment upon adult superstition. So Irene deposited all her lovely
peacock feathers — all but one — in the trunk of the car and
half-forgot them. It seemed to her that when Elaine urged them
on their way on Wednesday morning she might have shown just
a bit less eagerness to see their backs.

"Be sure to report to me what's happening at the farm," she
trilled from the veranda. "Daddy's been half off his head about
the pond."

"Why?" shouted Viv from the front seat.

"It doesn't hold water. Goodbye, goodbye."

Bronson, always a curious but irresolute motorist, found himself
obliged at every moment to consult the road map of the province
which lay open between him and Viv. He selected what on the
facts seemed the least convenient route out of the city, arguing
that such a traffic-bound artery as North Yonge Street (on a mid-
week morning after the rush but well before noon) would be all
but deserted. In this ingenious conjecture he was perfectly wrong.
He had to fight his way past huge earthworks and looming troughs
in the roadway at twenty miles an hour, all the way to the intersection with Highway 7 at Thornhill.

"Should have struck out for Highway 400," he mumbled.

The others spoke little. It was now terribly warm with temper-
atures of 34 Celsius (over 90 degrees Fahrenheit) predicted for
Thursday, Friday and the holiday weekend.

This was really unknown terrain for Bronson — he hadn't been
in these neighbourhoods for a quarter of a century. As they eased
past successive traffic lights along Highway 7 coming into
Brampton, he rotated his head and neck like an inquisitive seal
on a rock studying the impressive urban sprawl which lay roundabout. Realtors' signs, my God! So many realtors' signs. He had
not thought God had unleased so many. Pre-set traffic lights allow-
ing the cars to move in sudden startling unpredictable directions.
"Advanced green when flashing!" Shopping plazas of grotesque
proportions; little twinned movie theatres devoted to *Star Wars*
and soft-core porn. Here and there the dessicated remains of a

farm. At length they turned north on Highway 10 and headed off into the Caledon Hills and beyond them, Orangeville and lunch.

Immediately next to the Chinese restaurant where they ate (always the safest bet in a smallish city) stood a representative of a chain bakery into which, after lunch, Gary, Irene and Viv retreated in search of dessert. They came back with six light-grey cardboard boxes, tightly tied with thin string, containing doughnuts, sugar cookies, éclairs, date-and-nut loaf, sausage rolls and raspberry jelly roll; the smell of fresh baked-goods pervaded the family car like incense as the ride continued up Highway 10 to the intersection with 89, the Shelburne road, then jogged north on 24, a highway few people hear of. Here the tone of the day, the weather, the light began to alter most insidiously as they moved at a steady fifty-eight miles per hour or as Irene sagely observed, just under 100 kilometres per hour past Horning's Mills, Redickville and Maple Valley. Places you haven't heard of and neither have I. The country was void; on the right a vast falloff, the downwards slant of a moraine, began to trouble them obscurely.

Nobody has sufficiently investigated this groundswell of moraine. Why are they there? How is it that they give such a troubling air to the landscapes of this part of the world? They aren't very high. They aren't impassable. They are so familiar to us that we pay no attention to them. But get yourself out in a depopulated part of the province on a hot afternoon, with the land dropping away on your right hand like the trough of an enormous enveloping wave, with the next nearest swell plainly visible three miles away to the east and you may almost feel seasick. Turn off Highway 24 down a sideroad just before you get to Singhampton and even though you spot the comforting Bruce Trail signs, the sheer amplitude of the roll of moraine moraine moraine all the way to the sky will unnerve you. You bump down the road and realise suddenly you are on the sloping, quick-descending side of something enormous. It is a long long way down. You raise your eyes and away away away off to the east you can see the huge, hazily ill-defined flank of the next great whale heaving up at 4000 yards. That would be Creemore.

"We are descending the shoulder of the Mad River Valley," said the scholarly voice of Gary from the back seat.

"Gimme that map, stupid," said Irene. "It's *Mod* River, not Mad River."

They disputed the point amiably for some moments as the car jolted down a sharply increasing incline.

"I wonder if Gillette Foamy would stop us if the brakes failed here?" said Viv idly, almost to herself. Bronson threw her a reproachful glance. "No," she continued, "it wouldn't be quite thick and rich enough."

"Stop needling me."

"Needling you?"

"Horse's bum," said Bronson between his teeth. They passed another Bruce Trail finger sign.

"Hang a left," said an unidentifiable voice from the rear, "we're here." As they swung around and began to ascend an almost invisible rutted track, they spotted the mailbox, quite empty, its door hanging open, newly-stencilled letters spelling out the name *Freer.*

"We're obviously on the right track," said Gary, audibly more at ease with specific destination at hand. He was a young man who didn't care for feelings of disorientation, a practised reader of maps and encyclopaedias. "God, what a driveway!"

"Not a driveway; we haven't gotten to the driveway yet," said Bronson. "I think this is supposed to be a through road."

"You couldn't pass an oncoming car here," said Viv. "Collision would be mandatory."

"Now, we really are here," said Irene. "There's the gate. You can just barely make it out."

The grass and brush had been allowed to run quite wild where the gate was and the light metal frame, half unhinged, lay at a crazy angle, almost invisible in a criss-crossing weave of luxuriant tendrils.

"Strait is the gate and narrow," said Bronson. "I wonder if I can get the car up there. Elaine uses a four-wheeler, doesn't she?"

"There are good ruts," said Gary. "I'll give you a hand."

He got out of the car and by a process of signalling was able to show Bronson how to turn the corner and begin to negotiate the exiguous driveway. It took quite half an hour, in low gear the whole time, for them to coax the car up the final slope and around in front of the deserted farmhouse. It was like stepping slowly and fearfully into the frame of one of those Hopper paintings where grass grows up terrifyingly tall right next to the empty alien dwelling. They made their way carefully to the porch stoop and in a momentary return to calm lucidity discovered the front door keys just where they were supposed to be. From the elevated vantage-point of the stoop they were able to look across the waving grass to where the pond, or mere, was supposed to be located but they could see no sign of water, only a deep depression in which no grass could live.

Moved by joint impulse they set down their hand luggage and moved downwards through the weeds and shrubs to the edge of this formation; it was like peering into a moonscape. Some fault or fissure in the side of the moraine had split open wide enough to allow the mere or pond to drain into the recesses of the hillside. The superficial cladding of stiff clay which formed the surface of this recess was richly-etched with an oddly beautiful pattern of serpentine cracks extending from the upper edge to the bottom of the baked mud. At the brink a sizeable rubber hose, no doubt connected to the water supply in the house, showed how Elaine had tried, on her father's anxious and detailed instructions, to keep the pond replenished with water. She had burnt out two half-horsepower pump motors in the process before abandoning the enterprise; it had been a matter of pumping water up from the artesian labyrinth concealed in the moraine, pouring it back down and in (something like the actions of Sisyphus or another mythological personage), an unaccomplishable task.

At the very bottom of the empty pond there was a single dimple or pothole which had retained almost to the end some few drops of water; here the mud showed a darker brown than elsewhere and in the still-tacky substance sat a single old frog, flicking its tongue at passing insects in flight, once in a way hitching its haunches up and down looking thirsty. Inspired by this sight, Gary seized the front-door keys from his mother's hand and disappeared into the house. There was a pause. He reappeared bearing in either hand a brimming bucket of what seemed blood.

"What's that you've got there?" demanded his father.

"Some water for the poor frog."

"Why does it look so red? It's like some enchanted potion."

"All the taps in the house run red."

"Oh, God," shrieked Irene in mock-hysteria, "what weird fate hangs over us? Where have we got to?"

"It isn't us," said Bronson wildly, "it's this house."

"Will you stop all this silliness?" said Viv. "We've got to open the place up and get some air through it. Irene, do something! Let's move out! It must be over 100 in there."

"About thirty-eight. Celsius," said Irene.

"Hold it a second," said Bronson, watching as his son scrambled down into the pit with the two buckets of water he emptied carefully into the sucking mud puddle around the old frog. "That's a nice thing for him to do. I wouldn't have thought of it. Gary has good instincts."

"He gets them from you. Come on, we'll run the taps until the water clears; then we can all take showers and we'll feel better."

Inside the farmhouse they did indeed feel better momentarily, going around and casting open the windows, some of which were imperfectly screened. The house was a furnace. There was little breeze but at nightfall relief might be expected. There were only two bedrooms upstairs, facing north, with a storage attic running the length of the building on the south side across the rickety hall. Here and there were broken flooring and missing plaster. The second floor seemed especially charged with some strange sweet scent; there was another sensory element in the manifold of atmospheric impressions yielded by the darkened hall and bedrooms, some steady unidentifiable datum, whether heard, seen, or scented, it was at this moment impossible to say.

The ground floor contained the elements of civilised life: the usual kitchen appliances, a radio, an old 45 rpm record player with a single record (no others were found). There was a lot of food in the refrigerator and an enormous freezer in a kind of summer kitchen attached to the back of the house. In an attempt to cool the interior of the building, they opened this freezer (expecting to discover something quite nasty in it but there were only a package of frozen Niblets and some TV dinners). The freezer was useless as an air-conditioner. As soon as it was opened the frost on the neatly-wrapped packages melted and ran away through some concealed drain and the food warmed up. They slammed the lid shut and listened with relief as the freezer throbbed quietly.

"Maybe I'll just sleep inside it," said Gary.

"You and Irene get the bedrooms," said Bronson. If anybody were going to lie awake perishing with the upstairs heat, let it not be he. "Your mother and I will use the dining-room floor. We've got our sleeping bags."

"How foresighted!" said Irene. She was busy arranging peacock feathers in agreeable festoons around the bay window in the dining room.

"Are you planning a funeral?"

"Of course not; there's nothing to that old wives' tale."

"Elaine isn't an old wife," protested Viv.

Irene grew pale and Bronson eyed her keenly. "You didn't leave any feathers around the General's house, did you? By gosh, I'll bet you did. Idiot!"

"I only left one," faltered Irene, "for a little joke."

"Crazy nut!"

"It was just to show her that there's nothing to be afraid of."

"The only things to be afraid of are the things we think we've got to fear," said Bronson obscurely. He didn't follow up the inquiry, observing that Irene was genuinely alarmed about what she had done. They were all the more shaken when they turned on the six o'clock news during an impromptu supper (cold sausage rolls, raspberry jelly roll) to be assailed at once by an obituary:

> Major-General J.R.C. Freer, CB, DSO, MC, died this afternoon in Toronto's Saint Michael's Hospital where he had been undergoing tests for a circulatory disorder. After being returned to the hospital's intensive care unit, the General sustained a coronary infarction from which he was unable to rally. General Freer, who will be remembered locally as General Officer Commanding, Military District No. 2, during the period of World War II, served as Canada's ambassador to Brussels and Bonn in the late 1940s. He is survived by a daughter. The funeral, to be held Friday, will be private.

"You and your peacock feathers," said Bronson.

"I never meant any harm."

"And you haven't done any harm," said Viv soothingly. "General Freer has been sick for years. It's nothing but a coincidence, sweetheart. Forget about it."

Irene retired, half in tears, to her designated bedroom at the top of the house. At different times in the course of the evening discontented sniffles emerged. Darkness came on. It was impossible to leave the building for any purpose between 8:00 and 9:30 P.M. because of swarms of biting insects unfamiliar to the Bronsons whose summer home was hundreds of miles away.

"They can't be mosquitoes," swore Bronson, "not in late August."

But they were.

And in the house the swarms of flies grew intolerable; they began to get in their hair and up their sleeves. The bathroom was full of them and you couldn't run the water clear enough to take a bath anyway. Bronson drank a lot of coffee made from the clay-saturated water and felt as though his insides had been bricked or cemented shut. He and Viv and Gary were sitting around in the dimly-lit living room chatting about pioneer days in central Ontario (which they tended to dismiss testily as the Susannah Moodie syndrome) when the shrieks from upstairs began.

Irene, waking from unsettled doze, seemed to feel herself in mortal peril. With praiseworthy courage all the Bronsons charged up the stairs, Gary in the lead, to find Irene standing nude in the darkened hall. An immense thrumming noise now declared itself as the intensified source of the peculiar sensations felt earlier: the song of a myriad of honey bees. This perception at once clarified the origins of the powerfully honied scent prevailing upstairs.

"The whole goddamned wall is one giant honeycomb," said Irene, much moved.

"What?"

"Look!" said the astonished girl. She displayed an arm covered thickly with a clotted and viscous liquid. They rushed her to the downstairs bathroom, plunged the arm into the basin and ran the reddened water until it was full. Then they got the feeling they were looking at some wonderful painting. The arm, coated a couple of inches thick with gleaming golden honey, chunks of clear wax trapped in it, seemed to melt in the rush of reddened water, gold and red and waxy-white blending under the bare light bulb in the shadowy bathroom into a kind of art object accidentally discovered in the midst of life.

"Will you look at that?" said Gary reverently.

It took several minutes of running the water and flushing off the honey and wax to get Irene cleaned up before she withdrew the limb from the lukewarm flood.

"The wall's alive with them. It's one big bloody honeycomb. I could hear them getting louder and louder and they kept flying lower and lower over my face. Brushing it like a kiss. They didn't sting me at all. They might have done. I got up in the dark and like a dummy started feeling around the windowsill and then I slipped and my whole arm went down into the wall and it's nothing but a well of wax and honey."

Gary looked at her apprehensively. "And now I suppose you want my room?"

"Not on your life. I tried your room and it's like the crater of a volcano. I'm staying in the hive." A chunk of wax had adhered to the inside of Irene's left elbow. She peeled it off, inserted it in her mouth and began to chew and suck vigorously; she was regaining her composure. "I'll stick with the bees," she mumbled. "This is terrific stuff."

Somewhat later, the farmhouse quiet — except for the buzzing — and the scented night perfectly still, they retired to uneasy repose. It might have been the hottest night of the year, perhaps the decade. Towards midnight sounds of uneasy tossings and turnings began in Gary's room and his parents crouched apprehensively below, waiting for a loud crash from the second floor which never came. By morning all the Bronsons succeeded in achieving a troubled slumber. At breakfast the customary complaints began on all sides. Nothing to do. Too hot. Nowhere to go. Too hard to get the car out. Bronson, it should be stated, was not behindhand in the chorus. He didn't care for the sensation he now felt creeping over him of being held by some inscrutable sway against his will in a place from which he was not free to go at any time. A time would come when he would be at liberty to depart. Not yet. Something held him there. He felt a teasing thrill of dread when Gary picked up the single 45 rpm disc which lay forgotten on a window-seat in the dining room, found the record-player (a survival from the 1950s which would play only 45s) and set the little turntable in motion, dropping the record casually into place. Soon a peculiar duet struck up:

Hello Central, hello Central, give me 602 . . .
I want to speak to Margie dear . . .
Hello Margie, hello Margie, is that really you?
I've been trying hard all day
To get you on the phone to say . . .

Margie: (Spoken) Yes?
Man: Are you all alone?
Margie: Yes.
Man: All alone?
Margie: Yes, there's nobody here but me.
Man: And is the parlour nice and cosy?
Margie: Everything is really rosy.
Man: We'll have lots of . . .
Margie: Oh hurry up and get here honey.
Man: (Spoken) I'll take a trolley car.
Margie: (Spoken) Or you can walk . . . it's not far.
Man: But my time is all my own.
Margie: Then hurry up; there's something missing.
Man: We'll have lots and lots of kissing.
Together: Ma and Pa have left us all alone.

The Bronsons, trained textual critics, found this lyric utterly absorbing and passed much of the morning analysing its social and historical implications.

> Dates from the period before the introduction of the dial telephone; before the widespread predominance of the passenger automobile; depicts city life (trolley car, parlour, Central) but not metropolitan life; diction of 1910 to 1920 (Ma and Pa); sexual manners depicted those of that epoch (lots and lots of kissing); most likely some old vaudeville number.

They were unable to identify the performers even after repeated playings which took them down to about 11:00 A.M. Then, almost inadvertently, Gary flipped the disc and found another song available for their entertainment. Its title and the names of the singers were indecipherable because of long wear and much handling but the Bronsons thought they'd give it a listen. This is what they heard:

A Colonel from Kentucky who was as famous as a cook
Found a secret recipé and threw away the book.
The chicken was so tasty/tender and the spices were so great
That it soon became a favourite in each and every state.

(Mixed chicken chorus.)

Squawk, Squawk, Squawk, Squawk, Squawk, Squawk, Squawk, Squawk;
Squawk, Squawk, Squawk, Squawk, Squawk, Squawk, Squawk, Squawk!
Squawk, Squawk, Squawk, Squawk, Squawk, Squawk, Squawk, Squawk —
Squawk, Squawk, Squawk . . . Squawk . . . Squawk.

Both the words and the squawking chorus were sung by chickens — or by humans cleverly simulating chickens — in eerie four-part harmony. There was in the composition much of the classical tradition of choral writing for four voices, recalling the Bach of the Cothen period.

For some reason this anthem absolutely delighted Irene and Gary who had never heard singing chickens before or little-girl chickens (chickenettes?) or stalwart baritone chickens. The sound of the record conjured up a vista of lyric chicken performance: opera, oratorio, musical comedy. For most of the rest of the day, the kids lounged around the dining room in the awful heat refusing to touch food, refusing to venture out into the sun, playing both sides of the record over and over again, both sides, the chickens more often than the vaudeville duet. Their squawks began to etch themselves into Viv's brain. Around 3:00 P.M. she drew Bronson into the kitchen and pleaded with him to organise some sort of expedition into Collingwood, perhaps for the evening meal, if only for an hour or two to get them out.

"And, we haven't visited the beauty spots, the Devil's Glen, the Mad — or — Mod — River Valley. Don't you want to go there?"

"No," said Bronson.

"A Colonel from Kentucky . . ." sang the chickens, " . . . each and every state."

"I know exactly what sort of scene the Mad — or Mod — River will be."

"Squawk, squawk, squawk . . . scratch, squeak . . . Margie dear, Margie dear . . . nobody home but me. . . "

"Damn that record!"

"You've never been there."

Nevertheless I know what it'll look like. I mean, in this context."

". . . all alone . . . all alone . . ."

"It'll be a swift turbulent swirl of foaming cataract and whirlpool to which on some bleak winter night an abandoned housemaid, pregnant and alone, cast out from humble lodging by her overbearing mistress — a Joan Crawford type — wanders in the darkness and snow. How can she bear her shame? Is it all worth it? No, it is not. So she hurls herself and her unborn child into the raging water. And still, on quiet summer nights, if you listen closely in the Devil's Glen, you will hear her sweet voice calling."

"I see her as played by Bonnie Bedelia," said Viv.

"A *young* Bonnie Bedelia."

Viv knew that her husband so loathed the image of the young Bonnie Bedelia that nothing she — Viv — could suggest would get him out of the house for the remainder of their stay. The attitude wasn't rational or critical but it was an attitude by which her husband lived, a type of credo. If some conception fitted his imagination, he would never give it up. She grew fearful; perhaps they were destined never to leave the farm. She herded her little brood disconsolately to bed; they had come there expecting to stay until Sunday. Oh God, it was hot. She struggled into her sweaty sleeping bag and listened to the sound of the bees above and the flies all around her. The bees made the honey and the flies came after it and the chickens serenaded them. She drew the zipper shut across the top of her head; it was like being in hell. Later she dozed.

Towards dawn Bronson, who had likewise zipped his bag right shut, woke cursing and blaspheming. The heat and the swarming flies were driving him mad. He rose, tripping and stumbling in the half-light, and made his sweaty way to the windows, flapping his arms and groaning. He stood in the bay window and watched the early light move across the depths of the moraine. The grey unfathomable Ontario light. They found him there at breakfast time.

"I don't like to bring this up," he stammered. "I know we meant to stay out the week, but would anybody be interested in leaving now? I really don't think Elaine would . . ." He realised he was addressing empty air.

Half an hour later, approaching the car, he grasped that they had somehow teleported themselves into it. No intervening state of motion to and fro had been required. They rocked unsteadily down the drive and along the ruts towards the "improved" road which would bring them back to blissful blacktop. No sign came from the house. In moments more they were fleeing down Highway 24.

"We never visited the beauty spots," said a voice.

"Fuck the beauty spots," said Bronson. He drove like a man possessed. They decided to bypass Toronto by going east through Newmarket and thereafter along a sequence of unpaved township byways as far as Musselman Lake, a precinct recollected by Bronson from his childhood experience of Weekend Mystery Tours on Grey Coach Lines. They found that they couldn't bypass Toronto by doing this. Everything they passed through seemed to be Toronto sprawl, miles and miles of housing developments and light industrial installations which more and more induced the feeling of running and running and yet remaining in place. They descended Highway 48 through Markham and debouched onto 401 East into a frightening press of pre-Labour Day traffic which continued heavy and hotly-competitive as far as Trenton/Belleville. In the last of the afternoon the eastbound lanes cleared and silence filled the swaying family sedan. The constant swerve from lane to lane ended. Irene and Gary drowsed. Thoughts of chickens dwelt in their heads. They came to the Mallorytown exit and turned homewards north, and the high ridge which surrounded the lake came into sight and the Blue Mountain. Almost before the car was stationary all four rushed down to the water, tore off their clothes and hurled themselves in. Bronson retained his Jockey shorts in token modesty; the others went naked, sporting in the cool water like dolphins, like the Belugas, shining white as they surfaced and dived. How long they remained in the water they could not have said, but twilight came on as they gathered on the dock to examine the hull of the beautiful new boat. And though they sought for evidence long and anxiously, they found not the slightest mark on the paint.

In the Deep

THE ORE CARRIER *CHILORIA* of U.S. registry, home port Baltimore, Master, Samuel S. Ferguson, cleared Balboa early on the morning of Saturday, 16 June of this year, southward bound for Valparaiso. There she would load a cargo of iron ore, return after a quick turnaround via the same route to her home port where the ore was to be discharged. *Chiloria,* one of eight sister ships owned by a steel company, seldom or never carries any cargo southwards on her regular run and on this voyage was riding high in the water in light ballast. In summer these waters are normally calm; no heavy weather was predicted in the weather service bulletins. The vessel made good speed southwards towards the Equator, crossing the line during the evening of Sunday, 17 June.

Next morning found the ship off the Gulf of Guayaquil. At daybreak, the skies clear and the sun brilliantly hot, the usual coastal atmospheric disturbances caused a strong breeze to rise and freshen. By mid-morning, in coastal waters, a long rolling swell got up and the ship, riding high, with all her heavy machinery astern and nothing in her ample holds, began to yaw about, her bow swinging shorewards with each swell. The vessel was in no serious difficulties; her position and speed were being closely monitored by the appropriate onshore authorities. Captain Ferguson merely issued regular corrections to the helmsman as the vessel proceeded but the swervings to port and the series of course corrections continued. They were a function of the behaviour of the seas and the distribution of weight in the hull.

At noon on 18 June the vessel's position was fixed as Lat. 3°, 10′ south/Long. 82°, 35′ west, the approaches to the Gulf of Guayaquil just astern to port.

151

A few minutes after noon Apprentice Seaman Pedrecito Mariñ, a Chilean national who had joined the ship on its next-to-last call at Valparaiso (a competent seaman with an exemplary record of service during the short time he had been a crew-member) was ordered right forward by the bos'n to effect a minor repair to the retaining cables on the vessel's starboard bow which stretched from a stanchion abaft the foremast to a pair of eyes set into the plating of the bow.

There has been a worldwide slump in the demand for steel, consequently for iron ore, and the ships engaged in this service are not new. Their essential equipment, irreproachably maintained in all respects, has kept the small fleet to which *Chiloria* belongs in steady uninterrupted service. But there are some elements of the fleet's maintenance that are not perhaps quite all they should be. The safety cables, or retaining lines, which Pedrecito Mariñ was attempting to tighten were badly rusted, sagging, insufficient to prevent an accident if any heavy weight were applied to them.

The ship's position was fixed precisely at noon and Mariñ began to tighten the cables almost immediately afterwards so that we can judge precisely when and where his accident occurred. The vessel had continued to swing quite violently to port as the swell moved her; the helmsman continued to make the necessary correction. Pedrecito Mariñ now made a dreadful error. Ignoring the ship's abnormal and dizzying yaw, most evident in the bow, sea and sky rotating in a complex figure-eight, the seaman leaned well out over the cable in an attempt to place a large wrench over a rusted and greasy fitment so as to tighten it, reducing the slack in the cable.

At this moment an unusually heavy swell lifted the ship and swung it once more to port; the helmsman made an over-eager correction. The bow, very high in the water, shuddered under the opposing forces. The deck under Pedrecito's feet drummed and vibrated so that he lost his balance. His full weight landed hard against the upper cable which all at once went completely slack, snapping at a rusted point against the strain. Mariñ went into the sea at precisely 12:22 P.M.

In such a swell he ought to have been thrown against the ship's plating, flayed by the fouled surface of the metal, perhaps cut to bits by the revolution of the starboard screw; but it happened that as he went into the water he hit the undertow of a swell, sank far under the surface and was whisked a considerable distance from the moving hull as the following sea formed. When he surfaced, spitting and gagging, terrified and breathless, he expected to find himself on the point of being crushed against the hull and was amazed to find himself already far enough astern to starboard that it was almost impossible to sight the ship. She had been spirited out of his life. Then the next roller heaved him high up and there she was, already several hundred yards distant. He was being swept past her stern and in seconds would be able to see her port side. They would never spot him from her decks.

Unluckily for the seaman, it was another eight or nine minutes before his accident was noted. At that time *Chiloria* was already more than two miles removed from his position. In the heavy swell his body was being carried further and further away from safety. The onshore swell continued to rise.

In fact, there was at no time any possibility of Mariñ's being recovered by his own ship. His officers and crew observed every rule of the sea, took every measure they could imagine to rescue a crew-member. *Chiloria* hove to as soon as his loss was noted. She put over two of the ship's boats, both of them in excellent condition. A search was mounted which continued for the remaining daylight hours and for twenty-four hours afterwards air-sea rescue patrols were maintained from Guayaquil. None of these measures met with success. Nobody could survive for long in mid-ocean, not the most powerful and tenacious of swimmers. The young man must be presumed drowned.

In the water, in the equatorial afternoon, Pedrecito was not freezing to death. In most ocean seas the water temperature is sufficient at any time of year to kill a struggling man or woman in minutes simply from the effects of lobar pneumonia, a complete failure of respiration. Off Guayaquil the water seemed absurdly agreeably warm. A hundred miles further west it would not have been so warm; immersion would bring exhaustion speedily enough. In coastal water the survival of the struggling man was extended for valuable minutes, even hours.

He was courageous and intelligent and he realised the gravity of his position. He could die at any moment. There was no question whatsoever of his being able to reach shore; there were no nearby islands. The swell was taking him shorewards right enough, but land was more than eighty miles away. They would never sight him from *Chiloria*. A speck in an immensity, he would be invisible even in this glaring sun to aircraft or helicopters at any height. His life was ending.

He did what he could. He struggled out of his boots and trousers and with terrible effort managed to free himself from his clinging chambray shirt. Now he could move his limbs freely. He trod water desperately for several moments and fought his terrors. What should he do; what should he try to do; could he do anything by himself; was he not lost?

He gave himself up for lost.

Then, when he would have wept, though he could not weep, his eyes clogged and burning with salt, he felt solid footing beneath him. He kicked downwards, refusing to believe in the contact. A half-submerged plank or log? Not, God help him, a shark? He didn't kick again. Then he felt the waters underneath him move as though displaced by some sort of hydraulic elevator. A whole segment of the sea below him seemed to slip and pour away to either side of the force being exerted. He felt a surface moving up underneath him, a ridged, slippery, irregular platform of some kind like the deck of a submarine vessel. He found himself hoisted aloft, out of the water, sliding and slipping and trying to cling to whatever was supporting him. It rose. It floated. The waters poured away and he stared at the wet darkbrown woody fibrous resistant substance on which he lay unsteadily. He was sliding off; he scrabbled and dug with his fingers' ends at the surface. There was a thick edge. He stretched out his arms in front of him and felt in the flashing turbulence for this edge. He clutched and squeezed it. It was inches thick. He held on with his arms spreadeagled from the shoulders, clinging to the leading edge of the platform or whatever it was. He rose again, this time above the waves. He was almost clear of the water. Was it a raft of some kind? It was the size of a small raft.

At once he felt the equatorial sun begin to dry him and in a few moments his singlet and underpants steamed dry and stuck to him. He actually began to feel the heat, to fear the scorching rays. Water splashed over him now and then. The raft or platform rose and sank and thrust itself onwards in the water according to some powerful propulsive action of its own. Several times each minute the whole object below him lurched forward in a swimming motion. It must be a living thing.

Just as Pedrecito realised this the thrusting motion slowed and stopped. They lay at rest, rhythmically lifted over the surfaces of successive swells. The thing that was keeping him alive put its head up in front of him. Gnarled. Ancient. Washed very dark by streaming water, green and brown and a curious bruised blue, enormous, the size perhaps of a big pumpkin, a slowly-turning head. It was the head of a giant sea turtle protruding from the tough shell on which Pedrecito lay.

The head was articulated to the inner surface of the shell by immensely tough folds of skin which had the appearance and the texture of woven metal, hammered metallic cloth like the chain mail of mediaeval knights or the strips and ribs of Samurai armour, indestructible, resistant to all natural forces. The turtle turned its immense head slowly so that the sailor could see its right eye, shielded and almost invisible under a pouched and sagging lid. There was a visible pupil which moved sluggishly. Did the creature know that he was astride its back? Would it begin to plunge madly in the water to dislodge him?

He noticed that the sun had declined somewhat from the centre of the sky. They had come some distance and a considerable time had passed. From this moment of recognition of his terrifyingly lucky/unlucky position, Mariñ was unable to keep track of time. He could distinguish darkness from light and eventually realised a night had succeeded a day, a new day had broken; it, in turn, would end in darkness.

The first look into the slowly moving, deeply gazing eye of the beast underneath him was the end of Mariñ's youth. As he stared into the moving circle he felt like a mystic lost in concentration. His history, his old world, narrowed and focussed itself on that orb half hidden in folds of pouched skin. It was the colour of a wine grape, very dark blue-green; then it was the colour of a ripened olive, shiny black in the foaming water; then dull and opaque and unreadable. It seemed to show a small point of light, a gleam as it turned and took the sun of the summer solstice; they were moving again. The turtle had begun to thrust itself forward in a new direction. Its head turned away and Pedrecito was left to consider his plight. He could not drink the water which slopped over him and cooled him. He had nothing to eat. The turtle might dive at any moment. The shell was the most precarious perch imaginable but he had no choice, he had to hang on. Life reduced itself to his agonised grasp at the thick edge of the shell. Sometimes he was plunged in the water so that he could scarcely breathe; he felt as if he might drown while the turtle continued to hold him up. Could the inscrutable beast be trying to drown him to free itself from the unwelcome weight of his body? He thought so at first but slowly suspected that the turtle only wanted to balance itself in the waves. The forward motion was constant and powerful. Pedrecito grew accustomed to the deep and steady rhythm of the turtle's limbs which moved in a curious regular stroke, a deliberate gait. It seemed that there was a strong motion from the right shoulder, then from the rear limb on the left, then from the left shoulder, finally from the right rear limb. A cross-gait.

The shell planed and sailed and curvetted through the water, held steady by the powerful heavy body beneath it, the whole balance and thrust the product of thousands of years of evolution. It seemed to Pedrecito that the surface of the shell was much larger than men guessed. He couldn't judge exactly, but from its leading edge to which he clung so desperately to the tail, the shell might be ten feet in length. He was almost six feet tall himself; he could not find the trailing edge of the shell with his feet. He dared not change his position. He felt no assurance that he could safely sit or stand or kneel on the shell. Not in rough water. In a calm it might be possible for him to rest, to move his arms which now began to seem on fire from the long harsh stretch and clutch which kept him in place. The night came and passed and the following day, Tuesday, 19 June found them approaching the most eastern of the Galapagos group from the southeast.

For most of the next twenty-four hours, man and turtle were close to land though Pedrecito never knew this for certain. He felt that it must be so when land birds appeared in the sky, circling for fish, sometimes swooping down towards his tormented body as though they saw in him some strange inhabitant of the deeps, some gilled and finned human. But the birds knew as they wheeled above him, often not more than thirty feet above, almost within reach . . . if he could seize one . . . they knew that he was no man/fish. They never came in reach. He had had no food for thirty hours. He would grow weaker. He had to change his position. As they came closer to the shallows which surround the Galapagos, the motion of the water grew less turbulent and the swimming movement of the turtle's limbs became smoother and more effective. The shell rose and fell and rose and fell, lipping the water, flipping the foam high. Sometimes the turtle seemed to play with the waves. They flattened. On the afternoon of 19 June, to leeward of San Cristobal, the wind about three miles an hour from the northwest, the turtle slowed to a halt and lay rocking from side to side quite gently, almost if begging the struggling man to sit or kneel.

The rocking motion became almost imperceptible. Should he risk it? Pedrecito unclutched his tensed fingers, first one hand, then the other. He was afraid to let go with both hands. He held on with the left as he clenched and unclenched the fingers of the right hand. He moved his right arm and shoulder feebly. They felt as if he had been struck by a crippling arthritis. He could barely stand the pain of the overtaxed joints but he forced himself to move. Then he changed hands and worked his left arm, hand, shoulder, to loosen them. He kicked his swollen feet on the turtle's shell and tried to mouth a word or two of defiant song. The creature was now perfectly still. Should he try to sit or stand?

He let go his grip, the left hand first, then the right. The turtle made no move to dislodge him. Then he got very slowly to his knees, balancing on the gently-rocking shell. Some birds wheeled in the sky at a prudent distance. The sky seemed darker. He noticed something lodged in a crevice of the shell, something shell-like, ringed in green. He fell on his chest and stared closely at the crack in the horny substance of the shell. There were several mollusc-like shellfish, tiny, barely visible, stuck in the crack, partly-concealed by trailing green bands of weed. He thought of eating them, then decided that they would be unbearably salty and refrained. Rain would save him. It might yet rain.

No rain came through the second night and the morning of the second day, Wednesday, 20 June. The turtle continued to swim north-westwards. On the afternoon of 20 June they passed out of the Galapagos shallows to the northeast of Genovesa into the deep channel which separates the archipelago from the island of Cocos, about 400 miles north-northeast.

If Pedrecito had known this he would have resigned himself to death by drowning because their present course would take man and turtle out into the central Pacific. It seemed to the agonised seaman that he could not sustain his grip on life any longer. He had been borne up by the turtle for more than forty-eight hours. He had neither eaten nor drunk. The awareness of the small shellfish which he dared not eat tormented him. He prayed, sobbed and groaned; his wits turned. He felt certain that the sea turtle would now carry him away into deep water and there dive, leaving him to die after having endured so long. This might happen at any moment. He certainly could not last another day.

On the Wednesday night he was granted a respite for the rain began, softly at first, so that he could not distinguish it from the sea spray; then, much harder, sweeping across his dreadful perch, stinging his burnt and inflamed cheeks, washing them down. He opened his mouth in the darkness and swallowed convulsively again and again, his parched throat at first unable to accept the water. He thought that he might eat now and with his free hand dug and scraped at one of the shellfish lodged in the crevice beside him. He tore it free, ripping his fingernails as he did so. Then he held the small object up to the rain, hoping to rinse it free of salt. He held the shell to his mouth and sucked at an open end. A sweet juice trickled down his throat. He sucked again, rolling crazily to one side, holding on with one hand. Suddenly the meat of the shellfish came away from the shell and passed into his gaping mouth. He chewed, gagged, bit and chewed, swallowed. He had been nearly sixty hours without food. He managed to eat a second morsel before the seas roughened and the action became impossible.

Light came on the morning of the third day, the first day of summer, Thursday, 21 June. Strengthened by his two bits of fish and a little water, Pedrecito now felt that he could endure a final day but no longer. He knew he was starting to hallucinate. Once he was certain that he saw a ship ahead but the ship — if there were one — passed out of sight long before they drew near. Then for a long time he imagined that he was standing on the foredeck of *Chiloria,* moving quietly at three knots across the still waters of Gatun Lake; soon the ship would pass through a final lock and emerge into the Caribbean at Cristobal. He heard the bos'n shouting commands. He blinked and shook his head hard.

There was a ship nearby, not a mirage nor an hallucination. The turtle had come to the point where its course had neatly intersected the Panama/New Zealand shipping lane. The vessel off to port was the cargo-liner *Stronsay* of the Macdonald Line, homeward bound from Auckland to New York via the canal. Her position at this time was Lat. 3°, 55' north/Long. 90°, 15' west. Her Master was Francis Moores and she carried thirty-seven passengers as well as her crew, most of whom witnessed the ensuing rescue which was carefully noted in due form in the ship's log.

At 10:30 A.M. on Thursday, 21 June, the officers and crew of *Stronsay* sighted the body of a man floating face downwards in the water at a distance of perhaps 500 yards. Nobody could understand how he came to be there, so far at sea, nor could they make out what was holding him up. Captain Moores ordered his engines stopped and a boat was put over the side. This manoeuvre was accomplished in six or seven minutes. As the ship's boat came near the body in the water, her crew saw the man move. They realized with amazement that he was alive and witnessed a great splashing and foaming turbulence in the water near them. The man was suddenly pitched off his support, whatever it was; the movement of the water carried him, feebly struggling, towards the ship's boat.

He was safely taken into the boat at 11:00 A.M. having been in the water a little less than seventy-one hours. The turtle had carried him a distance of over 600 nautical miles in seventy hours. He was immediately offered water which he was just able to take. In another few minutes the boat drew in under *Stronsay's* sides; the falls were made fast and she was hoisted to the boat deck where her crewmen lifted Pedrecito Marin to safety. Then the rescued seaman, the boat's crew, the Master of the vessel, officers, seamen and passengers observed a remarkable thing.

The turtle, its shell more than ten feet in diameter, put its head out of the water and surveyed the ship. It then circled it from bow to stern twice, slowly, always looking upwards. Satisfied, it drew away from the shadow of the hull into the equatorial light of noon. And dived deep. Passengers, crew, Master cheered and cheered again, rejoicing.

Weight Watchers

1

PATSY LAMBERT KEPT A MIRROR from a burned-out apartment building hanging on her bedroom wall next to the sliding doors that led to the balcony. Much of her furniture had been obtained after the fire: her bedside table, the coffee table, an armchair whose stuffing retained the tang of smoke and charred wood. Friends of hers had owned the building. When it was destroyed by flame the insurance settlement with the tenants had liberated quantities of undamaged or smoke-damaged pieces, some of them of considerable value. Patsy, at that period establishing a first apartment, had been instructed by her contacts to inspect the ruins, take anything she pleased which might prove useful. When she sat in her armchair she rather liked the obscure odour of burning which the stuffing exhaled when compressed. She admired her big mirror because the water damage had streaked and discoloured its frame, conferring a striated effect on the wood not found on department-store pieces. In damp weather the dazzling apartment left lingering impressions of combustion so faint that only she noticed.

The glass in the big mirror seemed smoky or misty to her but this wasn't the effect of fire. Something had gone badly wrong with the silvering on the back of the glass after she'd dragged the heavy object out of the burned-out shell to a borrowed van then up the delivery-elevator to her twentieth-floor apartment. She had had no help when moving in, (kind friends otherwise occupied that weekend,) no boyfriend of record at that distant date almost two years ago. When I was obese, she thought. She remembered sweating heavily as she carried in the mirror, hoping that weight-loss would ensue, as indeed it had.

160

All she saw as she craned her neck around her left shoulder was a fleeting silvery vision of her left lower back and hip and then the reflection of the open closet door on the other side of the room: ranks and ranges of sweaters, shirts, scarves, skirts, of every hue, tumbling out of the wide space. A cat poster hung next to the closet door. Moving her eye up the reflected image she caught sight of the elegant carved figures atop the mirror, scrollwork supporting the form of some heraldic animal, perhaps a lion, which she had picked out in gold paint, giving the piece a Venetian air. Her reflection wasn't sharp enough to reveal the ghost of vanished flesh. She wound her neck around to the right and pinched the back of her right leg most painfully. Could she pinch an inch? She thought not but that impression might simply flow from foolish optimism. She stepped across to the side of her bed and removed the bathing-suit from its package. There wasn't much to it. But then, there wasn't much left of her.

Idling back to her post before the glass, she worked her arms through the nearly-invisible sling shoulder-straps, filaments of artificial fibre of great tensile capacity, feeling around behind her for the connection. A hook slid neatly into place. She squared her shoulders, confronted the mirror, admired the effect of stringently qualified modesty.

The other piece covered proportionately less of her than the top; it seemed little more than a bag for one's pubic hair. She examined her front, running her fingers along the edges of the triangle of scarlet material, checked for visible tendrils; there seemed none. The view from the back must be indeed persuasive but she could not quite register it. The mirror was too milky and she could not, after all, rotate her skull through a full circle. She padded across the carpet, pleased with her soundless footsteps, with her pretty bikini, her apartment, her bar setup in the dining area, her kitchen. She carried the back-of-the-bar mirror into the bedroom and poised it on a chair, arranging it at an angle to the bedroom mirror to achieve the fitting-room effect she required. Now she had an almost unimpaired view of herself from the back. She twisted and turned in slow movements suggestive of the moderately-talented topless dancer. What she wanted was a close estimate of the mass of her upper thighs and buttocks, their remaining deposits of adipose tissue, what remained of unwanted skin-folds. Correct evaluation was hard to establish, excess skin next-to-impossible to dismiss from consideration. Sometimes in older women, she knew, it had to be removed surgically or else it just hung there. Elephant-thighs, she thought. She saw that she had undertaken her corrective measures in time. No enveloping embarrassment of epidermis was visible in either mirror as she tugged vigorously at alternate legs. Nor were there any stretchmarks, and she was twenty years this side of varicose veins.

The back-of-the-bar mirror fell on its face with a loud smack, making her jump and jiggle. Fortunately the wide expanse of clear surface was unbroken. She carried the ill-balanced object back where it belonged and set it carefully into a pair of slots where the counter met the wall. She made a mental note to dust the bottles and decanters displayed along the counter. There was a troubling impression of chafing from between her legs. Could the new bathing-suit be too tight? How? Why? Still too much flesh next the crotch? Naah, couldn't be. She knew that at last she was bottoming out at the extreme low point of her cycle. She was almost where she wanted to be and her inner thighs certainly couldn't be chafing. She wiggled her fingers into the leg holes of the suit and couldn't detect any pinching in the material. Maybe the chafing was some sort of neurological phantom like that itch in the nerve ends said to remain after amputation. Chafe and crotch itch might be something she would simply have to learn to live with, no matter how much she took off. But no, there couldn't possibly be chafing where no skin surfaces meet. She would work on posture; when not in motion standing so as to give the warm sweaty area maximum ventilation. This could be mastered.

Satisfying herself that the mirror was correctly-positioned back of the bar, she passed through the living area and seized a copy of the March issue of *Shape* from the coffee table as she went. She took the magazine into the bedroom. Later she would visit the health club and the sauna in the basement of her building. Just now she wanted to review the article she'd been studying before her bathing-suit had been delivered.

"Great Glutes." She examined the text painfully for some time. Then she went over the instructions beneath each brightly-coloured photograph. Though much has been accomplished, she thought, much remains. She flipped the open magazine onto the bed and lay flat on the floor on her stomach. She placed her feet firmly together and joined her hands in the small of her back, stretching her arms slowly to loosen the shoulders and firm the chin. Then she raised her legs about eight inches from the floor; at the same time she lifted her head and chest to a corresponding height. She held the position, feeling a pull in her thighs and lower back. Then she lay flat for a brief moment before repeating the exercise. She continued in this way for some time.

Afterwards she stretched out flat on her back to execute the matching exercise for the lower abdominal wall. Thin, she thought, firm. Thin, firm. Thin.

2

Ethel sat sweating in Dr. Harcourt's office, suffering acutely from waiting-room nerves, tremor, fluttering pulse, butterflies, shame, remorse. Patients went in and out of various rooms and the phone rang and rang. Her blood pressure must be way up. This wasn't like going to an ordinary doctor for a checkup. This was a visit to her PSYCHIATRIST. Her first. A nut doctor, she thought; it had to come.

Dr. Harcourt shared space with three other physicians, an internist, an otolaryngologist (otolaryngologist???) and a practitioner of 'family medicine,' a very young man related to Ethel in an obscure way. It was through the good offices of this youth that Ethel had at last been persuaded to this extremity, consultation with a psychiatrically-oriented psychoanalyst. Or was he a psychoanalytically-oriented psychiatrist? She never knew. She was ignorant of the niceties of doctrinal and dogmatic definition so much insisted on in that profession, a rigour exceeding that of theologians, even that of Marxian socialists.

Dr. Jude Harcourt was simply an MD who had received the conventional medical training in psychiatry, then deviated into psychoanalytic practice as a result of an early flirtation with the thought of Harry Stack Sullivan. At the end of the 1970s he had undergone a thorough depth analysis — his second, revisionist, course of treatment — under a Montréal Lacanian who had unearthed in the recesses of his devotion to medicine an explosive anarchic rejection of analytic orthodoxy. He had then conceived an immense commitment to European analytic theory, most particularly that of the Hungarian school. He greatly admired Ferenczi. These new resources of diagnostic perception and understanding were about to be deployed for the benefit of Ethel Merriman as she was ushered by a grinning nurse into his consulting-room an hour behind schedule. One of the pragmatic defects of Doctor Harcourt's grasp of psychoanalytic method was his inability to judge when an interview should end. His sessions were invariably free-form, non-directive where therapist-anguish failed to interface with respondent-pain. In plain speech, he would take a great deal of trouble over consultation at every stage of a patient's distress, feeling that his own metaphors for the reality of the patient's self-perceptions were methodologically questionable. The dynamics of personhood grew less and less readable to him. He became aware of extreme turbulence in himself, grappled constantly with violent impulses, chose wilfully to babble nonsense. He may not have been the ideal practitioner for Mrs. Merriman, a circumstance which doubtless justified the nurse's smile.

What he saw, when this woman entered his room late in the afternoon, was somebody who at forty had allowed herself to grow very heavy without absolutely concealing herself in a fat-screen, something many of his patients had done out of profound hysterical self-detestation. One saw such people everywhere: on the busses, in convenience stores or just walking along eyeing the windows of dress shops blankly; they were almost invariably women. Twin sisters of the anorexics he thought as he covertly examined Mrs. Merriman. Poor colour to her eye-whites. Some true abdominal bloating. Not a case for ordinary medical treatment. He sensed great waves of disorientation and poorly restrained impulse thrusting towards him as the woman sat uneasily in one of the reclining armchairs which offered itself tactfully to interviewees.

"That thing goes back a couple of notches, if you'd be more comfortable that way."

There wasn't a couch in the room. The three recliners, his own and two for respondents, were perhaps a more subtle touch. There was no desk either, utterance-flow remaining non-impeded. The recliners and a few immensely-soothing and sober bookcases apart, there were in the space only a very thick carpet and a low coffee table with the equipment for the service of light refreshments displayed on it. Cups, butter cookies. The room exuded an over-whelmingly stagy atmosphere of silent calm.

Dr. Harcourt waited for the woman to make her move. He saw with pity that this move was already almost overt, immense slow tears starting down either cheek. In moments she would double up in non-physically-induced pain. Ah, there she went, the head bowing towards the abdominal cavity, the shoulders rocking slowly. Now she let her sobs become audible. There was a nice pace to the procession of anguish signals. He waited for the set to complete itself; it did so with classical precision. She straightened up, found a wisp of handkerchief and began to poke at her eye makeup.

"You'll think I'm just another hysterical woman."

He said nothing. She's about ninety pounds overweight, he thought, studying her bone structure carefully. It was a handsome face, the forehead and cheekbones retaining some definition above dependent fat. The nose was comely. But, oh dear, where was the lower jaw? Gone, quite gone. And the bustline. Here's a woman on the point of immolating herself in grease, thick lard, slipping and sliding in it. He could see the light shine of unhealthy perspiration on her palms and fingertips. What about the heart action, he wondered, strictly medical questions struggling to force themselves upon him. The dickens with her heart, he thought. The pain isn't coming from her heart; she'll outlive us all.

She acted out 'crying hard; unrestrained; abject' at this point. He decided to allow her another ninety seconds of this to see what else she might get up to. There were the predictable alternatives: a brief fainting fit; sudden abrupt departure; 'pathetic' attempts at humour. Then the manufactured introductory tale would begin; he would proffer the purely formal response, the perfunctory move of the queen's pawn at the beginning of the game. By the end of the first hour they might perhaps have reached the point of decid-ing whether to continue with the sessions. Or perhaps not.

Mrs. Merriman chose the most conventional opening, the 'at-tempt to be honest' though really fancying herself to be concealing realities beneath screens and layers of subterfuge. This was going to be one of the ones where the preliminaries were drawn-out, formal, hard for the poor analyst to get through. He would have to watch himself. He really detested these first seesawings.

"I'm so ghastly, so terribly ugly. I mean, look at me." She wept quietly. "I'm disgusting."

Remarks of this kind invariably reminded Jude Harcourt that he had patients both male and female (and professional associates too) who would kill to possess a woman with cheeks and hips and thighs like this, formed as she was like some Melanesian goddess. He could neither reply that she was indeed disgusting nor that many would adore her as she stood. Either response could prove disastrous.

"At this moment I stink of sweat," she declared roundly. "I itch in places I'm ashamed to talk about. Just look at my legs!"

She started to weep unaffectedly, perhaps remembering her girlhood and he judged it wise to make a formal move of his own. He glanced at the file card on his knee. Married, no children.

"I'm afraid I'll have to ask you to bring your husband to see me." He waited the usual five seconds for the bomb to explode.

She sat up in terror. "Oh, I could never do that."

3

"What? You did what?"

"I told you I was going."

"Bullshit you did. You never told me a thing about it."

"Oh I did, I did. I told you his name and where I got him from and I phoned your office right after I talked to him. I got through to Miss McIntosh and she put a note on your daily reminder pad. You'll find it there if you look."

"A note for what, for Chrissakes?"

"For our first appointment together."

....

"Frank?"

Harried pacings.

"Frank?"

"What the fuck do you mean, our first appointment together?"

"We have to be there together, Frank, or it won't do any good.

We have to share the experience. We have to work through it, the three of us."

"You and me and who?"

"Dr. Harcourt of course, Frank. He'd have to witness our transactions."

"Did he tell you that? Goddamn voyeur."

"Yes, he said that. Yes."

"Transactions?"

"I think that's the word he used."

"He can't have said that, Ethel, you've got it wrong. Nobody's done transactional analysis for at least ten years. You've got it all muddled."

"Frank, I swear to God, that's exactly what he said."

"And so you're seeing a psychiatrist? God, you should have your head examined!"

"He isn't just a psychiatrist, Frank, he's a psychoanalytic psychiatrist at the head of his field."

"How would you know? Just how would you know?"

"Denny Durfee recommended him, Madge's boy, and he should be able to judge, after all. He graduated with top marks."

"You've discussed this with Madge Durfee? Who else is in on the secret? I mean, have you thought of putting an ad in the personals? 'Woman, forty, lonely, miserable, fat, will consult psychoanalytic psychiatrist. For full reports, details, call Ethel, 925-0953 after seven.' I'm sure all our friends will want to hear about it. You could put it on video and market the cassettes. God, when I think!"

"But you kept telling me to get help."

"Well, help. *Help.* What else could I do when we haven't had a pleasant hour together in over a year? I get home and I find you bawling on the sofa, the house in total darkness except for the TV screen, nothing ready for dinner. Naturally I've urged you to seek counselling; but I didn't mean to drive you into the arms of a complete stranger whose professional interest lies in enticing as many unfortunates as possible into his lair to record their obsessive confessions. I meant you to see a clergyman perhaps, or a marriage counsellor, somebody you can rely on to be discreet. What about Father Essex at Saint Saviour's? He seems a decent enough fellow for an Anglican, with enough sense to keep his mouth shut. Seal of the confessional and all that shit. Keep it in the family. Nobody ever minds telling things to their ministers."

"But I need real help, Frank. I'm afraid of losing control of myself. I mean look at me: I look like the Goodyear blimp. No wonder you hate me."

"Now Ethel, I've never said that. I don't hate you. I admit I'm worried about you. I don't understand what's happening to you or to us but I don't hate you. I don't hate anybody."

"You're such a liar. Of course you hate me. You detest me. You won't willingly spend an hour in my company and why should you, after all? Who wants to be with me or look at me or touch me? I tell you, Frank, I've got to get real help. I don't need counselling and I don't need encouragement. I don't need to get a grip on myself. I'm afraid. If I don't find out what's making me like this I'll die."

"Oh no, you won't. Nobody ever died of being overweight. A little shortness of breath maybe, a bit of difficulty going upstairs. How much do you weigh anyway?"

"That's none of your business. Just watch what you say, Frank Merriman, or one of these days . . ."

"One of these days what?"

"You'll see."

"What'll I see?"

"You'll find me dead on the floor when you come home. It'll be good and dark and there won't be any dinner on the table for poor Frank and there won't be any more fancy diets for me: the broccoli diet, the thirty-day high-protein diet, the granola wafers, the fruit juice, the twenty-four-hour shape-up after a binge, the veggies, the laxatives, the square foods versus round foods controversy, the feminist approach to weight loss, fat as defence against the patriarchy, rejection of the ideal of femininity, the earth-goddess stance. I don't want to be an earth-goddess. I want to be little and slender like I was when we were just living together."

"I suppose now you're going to tell me that getting married caused your weight problem?"

"It helped. It helped."

"But it was what you wanted more than anything. We got married because that was what you wanted, didn't we? Wasn't it?"

"I can't remember. It's too long ago."

"We've been married fourteen years. Do you mean you can't remember that far back? You really can't remember?"

"I'm so confused."

"Fuck you are, you're doing this deliberately, Ethel. It's a whole series of self-inflicted wounds; can't you see that? It has nothing to do with me."

"It has everything to do with you. I'm what you've made me, Frank. I'm what you wanted and now you've got it. Look at me."

"I'm not looking, Ethel, so just stop it."

"You have to come with me, Frank."

"I won't and that's final."

4

Wouldn't you know this would be the season of the floppies? Baggy baggy calf-length trousers, blousy blousy blouses. She had a sweater which fastened down the back with a tremendous sweeping plunge between the shoulder blades almost to her waist. You wouldn't wear a bra with it, but superabundance of material in front made the bosom invisible (not that her bosom was very visible in ordinary covering). She had shrunk it down to a pair of tiny nubs. She giggled. Nubs.

Today was the day of the great celebration and if she had to choose between displaying her skinniness and following the mode, she would go for display and shame the devil. She had gone to the health club in the basement after work and there, *before* her workout, on an honest-weight balance scale, without cheating or kidding herself, she had weighed in at ninety pounds. She was where she wanted to be. She was as little as Karen the bird-girl, that notorious local thinzo. Ninety pounds. She went out and jogged five kilometres, finished the run with a series of wind sprints and went to the Nautilus and did her sets of presses, curls, leg-lifts. Worked on her quads, watched a man hitting the heavy bag, wished she had the courage to buy herself a pair of bag gloves and some tape. That might come.

She huddled in the sauna next to the hot rocks rapt in a high she'd never reached before. She couldn't quite bring the points of her elbows into view — it's almost impossible to see them without a mirror. She was sure that they would be a chalky blue-white, the colour of skimmed milk. If she dried herself out too much that surface, close to the bone, would get all chickeny-skin-like with dry flaky dimples. Body lotion, she thought, and went off to take her cold shower. Oh, I'm there, I'm there. I'll buy myself something fitted and go for the high-fashion starved look. A girl can never be too thin. She danced around on tiptoes under the tingling needles of cold water. She felt so healthy she could have shed tears of joy.

In the fitting room she examined one dress after another. She had once seen an oldtime movie star, Audrey Hepburn, in a movie whose name she couldn't remember on late-night television. She had paid no attention to the ridiculous story: what she did remember was the little basic black. Hepburn wore this little basic black number almost the whole way through and it gave her a look that would never go out or be forgotten. It had been almost sleeveless with a broad low neckline — not a décolletage, a very modest cut. Anyway, she had had no bosom to speak of — and the material was tailored at the shoulders so that it met briefly at the top of either arm. The shoulder blades were in full view and so fragile and the woman so small that the image of a little bird was insistently suggested. Patsy had never been able to get that dress out of her mind. It wasn't for today. It might be for the day after tomorrow.

The closest thing she found to the Audrey Hepburn look was a black wool in a length of traditional elegance, cut very narrow at the waist, a size 5, very expensive, but she took it. She had to have something new for this night. She took it straight back to her apartment to try it on above her best gunmetal pantyhose.

She stood as tall as she could in front of her cloudy mirror and hoisted the sheath above her head high on her forearms. She wanted to execute a specific trick she'd had in mind for months and years. She positioned her arms in either armhole. Then she let go of the gathered material and the dress flowed down over her head and neck and shoulders and ribs and hips and down her legs till it stopped with a whispering sound three inches below the knees. She hadn't had to move a muscle, to wriggle, to twist. It was like yanking a tablecloth from under the table-furnishings of a banquet, a stunning piece of sleight-of-hand, impossible to achieve unless a course of self-discipline so severe as to be unimaginable to observers had been undertaken. She had done the trick with her back to the mirror. Now she worked the dress back above her head and faced the glass. She let the material fall and this time it dropped soundlessly and miraculously past her hipbones without the least wrinkle or fold into the appropriate position for street wear. Naturally it had to be zippered up the back, but the sudden vision in the mirror suggested spontaneous clothing in a miraculous fairytale-armour descending from above. Patsy now saw herself as a character in a romance. She reached down her back for the zipper which snaked up between her shoulders. There was some difficulty about grasping it and the nylon track of the zip seemed inadequate when she remembered what the dress had cost. She slid it carefully up her vertebrae, changing hands to get a firmer grip on the tab. If she pulled a stitch anywhere on this night of nights she would feel agonies of frustration. No stitch pulled; the zipper closed at the nape of her neck. She didn't even have to smooth down the material; the half-lined wool hung perfectly, showed neither stomach nor bosom. Neither did it reveal the least protuberance when she turned sideways.

Size 5, she thought. God!

When she had finished dressing she realised how hungry she was. She had had black coffee, a slice of Melba toast and the juice of a lime at breakfast and some silhouette yogurt from a plastic cup about one. She decided to go down to the Riverrain, not more than two blocks away, for dinner and a drink. There might be somebody there she knew. Somebody had to see her tonight. She had to show herself to somebody. She was where she wanted to be. She might go lower she thought, get to eighty-seven, but what would be the point? She wasn't anorexic. She had it under control. She had come as far as she could reasonably hope to come. After all, she'd almost got there three times before.

Patsy was five feet, seven inches tall.

In the Riverrain bar she ordered an *Entre deux mers* as chilled as possible, taking it with her onto the terrace while she waited for her table. A lot of singles came here and sometimes paired off for a table when the restaurant was very crowded. She stood tiredly watching the racing dinghies performing their mysterious evolu-

tions on the river, expecting to see some larger vessel come sailing
by at any moment. Perhaps it would heave to, send a ship's boat
for her, carry her off to the land where everybody is a size 5.

Frank Merriman, whom she knew vaguely from the building,
came up to her and made a smiling invitation. Would she like to
share a table with him? They would be seated half-an-hour sooner;
the maître d' wasn't accepting singles till eight-thirty. She looked
ready to eat something. She could bring her drink along. Could
he get her something else? She sensed his eyes travelling up and
down her non-stomach and non-waist. He was simply gobbling
her down.

5

Like most whose emotional situation has grown desperate, Ethel
wondered daily how she could have come to be so transfixed. In
the beginning she and Francis — she had always called him Francis
then — had seemed to be creatures of complete accord: she had
delighted in his company and he had seemed to respond in a deep
quiet communion neither of them could hope to find elsewhere.
The beginnings of love (the first weeks or months) may hold hesi-
tations and moments in which our persons find their ways into
thickets of feeling and implication never to be revisited. There had
been whole hours in which she lay enrobed in his close touch,
silent, her face softened and nerveless, her eyelids motionless,
beneath them her slow eyes at peace beyond any need of blinking.

Those had been countries of love in which they might have
dwelt eternally had the smooth placid drift of her body been constant. She had been perfect mistress of herself, her limbs, their
forms, their movements. At such times she believed she possessed
some final self-awareness, some discovery of the way she went,
the way she moved. There had been a brilliant fitness to her sense
of union with her lover and his aptness of response grew with
her self-possession. It was as if mere flesh, that lovely healthy
existence in which ears and knees and toes in the tower of the
skin and muscles, singing with harmony and power, that adorable
realisation of well-being, might merge in pure love with the
radiance of the heart of the beloved. In his arms she was so very

much enshrined, throned, held in poised delight; their intense shared consciousness must have lasted forever; there was nothing in it but giving and rewarding. Each was the other's prize and pleasure. How could they ever stumble mistakenly out of bliss?

She imagined that the unutterable felicity of their union admitted of no lessening; their lives together must always allow the reflection of the other's eyes in one's own. She supposed they were especially talented for union, that something gratuitous, something given to them from unguessable distance, empowered them, raised them above the common necessities of understanding.

For understanding had come effortlessly. It delivered itself modestly between them, lying all around like a clear pool of blue light in which their little craft rose and fell soundlessly. She might turn in his embrace, raise her face towards his, beg for chaste salute, but the movement need not suggest hunger or any species of deprivation. They would persist in their stillness, the heart of each ready to quit the enclosing ribs, the twinned hearts to beat however briefly in strict time, mating in pulse and rhythm, closer than they might be in the original body. And this was what was implied in mutual succour and fasting delicacy.

Sometimes in his arms hunger became abstract, no longer sensed, attentuating its pangs as a finely-executed pencil line will fade, the forms given in the drawing reducing themselves to scarcely visible outlines of appetite; wish and flutter of the heart were drawn lighter and lighter. His eyes, slaty, flecked with dark points of gold, set in sockets of extreme subtlety and shadow, would darken and glow, assenting to long abstinence from nourishment but in the end the feast, the glittering range of set places and crystal, linens, silver, blue bowls lapping with berries in cream, the scents of flesh and adoration, incense of their shared altar, would rouse him and he might stir. He was invariably the first to grow anxious at undue drawing-out of the special tranquility which had become their signal. If my heart fail here, she would apprehend, let my right arm lose its power.

Then apprehension might grow since silence can remain unbroken only during times of untroubled heartbeat. After the first exhalation of breath, release of held stillness, which came with the ordinary, the daily, the sound of her own blood moving out of the ingenious pump which lifted her breast and let it fall began to trouble and at last to obsess her. She could hear her life beating away in strong pulses but felt no drumbeat of accompanying rhythm under her companion's rib cage. She felt he was living a muffled remote life, discussing her with himself.

"Why do you never speak?" she inquired gravely.

Flecks of gold danced in his deep eyes which seemed to concentrate his life in their steady shining admiration. She noticed nothing of the face which framed the profound sockets, neither cheeks nor lips. The blue gleam of the pupils was fired from within by a secret and consuming contemplation almost ready to transform itself into agitation too turbulent for ready expression.

He seemed to eye her with attentive misgiving. "I used to imagine you as a sort of dryad, a creature of myth, infinitely removed and ungraspable." He paused, listening to an internal voice that dictated to him in calculated periods.

She had a sense that he was about to throw open for her the fastened casket of his person. Perhaps she would know him as she was known, would console, would defend him from the elfish gleams dancing behind his eyes. With this conjecture she felt rising in herself giant yearnings for the true expression of her wishes. She wished — but here she stopped. What did she wish? A more perfect understanding of another's being? What, after all, did she know of Francis, his care for her set aside?

He was a clever fellow, had painted, sketched; there existed a pencil sketch of herself which knowing judges had praised perhaps too readily. At any rate it struck her as an achieved 'old-master' drawing. The flowers in her hair, her blouse modestly open at the brave throat, the hollows of the shaded cheeks, her widened eyes; all were delivered by the pencil with extraordinary subtlety on paper of such delicate grain that the movement of a dry finger over its surface might smear the soft fibres irreparably. This drawing hung above them now, giving her cause to plead, as she rose on an elbow and studied it, that after all we cannot remain as we were in perpetuity. Time doesn't concede the longed-for stop; when age comes it will speed on in a snowstorm of flying calendar pages. She begged him with her eyes for continuance of his address.

"I was destined never to possess you," he mused. "You sped through lemon groves and green distances on strong pinions, a woman of immense promise; there was limitless possibility in whatever you attempted." He paused.

She said, "I imagined you could accomplish whatever you chose." She struggled to form the conception. "I felt that life appeared to us as eternal, boundless. We were the first," the citation charmed her with its felicity, "that ever burst into that silent sea."

"I should beware that sea if I were you. Other beings sail there besides our poor selves."

"Poor?" she mocked him cheerily. "In what way poor?"

"In resource, in spirit."

"If in spirit, then blessed."

"Blessing must precede bliss but need not always bring it in its train."

"Oh, but it will," she declared roundly. "It must."

On that assertion she rose from their couch and almost acknowledged the impulse to turn her sketched visage to the wall. What she needed, she saw, was food. She understood acutely that romance turns to hunger as soon as the lover awakes. How often after entranced hours of stillness had she and Francis risen to raid the refrigerator. That was funny, she saw that it was funny, but for long she could not notice a damaging truth: when they woke from passion she was the one who went and ate. He would sit beside her or across from her at the midnight table, watching closely while she ate and drank. Sometimes he would appear to take nourishment but his feeding was birdlike, as it might be, hawklike. Birds, we know, do not 'eat like birds.' They eat continually, in each moment assuring themselves that starvation will not supervene in the next. But to the observer, unconscious of their impulsive pangs, the birds seem to eat little, to subsist on small crumbs flung to them by the charitable or the wind. Francis, Frank, as she now began to call him in the fourth year of their marriage reversed the pattern of birdlike snacking. He appeared to eat much and in fact ate little though he invariably sat with her after passion.

"Gives you an appetite," he said often.

"It increases by what it feeds on."

"Have I heard that somewhere before?"

"You may have done. But tell me, why should I want to fill

myself after lying in your arms all safe and sound? Why should I feel empty?"

"Hunger is only a metaphor," said Frank. "It means something else entirely than what it seems to mean. If you ignore hunger, then it disappears."

"And in the end you starve?"

"There is that risk, yes," he conceded gracefully.

"Or wax and grow fat?"

"Those seem to be the poles, as it were, of need. For hunger, you see, is the physical metaphor of need-in-general. Those who hunger and thirst after justice will be blessed; those who hunger and thirst after ham and eggs and beer will not; at least not necessarily. You had better put down that sandwich."

It was true, she humbly allowed. Ham sandwiches had always been a stumbling-block.

"Some of us," Frank went on, looking at his fingernails, avoiding her avid glance, "eat only to sustain life and these we recognise at once as gravely-deprived persons. They know nothing of the joys of life, of excess. 'Enough, or too much' says Blake. I think you must be in Blake's army. Nobody loves the person who eats only to maintain body weight. Moral beings must either starve or grow fat; there can be no middle ground."

She reached for more, thinking of Oliver Twist. "Calorie counting as the pre-condition of morals?"

"Get ye to a sauna, go," he commanded.

It was long past midnight. Their apartment, high in a high building, gave on the riverscape, dark tonight, speckled with gleams from the cuddies of small craft. Here and there phosphorescence flashed; otherwise smooth black lay on the water like a shroud. She felt slowly wrapping itself around her like a fine impalpable gas faint intimations of weight, heaviness, inability to move like the dryad she had felt herself to be. Tomorrow, she vowed, she would begin again with jazz dance, with yoga; tomorrow she would start to control her intake. When she turned back to the table the ham sandwich lay there, a single semicircle, her first bite, neatly removed from the form of the matched slices of bread and butter, the pink flesh glowing softly in the dim light. "I'll start tomorrow," she declared.

That night there was no question of resumed caresses, only

separateness; the next day was the first of many one-day-at-a-time ventures into deprivation. She would be at home in the evening, proud of a missed and needed dessert or glass of wine or second helping. During her recital of these small triumphs pressure from his nature, positive encouragement to reward herself for virtue would at last impel her towards a balancing-off of what had been left uneaten this afternoon against what might therefore be tried tonight.

"I guess I can risk this doughnut," she might hazard. His face would show nothing but the infrequent smile he gave at such moments.

"Can I?"

"What?"

"Eat this?" She held up the doughnut.

"What else have you had today?"

"I'm under my allowed intake by about 300 calories."

"And the doughnut —"

"— is about 250."

"Leaving you a net margin of fifty?"

"Better than fifty; maybe sixty-five."

"I dig your arithmetic," he said as he watched her weigh the doughnut on a tiny scale.

"Anyway, I'm ahead on the day," said Ethel. "Tomorrow I'll fine down some more."

"You have to build up some momentum," he said softly, for the first time betraying some commitment to what she was trying to do. After such an exchange his eyes would ignite, their gleams of precious gold evident, piercing. Bed was the invariable consequence, then snacking; in another year a terrifying and unappeasable appetite; in later years a thickening into solid matter of earlier intimations of flab. It seemed as if the impalpable airy fear that first fell on her turned over a decade into a compressed layer of smoky grease.

As a very young woman she had been a waitress in a hamburger joint — a summer task undertaken to help with college fees — and it had fallen to her from time to time to remove the collected fat from the flue above the large grill on which the various dishes were fried. Up inside this flue, her hair protected by plastic sheeting, she had to spoon out pounds of grease deposited by the fumes rising from the cooking surface. Some such deposit of fat now lay around her and she couldn't prove to anybody why this was so or what had happened to her. When she forced Frank to come to Dr. Harcourt's consulting-room, she saw the doctor was perfectly correct in his estimate of the situation. She had literally had to threaten suicide to persuade Frank to participate in the analysis, something he managed to sustain for one and only one meeting when he said the worst thing about her that she'd ever heard.

"I'm ashamed to go out with her. My self-esteem won't allow me to appear in public with her," he said to the doctor. "I can't accept that I'm responsible for that. Look at her!"

6

Nothing faked about this weeping. Ugghh. Oh, oh, OH! She had never been so cast down. Tears came without impulse and without restraint. She didn't seem to be there or anywhere. How could anybody talk like that about somebody else? I can't be seen with her, she puts me to shame. What could he mean by that? Only that she was so bloated, so misshapen, so disfigured by blobby wobbling meat on her body that no man could accept her presence or concede that she was with him or belonged to him. She sat huddled in her chair in front of the two of them across from her like inquisitors or some sort of jury and let herself go completely. She had never cried like this before, great convulsive sobs forcing themselves up from somewhere in her body, heaving and shudder-ing, leaving her abdomen stiff and hurting from their muscular force. She felt wracked, twisted; she knew she was no longer concealing anything or trying to convince the doctor that though she was fat she was good. She couldn't bear their staring, the pity, the contempt of their eyes fixed on her trembling body. Why should she be subjected to this? What harm had she done anyone? It was too much to bear. And for him to say — the cheat, the liar — that he would take no responsibility for what she had done to herself was wounding beyond imagining. How could he have said that; how could anybody say that about anybody else? It was all his fault: It was that holding back, that continual watchfulness, those little promptings about her self-indulgence which had brought her to this. How could he have said that about her? *I'm ashamed to go out with her.* My sense of myself won't permit it. She doesn't belong to me. I can't contaminate myself by being in her presence. Don't let any of her rub off on me!

Ethel looked for total self-abasement sitting there in Dr. Harcourt's office, a reality she had never pictured before. She wanted to go down on all fours, like some gross animal, parade her misery, strip herself, reach some zero-point of existence, cease to be herself altogether. She vaguely felt that the experience of true and effective cruelty would purge her of insincerity and trivial social guilt. Perhaps by being so humiliated she would escape into some gentle acceptance of herself for what she was. It wasn't her looks nor her power to discipline herself that were at stake; rather it was a need to be able to be with others in some way that did not automatically dictate calamity and suffering. Why could she not simply live quietly on terms of self-acceptance and regard for others?

When this question forced itself into her mind, she broke out again in sorrow and tears. She gathered her legs under her where she knelt stretched out on the floor and struggled first to her knees, then to her feet. Something seemed wrong with her physical balance and she felt a sharp pain just below her ribs on the right side. The two men rose to restrain her but she pushed passed them, moaning, and sidled awkwardly to the door; they stood and watched her leave. They exchanged critical stares.

"You shouldn't have said that."

"You shouldn't have insisted on my coming. What did you expect?"

The door swung shut behind Ethel; they heard her anguished cries retreating in the distance until the office was silent and the two men faced facts.

They would be taking stock thought Ethel as she ran; they would shake hands at parting and shrug her off as another hysterical female. How dare they? By what right? How could she ever go back to Dr. Harcourt's office when he had seen her make a spectacle of herself like that? And yet — she saw as she left the building — and yet she would have to see him again; she had no other counsellor. Whom could she turn to?

This perception made her cry again as she wheeled her car to the exit ramp and handed her ticket to the attendant. He seemed frightened by her appearance.

"You all right, Ma'am?"

"No," she said viciously, "I'm not all right. Do I look all right?"

She drove off, accelerating into traffic flow, leaving the attendant at his booth open-mouthed. She drove at once to the Peking Pagoda, impelled by an intense, unmixed desire for the humblest of Cantonese/Canadian food in massive quantities. It was almost five o'clock, nearly dinner time. She imagined chicken fried rice on a steaming platter and her mouth watered copiously but she knew she wouldn't have the guts to dine in public. She fled, still softly crying, into the darkened recesses of the restaurant. It seemed a long time but was actually about five minutes later when she emerged with an enormous double-lined paper sack stapled shut at the top held closely in her arms, her baby. The heat comforted her. There was a small bucket of boiling won ton soup in the bag which conducted an almost unbearable warmth. The men at the Peking Pagoda knew her well from previous furtive solitary adventures and this time they had done her proud. They knew she liked it hot. When she got back to the apartment the cartons of food were still much too hot to open and attack. She lined her little toys up on the serving counter, noting in passing their close resemblances to pillboxes or fortifications of some armoured line of defence. She played with them for a few moments impatiently as they cooled, lined them up in squares, in a circle, juggled them in her palms. She salivated in great showers, from time to time spat in the sink. She thought, to hell with the heat and ripped at the cartons to shovel masses of food onto a large dinner plate: sweet-and-sour ribs, pineapple chicken balls, fried rice, nothing recherché, nothing for the gourmet. She couldn't decide which to try first. The soup, the soup; don't let it cool. She adored won ton soup and felt that she never really got enough of it. The little won tons seemed to resemble the grey matter of the brain: wrinkled; fleshy; soft in the mouth. She ate two large bowls of the soup at once, speared other won tons from what was left in the bucket and swallowed them almost whole.

An hour later you're hungry. The conventional joke began to reverberate in her mind. Not this time. This time I'll get full. Her plate was empty; she took the cartons carelessly from the oven where she had placed them over a low heat and refilled. Two for the soy sauce, she thought; not on your life, this is all for me. Her abdomen grew heavier; the flavour of plum sauce grew more and more rank on her palate.

All of a sudden she hurt terribly in her middle. All that crying, she thought; you're such a baby. It was as though a huge metal weight were forcing itself up into her throat. She fled to the bathroom and collapsed weakly on her knees beside the toilet bowl which she embraced like a sister. She voided the whole contents of her stomach in an enormous vomit, lay prone on the tiles, slept.

7

Frank and Patsy met by appointment that night in the Riverrain bar where he told her about his adventure of the afternoon. "And then," he said with dignity, "I told her doctor that we shouldn't allow ourselves to appear in public together." That had an authentic sound. Like all fundamentally untruthful persons he had an urge to fudge his lie, make it resemble the truth as far as possible. "I said that being together constituted an endorsement of what she was doing to herself and that I could no longer be a party to it."

"That's what you said, is it?"

"Oh yes, yes." He struggled to adjust what he thought he'd said (the lie securely embedded in his recollections) with what he might have said or wanted to say. His treatment of Ethel began to seem more layered, as he thought it over, than he wished it to seem.

"I didn't accuse her of anything."

"Of course, you didn't," said Patsy, playing up loyally. "I'll have another of these things," she said to the barman, pointing to her glass; he promptly filled it with soda water and about a spoonful of white wine from a Niagara vineyard. The liquid in the glass shone with the faint yellow hue of a well baby's urine.

Frank eyed the wine glass with distaste. "What's in that anyway?"

"It's simply a spritzer, white wine and soda water."

Frank turned to the barman. "How many of these can you squeeze out of a bottle of that stuff?"

The barman knew Frank, considered him a dangerous man, perhaps a potential enemy. He decided to tell the truth. "I guess I could make maybe thirty drinks out of a bottle, Mr. Merriman."

"Closer to thirty-five, I should think."

"Maybe."

"At three dollars a time?"

"Yes, sir."

"About a hundred dollars worth of sales from one bottle."

"Well, there's the soda water too."

"Indeed there is, about five bucks' worth; the wine might cost about the same. Tell me, son, who owns this place?"

"You know who owns it, Mr. Merriman."

"Does he need any further investment capital, do you reckon?"

"I couldn't say about that, sir. He may do."

"This place must be a gold mine," said Frank discontentedly. "They sell ten dollars' worth of water for $100. All at once he seemed to weary of the inquiry and turned back to Patsy to offer her further treats. "Why not try something with a bit more zing to it?"

"This will do me fine, thanks."

"Might as well be drinking from the tap," he grumbled. He looked at her elbows in the ambiguous light of the lounge; the points of the connecting bones seemed on the point of forcing their way through the skin. You could see — even in this semi-darkness — the ridges and knobs at the tip of the ulna where it fitted into the joint. Muscle strings were visible too. He could see how the arm worked as a lever when the fibres contracted. He had a sudden bleak vision of Patsy as a living dancing skeleton or victim of the camps, all her parts activated by an invisible will, all traceable under the papery blue skin. If there were any the less of her, she wouldn't be here at all; she would simply grow finer and finer and disappear. The tips of the folded arms, just at the joint, were purple and pale grey and they seemed dusty.

"We'll go eat," said Frank. "If necessary we'll insist."

"I expect they're ready for us now," said Patsy, trembling with anticipation. She had not quite gone to vegetarianism but was very close to it. The Riverrain operated the best salad bar in town, was famous or notorious, depending on personal tastes, for its broccoli, snow peas, lentils, bean sprouts; these foodstuffs were kept tactfully to one side of the long table where the other vegetables and the dressings were displayed. You could make yourself a fruit salad if you chose. The usual potatoes, macaroni, rice, pickles, cole slaw and so on. Or you could edge unobtrusively along to the end of the table where the broccoli was and make a bulky plate out of things that wouldn't, couldn't, manufacture fat.

Most men who escorted Patsy hither and yon paid no attention to what she put on her plate, never felt criticised by implication or reproached for their feeding habits because of cunning arrangements like this. These men never accompanied her to the far end of the salad bar and when she set her plate down across the table from them, they saw simply that the plate was full. It usually had one or two enormous dark-green leaves stretched on it as a base, forming a bed for the deposit of quantities of beans, peas, spinach, sprouts, carrots, broccoli spears. Once, she recalled, she had fastened too liberally on the Brussels sprouts and they had undeniably smelt strongly. A short-term boyfriend sitting across from her had obviously been mystified by the sulphurous odour. He had been much too tactful to inquire into the source. She remembered he never called again. Very silly and inconsiderate. Fish smells strong. Broiling or frying meat certainly smells strong. Onions. Why must anyone object to the odour of Brussels sprouts? She was not sorry to have seen the last of that young man.

She put another serving of raw carrot on top of her plate and turned to go back to their table. Frank materialised beside her before she had taken a step. He extended his hand in which he clutched a fork. On its end, insecurely impaled, lay a canapé, a Ritz cracker thickly smeared with cream cheese and topped with a slice of pepperoni.

"Eat!" he commanded. "Enjoy!"

Without thinking she opened her mouth wide like a feeding nestling, an action which made Frank's heart leap in his chest. He thrust the morsel at her lips unsteadily then popped it into the open place. She chewed and swallowed obediently.

"That good?"

She nodded, unable to speak.

8

What is there to say to yourself when you wake up on the freezing bathroom floor with your head wedged in behind the bidet and your feet wrapped convulsively around the broad base of the toilet? That you've hit bottom, that you've got nowhere to go but up?

Ethel lay trembling on the spreading lanes of small hexagonal shapes, counting them mechanically over and over as they tracked away from her eye, the right eye. The other eye was still stuck shut. She had cried long, had lapsed into a peculiarly distorted state of half-consciousness that resembled, but was not, drunkenness. Could she have been poisoned by something in the plum sauce or the dressing on the diced chicken and almonds? Maybe it was the monosodium glutamate which always left the inside of her mouth puckered and dried out, cankered. She ran her swollen tongue painfully around the lining of her cheeks and palate; they felt as if they had been burned or raked over by a sharp small instrument, a too-stiff toothbrush or one of those rubber gum stimulators.

The other eye came unstuck with an audible pop, completed binocular perspective on her position. The lower depths, she thought, down the tubes; with difficulty she unwound her calves from around the bowl and extricated herself from her resting place among the bathroom fixtures. She banged her elbow painfully on the projecting china lip of the bidet as she got to her knees. She felt drunk; the effort of standing erect was almost more than she could handle. She swayed uncertanly. Had anybody ever actually killed themselves by an overdose of food? Was that possible? She remembered certain cases of suffocation by regurgitation while semi-conscious, but to the best of her recollection she had completely emptied her stomach before passing out. The muscles in her abdomen ached and throbbed rhythmically. Some rock star had died of a blocked respiratory tract, she knew, choking on a half-consumed sandwich which had found its way down the wrong passageway.

She cleared her throat convulsively then spat into the washbasin. The obvious thing to do was to get out of her clothes, rinse her burning mouth and brush her teeth about a thousand times, relax in a tub bath, sleep again in a freshly made bed with clean sheets.

She began to remove her clothes, collecting them together for the laundry hamper. Her nose wrinkled convulsively with distaste as she peeled off her laddered bagging pantyhose which she simply threw into an already overstuffed garbage bag in the kitchen. Her other clothes were in scarcely better state but were perhaps worth retaining for possible cleaning. She bundled them into the laundry hamper, hid it in an obscure closet, returned to the bathroom and ran the water into the basin as cold as possible.

She gargled first with a potent mouthwash whose flavour made her gag but which tasted totally unlike a mixture of vomit and plum sauce, thank God. It took some time but her mouth grew refreshed and her sense of smell began to resume its normal accuracy. She brushed her teeth repeatedly, found the gum stimulator she had been imagining, attacked the spaces between her upper and lower front teeth. Where was the dental floss?

It took quite an hour-and-a-half before she succeeded in eliminating the disgusting aftertaste which haunted her. All these activities served merely as distractions, modes of concealment of her awareness of the complete silence which reigned in the apartment: the phone didn't ring; the radio didn't automatically come on at 7:30 A.M. (nobody had set it); no lights shone except those she had turned on and she could almost hear dust falling on her. How long had she been alone in the apartment? What time was it anyway?

It was 4:45 P.M. and it must be Saturday.

Where could he be?

She didn't want to think about this or draw any conclusions. She ran her bath as hot as she could stand it, added a consoling dollop of scented bath-oil and lowered herself into the steaming water with care. It was almost too hot; the mirrors clouded over at once. Her feet and ankles turned a dangerously bright red. She didn't want to die by scalding so she took her descent very slowly and in two or three minutes had managed to ease herself down on her back in the large comfortable tub. One of her favourite places, she decided, letting her head rest almost beneath the surface against the slope of the tub. She inhaled the steam and the bad smell seemed to melt out of her nostrils. Now she could smell the bath-oil. She opened her eyes and saw directly in front of her the sagging heavy abdomen, the blue veins, the rolls of fat rising out of the water, an island of floating flesh bobbing gently as if independent of herself, as if her body were no longer her possession but something that enshrined an independent will and existence of its own and held her prisoner. As she stared, her stomach muscles contracted and a long rumble twisted her insides, varying in pitch with a gurgling timbre which had its own absurd music. Beneath her stomach her knees stuck out of the water, her thighs resembled the slopes of sugar-loaf mountains covered in dirty snow. She stretched her legs out abruptly, submerged her knees. This vision of independent existence of flesh frightened her, the continued silence in the apartment frightened her, the sound of dust falling, the light changing as the day came to a close. There wasn't even the familiar comforting sound of Frank's travelling clock ticking on the bedside stand.

She was going to have to go back to that doctor and confess that Frank had walked out on her at last. No doubt about it. He had taken everything he wanted and would not return. Her bath water cooled as she lay there. A self-tormenting impulse seized her and she jerked the stopper out of the drain-hole, stretched out full-length in the voiding tub as the water receded around her. Lower and lower fell the water level. Streaks and rivulets appeared on her breasts, her stomach. The grit and dirt she had soaked away from her skin lay deposited beneath her.

I look like a beached whale, she thought savagely.

He came for his stuff and he just buggered off.

My husband has left me. Doctor, I think it's definitive.

Frank's on an extended business tour of the northeast.

I don't know where he is and I don't want to know.

I'll sue for alimony and I'll take him to the cleaners.

Doctor, my husband has left me. I think it's definitive. I could care less.

The look on doctor's face, the pretended indifference, the crude male triumph underneath.

No man could have any real sympathy for her.

My husband has trashed me, Doctor, used me and stuffed me down the tubes.

I'm too heavy.

9

Jude Harcourt parked in somebody else's space in the barristers' lot and walked around the side of the courthouse to the administration wing where the judges' chambers were located on the top floor. His appointment was at 2:30 P.M. and he noted with professional pleasure that he was not kept waiting. He had often used unpunctuality as a professional tool for which there was no excuse. He knew psychoanalytic opinion stigmatised habitual lateness as an indication of grave personal malaise while psychoanalysts remained the least punctual of professional people. The usual excuse was excessive compassion for the incumbent patient but it was, at best, a lame one. Dr. Harcourt preferred to accuse himself implicitly of inner ruin.

Judge Le Mesurier threw open the door to his office and beckoned his professional associate inside. The room displayed the customary signals of power, influence, opulence, formal allegiance to an ideal conception of justice: the oak desk, the heavy dark carpeting.

The two men sat facing one another across that desk on that carpeting. Neither was quite certain of his position in the order of this arrangement. When psychoanalyst meets judge . . . what do they talk about?

Indeed, when any two professional men of high qualifications, each accustomed to immense respect from associates and friends, each a learned consultant approached at times of crisis for the blessing of his counsel come together to solicit each other's opinion (perhaps even to act on it) neither can judge accurately where he ought to sit, how he ought to frame his questions. Should one abandon the detached air of the formal inquirer, the posture of learning and robes of discipline, for an air of sociable informality?

This was a professional occasion; not an informal sounding.

"Jude," said Judge Le Mesurier cautiously, "I want you to bill us for this consultation. I'll have my secretary give you the address and the dossier number as you leave. The bill goes to the Master and he will make a purely formal assessment of it. You'll be paid in full at your normal professional fee. I didn't expect you to come and see me during office hours for free."

"Justice is blind but rich," said Jude airily.

"Perhaps not rich, but able to pay for top talent. The thing is, you see . . ." The judge groped for words.

"Yes?"

"This is a first-time thing for me, Doctor. I haven't done this sort of proceeding before and I should explain what the problem is; problems *are,* plural. There's a professional problem for me and for all of us on the bench in this jurisdiction. Then there's the humanitarian aspect of the matter; you could almost say the religious aspect of it if your opinions ran in that direction."

Doctor Harcourt said nothing; his expression was one of incomprehension, bewilderment. More and more as time went on he found his understanding of social principle and the foundations of social institutions sapped. Immensely solid institutions which had seemed founded on rock in his youth were being swept away in floods of innovation which terrified him. The pace of change had accelerated so rapidly in these last dozen years, almost these last dozen months, that he could not perceive any firm base for permanence. What became of a form of psychotherapy which could propose no permanent underpinnings for the self? What, indeed?

"You see, Jude . . ."

Back to the first name and the informal chat. ". . . you see, we've just rewritten most of the enactments covering divorce proceedings in this country and now we've got to determine in practice what our new code allows. We've done away with the notion of a divorce proceeding as a civil suit where one party proposes to show fault in the other and receives the divorce decree as a kind of damages. A hundred years ago you couldn't get a divorce in this place. Fifty years ago you had to prove adultery — there were almost no other grounds. Oh, there was refusal to consummate; there was duress; there were a few other freakish grounds which nobody ever brought. Adultery was it and you really had to prove it; there could be no hint of connivance or complicity or else both parties and their counsel would find themselves in serious trouble. Desertion was later accepted as a legitimate ground, then cruelty; then the gates opened and the divorce rate zoomed to about one marriage in three. Fifteen years ago our legislators in their wisdom decided to revise the whole legal foundation of divorce law and remove it from the purlieu of my Lady Justice who, as you may say, is blind or at least temporarily blindfolded. She may weigh what is in the balance but she may not read the precise quantity of the balanced matter on any sort of numbered dial. Hah hah! What we mean by weighing the evidence. Little legal joke there."

Dr. Harcourt nodded politely with a smile of dog-like intelligence.

"Well, then we were instructed to proceed on the principle of 'no fault' divorce, much as insurance companies now treat automobile accident claims. That is, neither party to the proceeding needs to be proved wrong for which he or she may be pursued in order to obtain redress. Settlement of the issue, quickly, without fixing responsibility for the breakup and without assessing damages — that's what is wanted nowadays. Ten years ago a 'no fault' divorce could be had almost automatically if the parties were careful to live apart for three years; the decree followed almost without exception. In the last few months, as I'm sure you know, the period of separation has been reduced from three years to one year. Now if a husband and wife wish to dissolve their marriage, all they need do is live apart, provably, for a twelve-month period and then their union may be dissolved on the grounds — if you wish to call them grounds — that they are unable to live together conveniently. And, mark you, the application for divorce may be registered as soon as they begin to live apart. A man or woman or both may file for divorce as soon as they part and observe a few formalities: They must not meet or 'socialise', as we say, during the waiting period; neither may offer the other financial assistance during that time; they may not cohabit in any sense; they must be present, twice separately and once in each other's presence, at counselling sessions conducted by the presiding judge in the case; and, they must be prepared to consider his remarks seriously. The counselling sessions are to be held during the fourth, eighth, and eleventh months of the waiting period; the middle is the session at which both must be present. I see each separately; I see both together (that'll be a jolly time); I see each separately again; I issue the decree a month after the last session. There are a few ritual observances at the final court hearing. Bingo! They've got their divorce. How does that sound to you?"

"I believe," said Dr. Harcourt meditatively, "under classical Islamic law — religious law, of course — a man needed only to point at his wife and repeat 'I divorce thee' three times for it to become fact."

"We're coming to that for both parties," said the judge. "Already there are voices proclaiming that inasmuch as the parties are going to get their freedom in a year, why not give it to them at once; make the whole process as pure a formality as the issuance of a marriage licence. And this argument has weight in the prevailing social climate."

"The prevailing social climate," repeated Dr. Harcourt.

"What I said. The prevailing social climate which is . . . I don't know what it *is* but it isn't what it was. The effect of all this tinkering with divorce law is that the judge, hardworking and preoccupied already, is made over into some sort of legal caseworker or marriage counsellor which none of us was trained to be. I'm not really qualified medically to advise people on the conduct of their relationships and I don't want to do that. Result: as soon as I begin to preside in a divorce case I'm way out of my depth. There may be very good and sufficient reasons why two persons should not continue to live together. It may not be safe for either, perhaps both. They really may be incompatible. On the other hand, to continue the marriage may be the right course of action. You understand me, I'm not introducing the religious aspect of the matter; I'm trying to evaluate the lines of conduct available in the ordinary unilluminated secular world."

"And what do you wish me to do?"

"I thought you might be able to advise me about this first case. It's the first divorce I've done since the latest legislation came into effect: the one-year wait, the consultations in chambers, the review of information submitted by respondents nominated by the parties. Both husband and wife have the right to name observers who can be required to make depositions before the judge on the conduct of the marriage and the facts of the separation. There are certain statements about property, for example, which have to be considered in preparing the terms of the decree. In no-fault divorce legislation, of course, the distribution of property becomes the main matter of fact in the case. Who owns what; how it is to be apportioned; whether the party who has no gainful employment or other source of income is entitled — as he or she usually is —

to payments from the salaried partner. If there are no children involved, this matter may have surprising aspects. Where there are children and the mother retains custody, with rights of visitation, the father is normally responsible for the support of the children or at least for substantial support payments and he must be encouraged to make these payments. And so on and on. The core of the matter, for me, is the question of counselling. Are we to assume that marriages, on the whole, ought to be sustained and continued wherever possible? Even under conditions of grave stress? Or are we to take them as more or less temporary arrangements which may be discontinued at almost any time upon legal notice? *That's* the real point. And that's where I need advice."

"You want me to answer that question for you?"

"And other questions. I'm sure you know why I've asked you to come. I haven't subpoenaed you as you know. You are not under any legal obligation to furnish an opinion but one of the parties in the action I have on my hands at the moment, Merriman and Merriman, has named you as a potential observer and consultant."

"Ethel?"

"That's right. In a couple of weeks I'm going to have to meet her and her spouse separately for the first of the conferences. These have to be recorded. I can't treat them as purely conventional. I have to make at least one hour available to each of them and I have to give them two hours when we all meet together — something I'm not looking forward to. I haven't met Mrs. Merriman. I'm seeing her first and I need to have some sort of line to take. What am I to tell her?"

"The ball's in my court?"

"It certainly is."

"Do you need to make a record of my remarks, tape them, or have them transcribed? I mean, is this officially on the record?"

"No, we haven't reached that stage yet. This is a preliminary consultation with a relevant authority undertaken by the presiding judge as a means of informing himself in the cause."

"It seems slightly irregular."

"It might be slightly irregular if there were any established rules. Meanwhile, it'll stand up in court — to use a somewhat tasteless

metaphor. We're all feeling our way through these new enactments."

"Then I will make some sort of statement but I should say that
I'm as much in the dark as you are. I think you put your judicial
pinkie directly on the centre of the problem when you ask about
the status of marriage today. Are there any remaining grounds
for treating it in the traditional Christian terms as a sacred relationship which is supposed to endure forever, even beyond the grave?
Can that be our view of marriage? When two people marry, what
are they doing? Are they making a final commitment to one another
for the rest of their lives which may only be terminated by death,
perhaps not even then? Or are they agreeing to some other, less
permanent arrangement? Or are they making a short-term agreement in which permanence is not in question, simply an agreement
to share the use of a dwelling, certain property and each other's
sexual favours, these not necessarily given exclusively to one
another? What used to be called companionate or open marriage.
Now the thing is, Judge Le Mesurier, we can't even take a step
in the direction of asking these questions seriously, much less
answering any of them, unless we have to hand some reliable
index of contemporary society's view of marriage. And I do not
know where such an index is to be found. I really don't know.
There are some statistics available but you know what 'statistics'
are. No matter how the inquiries are framed and no matter how
the responses are interpreted — as long as they are given a reason-
able and fair reading — the most contented and functionally well-
adapted members of society invariably turn out to be men over
forty who have been involved for some time in a happy marriage.
Happily married women over forty come second in these assess-
ments. Single men between nineteen and thirty invariably turn
out to be the least contented members of a given social group.
The crime rates show this; so does the suicide rate; so do several
other of the usual indices. Further to that, whenever serious studies
are made of the career choices of young women in the late-adoles-
cent years between sixteen and nineteen, a permanent marriage
and motherhood in a loving relationship — whatever that may be
judged to be — leads all other options by more than two-and-a-half
to one. What are we to make of this?"

"I don't know," said Judge Le Mesurier. "Are we to take it that marriages are still being made in heaven?"

"Not the Merrimans' marriage."

"No."

The doctor said, "I really don't know what to think. The people who come to me are ravaged by continual firestorms of passionate hatred of themselves, their partners, their parents, their children. A happy and loving marriage. What the hell is that? I don't see any. I see uninterrupted suffering, eternal pain, egotism, self-will, a total breakdown of the notion of charity or compassion or self-sacrifice. I suppose we can do without these things; I just don't see how."

"You . . . don't . . . see . . . how," repeated the judge, licking the point of a pencil, writing these things down. "Firestorms of passionate hatred. Yes, I see that."

10

"I don't need medication," said Ethel, "I don't want it. I've got to try to do this on my own. I've seen too many of my friends on Valium. I think you people hand them out like jelly beans to poor sick women to make us feel good while we get deeper and deeper into trouble. I know I've got to get my weight down someday but I can't even think about it now."

"No, much better to take things one at a time. The thing for you to do now is to carry on with our analysis. It must be evident to you, Mrs. Merriman, that we've turned the corner from psychiatric counselling into deep analysis. We've got to go on with it now. I know that analysis has certain comic aspects. I see our movement caricatured every day in newspaper cartoons and on television comedies. I've even had people refer to me to my face as a 'shrink.' There seems no end to the vulgarity with which foolish people will treat matters they refuse to understand."

There, he thought, that should encourage her. Make her feel that I've got my own problems and my own vulnerabilities. Goodness knows I have. I wonder if there really is any way to make analysis reciprocal. Perhaps my patients could reveal me to myself. He began to lose his concentration and wandered off down tricky theoretical slopes. The voice of his respondent settled into an easy drone, a vocal jog-trot, and Dr. Harcourt entered a familiar mental landscape where blasted stumps of once-great oaks and pines, pocked and seamed mud flats, arid watercourses and dead animals' bones lay all around. If I'd been a painter, he would tell himself at such times, I'd have been a surrealist in the manner of Dali. Everything I can imagine lies on a flat endless plain receding to the empty sky, concealing and revealing nothing. Only now and then at some unimaginable distance flashes of firelight expose the sky.

Apocalyptic thought, characteristic of the late abreactive phase in the manifestation of schizophrenia, additional drug therapy indicated. Bleahhh. He shook himself mentally and tried to dismiss the words he had been taught from his mind. The trouble with psychoanalytic method, he saw, was that it could not be taught; it could only be learned, could never be codified in the framework of institutionalised language. Nor could its technical vocabulary be of much use in the consideration of individual cases. There seemed no way to rejoin the universe of the suffering other person; yet it would be a grave error to conclude, as certain practitioners had done, that analysis was an assumption of the classical rôle of the scapegoat, the *tragos* of early ritual.

"We've got an agreement," he heard Ethel Merriman declare from far off, "on the use of our summer home. Of course, there could not have been any question of sharing it or joining each other on weekends or of my meeting his new friend, friends. We had to hammer out a binding agreement. My husband has it in June and August; I have it in July and September. He got the better deal for himself. I must make certain that I get the cottage in June next year. June is heavenly there. There, you see, he's always managed to hand me the shitty end of the stick. I'm always the one to be cheated out of my rights. I think I'll go out of my mind. I can't put up with that chiselling sort of treatment. It's the pettiness, the malice. It's the latent hostility."

She looked at her analyst brightly, a child hoping to be praised for some mnemonic feat. Latency, she was plainly thinking, latent. Toy words. How peel away these layers of performance, how cast off his own? He bore his patients no love which might justify sudden drastic self-revelation. All he could do was hint jokingly at his own soreness. The practice of analysis was described in overabundant literature as an action which was almost impossible to discharge perfectly. The analyst must perpetually walk a knife-edge between dispassionate critical evaluation of the respondent's character, nature, person, 'personality,' truthfulness, elegance of behaviour and passionate identification with the patient's grievances and sorrows. He stirred himself and looked more carefully at Mrs. Merriman. What could be found in her to love, to respect? What elegance was there in her interminable recital.

"At least in June there are the small birds but by September they've all gone away. It's so sad. When we were at the lake together in June I used to enjoy them so much. They seemed so happy and they had their new nests and young. You could watch all that from where we were almost as though their nests were in the house."

Dr. Harcourt made a mental note of this imagery. To make sure that he had preserved it, he wrote down some of its suggestions.

". . . in September they're gone, all but the crows and the starlings and the sparrows and who's interested in them? They have no colour but grey and black and they never go away; they're always there. I miss the little orioles, the buntings, the grosbeaks."

She wept again, dolefully, at length.

"Mrs. Merriman," he said.

"Call me *Ethel.* Nobody else does."

"I don't think we're quite on that footing yet."

"We certainly ought to be by now," she said tartly.

She was implicitly rejecting the size of the fee, a common occurrence in the early stages of analysis, a necessary element in the groundwork preceding the transferential state. She must resent him terribly. He would clearly have to assume everything she felt about her husband, never a pleasant undertaking.

"And after cheating me out of the happiest month at the cottage, what does he do? He doesn't use it and I'm barred from it. In June he was off on a business trip and now in August he's boating on the canal with that woman. I've seen those locks at this time of year. When you're down inside them and you have to wait for other boats to come along and fill them up, it's like hell. No air, no shadow. I hope they fry. I hope they burn themselves on the building blocks. I hope they get stuck in there and never get out."

You could scream as loud as you liked in Dr. Harcourt's office and nobody but the doctor would ever hear. Scream, he thought, scream louder, louder. His head throbbed rhythmically and made him feel he was making progress. The noise went on.

11

At Cherry Island in the canal system there's a huge old summer hotel founded by Americans who used to come here in the 1870s, one of those extravagant wooden follies with wide verandas, sagging staircases, expansive galleries above the verandas along the second and third floors. In the lobby there's a display of historic photographs of the hotel as it was about 1895 with steam yachts in the background and ladies in shirtwaists and skirts that reach their toes standing in elegant attitudes around the clock-golf layout. Sometimes they carry oddly-formed tennis rackets and are all in white. We can spot canoes and four-oared skiffs at some distance down the river where it widens into a near-lake and the approach to the locks. This old place has been a centre for family vacationing "in a woodland wonderland of parks and recreational facilities for Mom and Dad and the kiddies, featuring horseback riding on forest trails, hiking, tennis and all the traditional aquatic sports and the best game-fishing in North America" for the whole of this century. People started going there for the innocent family fun heralded by the brochure. Now they come for the cuisine which is remarkable.

You can still dine off your day's catch (prepared for you in the cavernous echoing kitchens) at dinnertime of the day you caught it. Pike, bass, an extraordinary perch fillet that simply turns to pure pleasure on the palate when served in little nests of buttered greens as an *hors d'oeuvre.* Those who do not love fish will find their wishes are equally well-served by the huge range of the menu. On the American Plan you might eat yourself into insensibility should you so wish, two or three times a day. Vacationers often return to El Paso and Cleveland and Indianapolis to face the unwelcome fact of substantial weight-gain even though plenty of vigorous physical activity is available to guests. There is something about the old place that encourages long sitting on shadowy galleries and verandas talking business to that nice gentleman from Toledo in Suite 306. You send the kids off somewhere and you sit and you eat, feeling like a minor figure in some satire of American manners by the middle-period Henry James. And some-times there are agreeable droppers-in whom you enjoy meeting. They have mounted the slight rise from waterside from their luxury cruisers tied up below the docks for a day or two. These folks are apt to seize the opportunity to don their most fashionable attire (dinner dress, slightly wrinkled tuxedo) and at such times the long graceful dining room echoes with happy chatter and very good cheer.

It was to this testing atmosphere that Frank and Patsy presented themselves after a week aboard *Pretty Colleen,* the sizeable un-handy inboard cruiser which Frank had chartered for the summer. The old boat rented completely-equipped for $750 a week plus operating costs.

By the time the couple had successfully made fast their mooring lines at Cherry Island locks they were ready for a night of onshore gaiety, time spent away from the exigencies of inland navigation. The place to really get to know somebody is your 1950s power cruiser with its unresponsive steering, huge fuel consumption, questionable constricted head, inadequate hot-water supply, con-stant drain on the attention. Patsy and Frank had imagined them-selves lounging on the afterdeck in picturesque yachting costume but, in order to manage this, a crew consisting of a skipper and paid-hand would have to have been recruited. *Pretty Colleen* pos-sessed two large and comfortable staterooms with other accommo-dation right forward under the forepeak, but neither vacationer wished to forego the romantic privacy which was the chief and perfectly genuine attraction of a cruising vacation. Once or twice they had made up their love couch on the afterdeck. It was now late in July and the worst of summer's biting insects were dead or flown away. Moored in some safe anchorage at a discreet dis-tance from prying eyes they had lain in close embrace listening to the few obtrusive sounds of the river night, a great pike leaping close at hand, a crying loon on a nearby lake, one or two uniden-tifiable buzzing sounds (possibly motors of lost night trippers).

And once, while they lay out aft in the cool beauty of this vacation paradise, the moon had risen full above them and for a time calmed their beating hearts with its splendour and its soft pace.

Other nights it rained and they used the two big staterooms. Sometimes they slept apart, enjoying the wide spread of the big bunks. Sometimes they used the same room. They were often tired because the big cruiser, though it could never run into any danger worse than possible grounding on a mud flat — not in these waters anyway — nonetheless required constant helmsmanship because of the danger of collision with downbound craft, many of them in the hands of persons unskilled in their management and ignorant of the elementary rules of the sea. Frank was a gifted skipper under sail or power and had often competed in ocean races. Navigating a cruiser from the Cataraqui to Poonamalie was child's play to him. At the same time *Pretty Colleen* manoeuvred slowly; a responsible crew member was a necessity. Patsy was very good at this. Nothing escaped her; no half-submerged deadhead eluded her vigilance. They arrived off Cherry Island without so much as a scratch on the boat's gleaming hull, pleased with one another but fatigued by this constant lookout and ready to howl on shore-leave.

They presented themselves at the reservation desk of the hotel dining room at about 7:10 P.M. Patsy clad in a wisp of chiffon that just kind of hung around her like a little pale-blue mist, Frank in some sort of exquisite yachtsman's blazer improbably imported from Italy. They looked like a layout in some thoroughly unpleasant fashion magazine. They made a reservation for eight o'clock and were reminded that the hotel served no liquor. Hotel guests could and did prepare *apéritifs* in their rooms but there was no other liquor service available nearer than Elgin or Westport. This wasn't exactly a disappointment; it seemed unnecessary to retrace their steps in order to have a drink. They asked for soft drinks to be served on one of the verandas and passed the time before dinner drinking Cokes with that real old-fashioned summer-hotel crushed ice swirling in tall glasses.

When at length they were seated on the veranda annex to the main dining room, next to a rumbustious family party of ten (Americans they were, apparently all from Dayton, Ohio), they were served at once with their little dishes of perch so delicate as almost to seem to be breast of guinea-hen. Their neighbours observed their relish with approval and began to address them in comradely terms.

"Have some of our pike," they invited largely. Their party consisted of three married couples and four grown children plus a squadron of youngsters who had been banished to outer tables. They were eating their own catch — magnificent pike which they had taken early in the afternoon — fried in batter in very sizeable quantities.

"We know all the good spots; we've been coming here for thirty years," they chorussed.

Frank and Patsy accepted the kind donation of pike, found their helpings absolutely delicious and were by degrees drawn into conversation with the veteran married couples of Dayton, O. It grew dark; six children began to romp between the tables, drawing forced smiles from the college-girl waitresses who helped to give the dining room so much of its nineteen-forties atmosphere.

All at once Frank and Patsy withdrew from the hilarious exchanges of reminiscence — after inviting all adults at the neighbouring table down to *Pretty Colleen* for after-dinner brandy — and turned back to their own table to find the beginnings of their meal waiting for them: hot buttered breads of various kinds, smoked salmon, fruit salads made from pears, apples, oranges, peaches and gooseberries which had that morning been nestling in their own skins, *fresh* fruit.

Perhaps it was the omission of the usual two cocktails before dinner which sharpened their appetites but Frank and Patsy ate their perch fillets, double servings of pike lightly sautéed in butter, smoked salmon in quantity, bready rolls and fruit compôte without pausing to register intake. At length their main courses arrived at the table. Lamb for Patsy; thickly sliced beef for Frank. Their appetites had apparently been inflamed by feeding; the meat dishes with accompanying vegetables vanished as if they had never been. Then came tall frozen mint parfaits for dessert, crisp biscuits, mint chocolate slices with excellent coffee and a running conversation laced with much good cheer with their fresh-faced waitress who professed to find Frank 'criminally handsome' (or so she averred).

They tottered out of the hotel about ten-thirty and led a small raiding party of Ohioans down to their mooring where soft lights glowed and the sound of the boat's radio, tuned to CBC-FM and the dulcet tones of Bernie Yablon from St. John's, Newfoundland cast music on the sweet night airs. About a dozen revellers — including the fresh-faced waitress — perched in various spots on the afterdeck. Patsy served brandy in balloon glasses and wished that some fashion photographer were present to shoot the scene which had an undeniably picturesque charm. From brandy they moved on to other drinks; the customary pairings-off ensued. Sometime after midnight Patsy found herself fending off the cheery embrace of a Dayton ball-bearing manufacturer crowded in with her in the exiguous cubicle enclosing the vessel's head. At last their guests took their departure, their waitress — sweet sophomore — last of all. That night Frank and Patsy slept in separate staterooms for the sake of their peace of mind and at noon next day had no difficulty in agreeing to proceed upriver. Too many distractions at Cherry Island.

Patsy strolled over to the lockkeeper's office and checked on schedules; they could occupy first place in the vacant lock immediately after the last of the downbound boats had cleared in about an hour. She and Frank passed the time warming up their engines, straightening up the staterooms and the saloon — which was in a mess — and making notes towards replenishment of their liquor supply. Just after two-thirty they were able to see *Pretty Colleen* into position on the starboard side of the lock in the forward position. They passed their season's permit up to the lockkeeper on the end of a pointed stick which he thrust down at them. He returned the pass, waved at them in comradely style and pointed out the dangling pulleys into which they must feed their lines to be taken up carefully as the vessel rose in the water. They put over their fenders and sat back to wait for the other positions in the deep lock to be taken up. A two-hour hiatus ensued. It grew fearfully hot; the sun glared down into the well of the lock quite dizzyingly. Frank reclined in a chair on the afterdeck, shielded his eyes and gazed bewilderedly at Patsy's protruding rear-end as she bent to take up slack. She reminded him vaguely of somebody.

12

In September Patsy sat sweating and terrified in her apartment; appetite tore at her will. When the second payday in the month came around she went to the medical pharmacist's on the ground floor of her office-building and put in an order for proper balance-scales. Always before she had made do with the usual cheap bathroom scales, the kind that go out of whack when an area of low pressure moves in with rain. She had often mounted her bathroom scales assured in the conviction of achieved weight-loss to find that they showed a small gain. Then she would realise that it was raining heavily and her scales simply could not be trusted to give an accurate reading in wet weather. The best she could hope for was a more or less consistent reading which would bear a fictive or conventional relationship to her true weight and mass.

She had the medical scales delivered. They came in pieces and she assembled them. Here neurosis and anxiety supervened. Forever after, when she used these gorgeous scales she was as-sailed by doubts about whether or not she had assembled them correctly. She had had two pieces left over that did not seem to appear in any of the diagrams found in the instruction leaflet. One was a long slim metal rod, perhaps aluminum, perhaps some light alloy, notched at both ends as though it ought to fasten into place like a connecting rod but nothing on the upright post of the scales seemed notched correspondingly. And there was a peculiarly heavy, nearly square Rubberset pad or platform which seemed designed to fit on top of the weighing platform where one stood but there were no visible screw holes anywhere.

She simply had to discard the two superfluous pieces and hide them from herself at the back of her walk-in clothes closet behind a pile of twisted and knotted discarded pantyhose. She tried to forget about them but they haunted her; she always remembered where they were.

The scales appeared to function perfectly well without the pieces when once she put them together. They seemed to give a true weight, a circumstance that yielded mixed gratification. They were far too true for her to dismiss the evidence they proffered. She was on the upswing side of her cycle; she knew it; she'd always half-suspected that this would happen. The first time she'd mounted the (terrifyingly expensive) new scales, they had shown her at 128.

It was true that she had let herself go a bit while on that god-damned boat; the trip had been one continuous pig-out and there had been no way to take any exercise. For a day or two they had jogged in place together on deck but Frank had hated it. You can't keep your weight down by swimming and certainly not by fishing. All she had done on *Pretty Colleen* was lounge around on her butt and break her fingernails on the mooring lines.

She cursed desperately to herself and rang up her doctor's office to persuade his nurse to allow her to drop in two or three times weekly to get a true reading from his scales from which she might calibrate her own. No matter how many times she sneaked into the doctor's office, approaching his scales with the greatest cir-cumspection, she got the same read-out . . . 130 . . . 131½ . . . **135** . . .

Oh god oh god . . .

13

Following the example of their lawyers, Frank and Ethel got to their feet when the judge came into his chambers wearing robes of some sombre silky stuff. There was a protracted silence as Judge Le Mesurier stood behind his desk and shuffled through the papers spread abundantly over his blotting pad. He seemed burdened by notices of many causes. Dossiers and dockets and briefs and appli-cations and transcripts, the apparatus of reported or impending procedures and proceedings, all neatly-fastened together by pecul-iar brass clips lay in piles on the massive desk and the adjoining side table. There was no telephone in the room, a curious fact which impressed the Merrimans without their being perfectly aware of it. Not many serious conferences go forward today away from the potential summons of the telephone bell. Nor was there a visible clockface anywhere.

Judge Le Mesurier did not, however, scruple to wear a wristwatch; he glanced at it as he located the papers which bore upon the present case, sat down behind his desk and nodded authoritatively at the quartet who stood before him. After an almost

imperceptible pause the lawyers sat down, and in another moment, flustered, somewhat irritated by the formal air of the meeting, the Merrimans sat down too, as far away from one another
as the arrangement of the chairs in the room allowed. It was
curious to observe how their personal hostility and reciprocal dis-
like were muted and civilised by the official and judicial atmosphere of the proceedings. A silent man came unobtrusively into
the room and stood beside the door; he would remain there until
the conference was over in seemingly official status, doorkeeper,
bailiff of chambers, what? This was never revealed. No record of
the conference was officially preserved although both lawyers took
occasional notes.

At one point early in the hour Frank Merriman foolishly took a
small brown leather-covered notebook from his inside jacket pocket, opened it and made one or two notes in ballpoint. As he did
so, he had a powerful persuasion that he was being watched. He
glanced up to see the judge staring at him so balefully that his
body jerked involuntarily; he dropped his pen; thrust the closed
notebook into the inner recesses of his jacket, felt around on the
floor for his pen and wondered if he were perhaps in contempt
of court or something.

Like most of us, the Merrimans knew little of the precise nature
of court proceedings. As children each of them had been taken
on a 'field trip' to Magistrate's Court in the town in which they
had grown up. This was a regular feature of the Social Studies
curriculum in all local primary schools, the product of strong con-
victions held by one particular magistrate who had presided during
the middle years of the century. Old Judge Wright had died a few
years' since but local schoolchildren still trooped down in the
dozens to attend a sitting of Magistrate's Court when they were
about halfway through grade seven; the visit was a hallowed civic
institution, something the whole of the citizenry had in common:
the day they visited old Judge Wright's courtroom.

All those generations of children could remember the way the
courtroom was divided: the judge's high bench raised on a kind
of dais at one end of the room under the coloured photograph of
Queen Elizabeth, the flags of Canada and Ontario standing next
to the bench with an arrangement of fat leather-bound volumes
atop it; then the well of the court in which stood a long heavy

table and some uncomfortable-looking chairs; a witness box; a place for the accused to stand. (A bar? Prisoner at the bar? Could be!) Then there was a railing like an altar rail in an Anglican or Catholic church with a little swinging gate in it and rows of seats stretching away to the rear of the room. These images remained fixed in all the citizens' imaginations as 'court.'

Not one in a hundred ever recognised that Magistrate's Court was presided over by an appointive Police Magistrate and not a judge at all; nor did they grasp that old Judge Wright was not a judge. He was a magistrate and a justice of the peace; his courtesy title of 'Judge' was a sign of the fondness with which his fellow citizens regarded him.

Nobody ever seems to know anything about courts and court proceedings beyond that childhood field trip; the intricacies of legal procedure remain a closed book to all but those learned in the law. Certainly Frank and Ethel Merriman were thoroughly-cowed by the powerful and ponderously somniferic trappings of their suit for divorce. They had been served with legal notices of this conference at which their attendance was obligatory if the proceeding were to go ahead. If they failed to file notice of non-attendance which would have the effect of arresting or annulling the suit and subsequently did not present themselves at the appointed time and place of the conference, they would be liable to be held in contempt of court and become subject to the prescribed penalties and so on. They had both examined their notices with misgivings, indeed with trepidation, and had equally considered giving up the whole thing.

A few months before, each of them had been summoned to a conference at which the other party had not been present. Each had spoken to the judge about the other party in heated terms. Naturally they now wondered equally what their former partner had had to say about them. Had there been any scabrous revelations about specific sexual adjustments? Every married couple deviates now and then into practices which they consider peculiar, perhaps blameworthy, practices which — did they but realise it — are as common as the air we breathe. But they don't know that. They fancy that this action or that is something that no lovers have ever imagined. Maybe it's against the law. They then remember that in some jurisdictions certain common sexual practices are still technically illegal and may upon discovery be visited with extreme rigour under the law. And they begin to bubble and ferment with anxiety, bad conscience, feelings of guilt and shame which surprisingly they may rather enjoy.

That must be why the parties in a divorce action invariably look so unsure of themselves, thought Judge Le Mesurier as he seated himself, especially under these rules. Neither of them knows what the other has told me; they guess I've been the repository of some pretty menacing confidences. The judge had one old friend in particular, a Catholic priest, a veteran hearer of confessions and he had many friends like Dr. Harcourt who practised one form or another of psychiatry. From what they had told him and from his own experience the judge concluded that human conduct moves as if on rails, on predirected paths which may seem to those who take them as freely-chosen as any other conceivable way. But observed, say, from the air, all travellers will be seen moving in closely organised patterns like those of the anthill or colony of bees. Even those who "go off the rails" are not so much suffering the consequences of derailment as simply following out branch-lines and obscure country rights-of-way with spurs and sidings almost hidden by tall grass which have nevertheless been followed many times before. It is true that there is nothing new under the sun. Neither Frank nor Ethel had invented a new vice, new sexual kink, new method of acquiring weight. Neither suffered from mental disabilities not known to cave-dwellers; and, though their defects, fears, confusions, were of ancient lineage, they were not simple. It was as open to cave-dwellers to succumb to anxiety and repression as it is open to baby boomers. Complexity of character and depth of emotional stress were not invented after the second World War.

So the Merrimans suffered from old and complicated diseases: proneness to self-indulgence, idleness, luxuriousness in the husband and self-pity in the wife, untruthfulness in both. Ought he to counsel such a pair to remain together? Would they do better apart? The man was close to forty-five, would evidently not change his ways and had done nothing, would do nothing, unlawful. It wasn't illegal to tire of your sexual partner, goodness knows. Most of the adult population of the globe would otherwise be in jail. And Ethel, the no-longer-cherished wife whose crime in her husband's eyes seemed to be her mere physical bulk, could she possibly wish for the return of someone who had publicly humiliated her often? Were they not much better apart? The judge examined Ethel Merriman closely while seeming to continue to shuffle papers about. He considered this a shrewd stratagem, one that no observer would ever notice. In this he was quite mistaken: most people realised at once that when he shuffled his documents and appeared somewhat at a loss, old Le Mesurier was about to transfix you with a basilisk stare and ask some peculiarly embarrassing question. We all imagine our most characteristic social strategems are invisible to others but they are the more visible as they are more characteristic. This foot-dragging of the judge's was well-known to both counsel present and readily grasped by both Mr. and Mrs. Merriman.

Ethel was in fact encouraged by the judge's laborious preparations for discourse. She thought he was a fine man and a fair man and wished he would take some notice of her beyond what was strictly required by the evidence. He would certainly prove more forbearing than her rotten stinker of a husband . . . (Here her fancies turned into private thoroughfares where perhaps she ought not to be followed.)

"This is the second, and perhaps the most important, of the three counselling sessions which our divorce laws require me to convoke," said Judge Le Mesurier at large.

There was a murmur of assent from the four participants in the session; the man who stood next to the door at the back of the room shifted nervously from foot to foot and said nothing.

"And I must say that the final session of three is slightly less than three months away when you will be conferring with me for the last time, separately, as you did some months ago. This particular session is the only one in which the parties meet together with me for a tripartite examination of views, claims, grievances. Now I must ask you first to dismiss from your minds the many particular offences and slights, the unfriendly actions which you may imagine yourselves to have suffered from your partner. Put all this out of your minds and try to look at the circumstances of your lives together as if you hadn't been husband and wife. That is, you must ask yourselves whether or not your partner's conduct to you was more or less offensive than that of the ordinary person whom you might meet on the street or in the department stores or in some office or resort. Isn't it the case that your partner was many many times a comfort to you and a resource which no casual acquaintance or passing stranger could ever be? I ask you to think back to the earliest days of your marriage when every possibility seemed to broaden before you and your path, as the poet says, "was through roses."

The others in the room gasped inwardly at this apt citation.

"Then, every casual aspect of your spouse's conduct seemed especially considerate, framed to cheer and hearten you. The tender attention, an arm proffered on a staircase, a door held open, some special meal prepared with loving liberality. All such things were shared on a footing of intimacy that you have probably never achieved in any other human relationship. For who can have been closer to you than your marriage partner of fifteen or twenty years? Your mother, it is true, may have cared for you in ways not expected of husband or wife but the mental communion between mother and child can never be as fully understanding on both sides as that between free adults. No. I must urge you to consider that you will in all probability never know another human being as well as you know the person sitting opposite you to whom you have been married for so considerable a time?

This was perhaps a somewhat tactless reference and the judge passed quickly on to other considerations.

"Such a relationship probably comes but once in our lives. There is a profound sense in which it is true to say that one can only be married once. One is not given enough time in the years from twenty to forty — the years when a mature and loving relationship with a person of one's own generation, one's own historical moment, becomes possible — to form as many as two profound emotional and moral unions. I am not here to preach at you. I am directed to urge upon you the consequences of your divorce. You will be putting aside all that you have shared, all that history, all those small acts of mutual respect and consideration. It is not simply a question of the distribution of property."

Here the judge paused to study some other documents.

"I am happy to note in this instance something which is very seldom the case in such proceedings. Questions of the distribution of property are not at issue. Arrangements for division of goods and income have been arrived at which are satisfactory to both parties. That shows a generous breadth of mind on both sides which I must commend. At the same time I put it to you that accord on this relatively minor question suggests that compromises and accord might be established on the greater matter."

This isn't doing one bit of good he thought as he paused to clear his throat. There's nothing to be gained by addressing them in elegant periods as though I were summing up in a murder trial. They've made their minds up; this counselling stuff is a charade and a waste of my time. Shook 'em up a bit with that line from Hardy though. He let his eye fall once more on Mrs. Merriman. Probably weighs a solid 185. May take an occasional drink. Not a drugger, I should say, and younger than hubby. Good stuff there. Some people like a good armful. The Italians do. Just the way some people always buy the extra-large size in sweaters thinking they may as well have the material. I don't mind big women, not a bit. You can see what you're taking hold of.

"Now Mrs. Merriman," he said aloud, encouragingly, "aren't there serious grounds for reconciliation?"

He thought he could predict precisely what look would now cross those pleasing features and here it came, the poor cat i' the adage: disgust.

14

"But I've only got the one bedroom," said Patsy.

"That's all right, we'll only need one. Hey, I like the mirror. How much can you see from there?"

He made her lie down on the clean bedspread and kick her heels in the air.

"Can you see yourself?"

"Ye-e-ss. But I get a better view standing up."

"That's what you think."

If what crossed his face wasn't a leer, then she didn't know a leer when she saw one. A leering man, she thought; I'm involved with a leering man. Everything she'd read about people like herself seemed to come back to haunt her from the recent past, articles in *MS* and *Cosmopolitan*. What does a leer signify anyway? Mere rude desire? Frank wasn't such a bad guy.

"Have you ever balanced a mirror in the doorway?" he asked, interrupting her train of thought. She blushed.

"Aha, you have, eh? Why, you bad little girl!"

Can he really be an awful creep, she thought; sometimes he says such awful things, other times he's very liberal. He doesn't care what he spends on me. This was true. Frank had no responsibilities apart from his own maintenance. No system of support payments had yet been dictated to him and there were no children from his marriage. His income continued very high. With their two incomes, Patsy figured, and only this little apartment to keep up, they would have over $100,000 a year to spend. It *was* true that a dollar was no longer a dollar and would very soon not even qualify as paper money any more; still 100,000 of those little metal pieces would form a very comfortable income for a youngish couple in a small city such as this. Or at least, a young woman and her middle-aged boyfriend. She might get rid of the furniture from the firestorm; the scent of the scorched curtains was beginning to make her feel just a little nauseated from time to time, around breakfast when the weather grew Novemberish. Frank liked the smell of burning, claimed it was a turn on; she didn't know; she couldn't really tell. There was no doubt he was generous enough.

"If you're tired of the furniture we'll refurnish. I like the carpet though."

He had his shoes off and was drawing his feet against the lie of the nap, making big streaks where the pile lay the wrong way.

"Look," he said, "I can write my name with my feet."

He began to stride around the bedroom as he unbuttoned his shirt and made wide sweeping motions with his legs like a hockey player. In moments his name stood out against the deeper background hue of the shadowed strands of fibre in writing that closely resembled his handwritten signature. The body has its own severe consistencies.

"Do you know," she said, "what you've written on the carpet with your feet looks exactly like your signature on a cheque." She blushed. It was true she had taken money from him.

"That's because I'm a monster of principle," he said, "that's what Ethel could never learn or if she could — maybe she did —

she couldn't accept it. Consistency, the hallmark of champions."

"I don't understand."

"It's too simple," he said. "Now if you're building a ballclub from scratch . . ."

Patsy hated his analogies drawn from the summer game.

"I know, I know," he said, "all women find baseball incomprehensible. There's something about it that offends the inner core of their being. But let me finish. If you're building a ballclub from scratch you look for the kind of player who has the same good stats every year for six to eight years. Five-hundred-and-sixty appearances at the plate."

Appearances at the plate kill you, thought Patsy.

"A hundred-and-seventy-five hits, thirty-two doubles, four triples, twenty-four HR, ninety RBI, a .314 average. Every year. That's the André Dawson type of year."

Patsy had no idea what he was talking about and by now he had all his clothes off, neatly folded on a Sheraton reproduction she kept standing in the corner next to her closet. That was where she set down underthings for the next day when she retired. There would certainly have to be many minor adjustments.

"Do you really think this place is big enough?"

"Come to bed," he said and she did.

Afterwards, he left her lying there and went naked into the adjoining room; she could hear him in there poking around at objects she wished he'd leave lying where she'd deposited them. Nobody wants to have her cherished personal arrangements disturbed by guests (no matter how generous or how welcome). He was experimenting with the decanters. She could hear him extracting the stoppers, sniffing, re-inserting them; there were occasional chimings from the fine crystal. She waited for the sound of breakage but it didn't arrive. He reappeared briskly, carrying the mirror from back of the bar which he poised at a lascivious position in the doorway and immediately returned to sit astride her.

Nothing covered them. All at once she spotted herself in the doorway mirror from an unfamiliar angle which accentuated unsuspected roundnesses. She hid her head in atavistic surprised modesty deep in the pillows but he drew them away.

"Come on, be a sport."

Finally she was obliged to plead a compelling physical need and broke away from bedside to conceal her anxieties in the bathroom. She could hear him parading around in the bedroom talking to himself in a pleased way while she stealthily slid the weights back and forth on her beautiful scales. She muffled the sound of the weights by running water copiously into the basin.

"No-fault divorce," she heard him say. "Hell of an institution."

The balancing arm moved leisurely up and down. She nudged the smaller weight and stood on tiptoe.

"In another two months the divorce will be final," he exulted outside the door.

148½.

15

There was a dark tunnel which ran between the administrative office building and the courthouse, always stifling, always swept by currents of heat emitted from the adjacent boiler-room and the labyrinthine system of duct-work which traversed those precincts. The place inspired Judge Le Mesurier with his ordinary banal — as he felt — reflections on the law, its course, its consequences. He had ended one marriage twenty minutes before by the stroke of a pen (let no man put asunder?) and now he was about to terminate a second. Sometimes he could get through four in a day's sittings. The fact depressed him. Once he had seen in a popular magazine a drawing of two woodsmen standing among ranks of enormous stumps which stretched as far as the eye could follow into a far background. One man carried an enormous double-bladed axe. The other supported one end of a vicious-looking crosscut saw. The stumps were obviously those of redwoods or giant sequoias or some other monstrously long-lived tree and the caption of the cartoon said succinctly, "We may not be able to grow them, but we can sure as hell cut 'em down."

This cartoon with its moralising caption had remained in the Judge's mind ever since, communicating to his judicial acts an undertone of discontent and perplexity. He did not like to bring to an end a partnership of any kind either in business or private life. For when two people, or ten people, have struggled together to encourage a stately growth (some stockbrokership or pride of lawyers or even just husband and wife), he hated to be the one to put the axe to the trunk, bring the tall growth to the ground, root, branch and corona. It was hot in the tunnel; his robes were binding; another decree to sign into effect; sweat under the arms. We must suppose that even judges have their moments of queasiness when they understand they are bringing down what they could not have grown or even erected. Discontents of the judiciary.

All stood as Judge Le Mesurier re-entered his courtroom. 'All' was a very small number: the court clerk, a bailiff who stood in a stunned and somnolent attitude at the rear of the room, the court reporter who began to hammer away at her word-processor as soon as the judge had seated himself, the petitioners, their counsel, an official witness for each and a light sprinkling of the vain and curious who invariably turn up in such places at such times. Kites gathering in the sky . . .

'Kites gathering in the sky,' thought the judge, checking this line of reflection with amusement. What's gotten into you, Norman me bucko? Liver trouble? Advancing age? The effects of solitude? Mere randiness? We can sure as hell cut 'em down!

He turned over the papers in front of him oblivious to the murmurings of clerk and counsellors who tried repeatedly to gain his attention. One of the first rules — in fact the most important of all — is to make sure that ALL the pieces of paper which should be in the file are really there. Rulings have been overturned and careers ended because a doctor left a sponge in the patient and because a judge left an affadavit or a notarised deposition under his desk blotter or in a wastepaper basket. Everything was there: Merriman and Merriman. Property settlements? Yes; Applications? yes; Dates and places all consistent? Names of deponents? Hum, hum, hum; what else? Anything missing? Decree forms on top of the pile ready for his signature in seven copies. He glanced up from under bent brows. Yes, the two witnesses about to give evidence of non-cohabitation for the stipulated time were certainly present. One of them looked like an apartment-house superintendent and the other — he saw with great surprise — looked like a clone, an identical twin, of Mrs. Merriman. And yet — this was a puzzler — she seemed to be the husband's deponent. He raised his head and the murmuring stopped abruptly.

"Are we ready to proceed, Mr. Conboy?" he asked the clerk.

"We are, my Lord."

"Then call deponent for the first party."

Foot shufflings, somebody tripping over a chair. The apartment-building superintendent (for such in fact he was) came to the stand, was sworn in, turned to face the judge. The fixed series of questions ensued.

You knew both parties familiarly? Yes. You were in a position to witness their movements and their domestic arrangements routinely? Yes. And you would naturally have reason to remember and perhaps even record the dates and times of their movements? Yes. On what date did Mr. Merriman remove his effects from the Merriman apartment? Did he at any time resume residence? I see. Did Mrs. Merriman continue to dwell at that address as stated here? Yes. In daily occupation? Yes. And you have no reason to believe that the separation of the parties wasn't final and uninterrupted? No. You understand these statements have been made under oath, that any wilful mis-statement renders you liable to pursuit under the law? Yes. That's all, sir. The clerk will show you where to sign your statement.

Now let's have a squint at this lady? Who can she be? She's the image of the Merriman woman only younger. Maybe ten years younger. They're both a good solid size. I do like big women thought Judge Le Mesurier wistfully. Tell you what, my boy, this woman is the girlfriend of the party of the first part. That's who she is. Well, I'll be damned, the old roué. He doesn't mind at all if they're fat; he just wants them young.

You are Patricia Alice Lambert? Yes. And you have a close and familiar knowledge of these persons? Yes.

I'll bet she does, the barefaced creature. She's going to swear to what she knows first-hand.

Judges must laugh sometimes.

And you have had sufficient reason to remember and even re-cord the dates and times of their movements, might even, for some reason of your own, have taken a note in writing of some of them? I see, you did. In writing? Uh-huh. (And so on and so on.) You may stand down now. The clerk will show you where to sign your statement.

Cut 'em down, cut 'em down. We'll get through two more today if we're lucky.

As Judge Le Mesurier began to read his decree aloud, he could feel his eyes flicking back and forth in puzzlement between Mrs. Merriman and Miss Lambert. They looked so much alike standing to either side of the shadowy room that for a second or two he felt obscurely frightened as if by a suspicion of ghostly presences or unlooked-for changes of state, transformations against nature.

"And I therefore declare that the divorce is granted unconditionally as from today. There will be official publication of this decree. You may now leave."

He followed the two women with his gaze as they passed out of the room. Seen like this, at some distance from behind, they were identical.

16

Frank had now reached a feverish trancelike state of illumination. The room in which he sat had gone all misty, its upright lines where the walls met at the corners seeming wiggly and bent, windowframes skewed to one side or another. He was breathing very deeply, perhaps hyperventilating, in a state of intense but controlled excitement. He kept blinking his eyes and the mists would thin momentarily, then swirl and confuse him. He could see the figure of the judge well enough. The judge seemed to be half-standing or leaning well forward as he traded mumbled sentences with the old fink from the apartment building. Patsy replaced the old fink in the dialogue and Frank had to struggle to contain himself. She would make it all right; she wouldn't let anybody find out anything about him, any of the vertigo that circled around him. He never understood how he had come to want the things he wanted and how it was that he couldn't seem to lay his hands on them. It was his swing he thought; he didn't seem to have his rhythm; he wasn't swinging down on the ball. Everything he tried to do went slightly wrong, fouled off to left or right, never properly in play. He shook his head and some of the mistiness disappeared.

The judge had finished with Patsy. She stood down from the little square platform she'd been perched on. As she came down she vibrated all over. He had had to help her into her dress that morning, had had to work it carefully over the broad shoulders and down to where she narrowed slightly in the middle then flared widely. The waistline of the dress was very snug. He had to bunch the material of the skirt in his hands while he tugged the sleeves and bodice into place. (Once upon a time that dress had been too big for her.) Then he'd eased the skirt down over the sheer, deeply dimpled panties. There had been an unfocussed lewdness in this act. And here she came, wobbling. He saw the judge glancing from Ethel to Patsy with uncertain eyes and he knew what the man was thinking. What's the difference? Why this one instead of that one? He came out into the light at this point, saw who he was and what he did. He was the man, the miracle catalytic man who, when added to a woman, produced fat. He held out his arms and stretched his legs in front of him, looked at them in amazement and fear as if the flesh on his bones might now start up like rows of little fingers and dance. Everybody was leaving. Only the small stuttering rattle like jiggling teeth on the word-processor keyboard disturbed the thickening silence. Finishing up. He looked across at the court stenographer bent over the ivory keys. Rather a pretty girl, thin.